TERRORS &
LONGINGS

Robert Hutchings

A Bright Pen Book

British Library Cataloguing Publication Data.
A catalogue record for this book is available from the British Library

ISBN 978-0-7552-1412-9

Authors OnLine Ltd
19 The Cinques
Gamlingay, Sandy
Bedfordshire SG19 3NU
England

This book is also available in e-book format, details of which are available at www.authorsonline.co.uk

Dedication:

This is for my late father Spencer Hutchings, who survived two years of trench warfare on the Western Front.

Chapter 1

He had only dozed briefly and fitfully. Yet still, it had been impossible for him to escape another failure dream.

His weapon had jammed, his gas mask had been lost, his efforts to staunch the blood haemorrhaging from the sergeant's throat had been futile, and he had found himself alone. Alone, that is, except for the piles of dead bodies all around him. Then the darkness had begun to fall, and rats had started to panic as the water rose above the duckboards in the bottom of the trench. Next his nostrils had begun to twitch at the first whiffs of chlorine gas. His anguished cries for help had met with no response. There were no stretcher bearers to help the sergeant, and by now the blood had ceased to pump from the victim's throat…

But then powerful hands were shaking his own shoulders. 'Come along, sir, wake up. This is the end of the line. We're in Folkestone and you've probably got a troop ship to catch – just like the rest of us.'

Before he could even begin to reply, the corporal who had roused him had disappeared from the train. He rapidly blinked his eyes, gathered his thoughts, grabbed his valise and stepped out on to the railway platform. Thankfully, he had but a short walk ahead of him.

As he approached her front door he realised that his aunt was looking out of the window. The tears streaming down her face mirrored the raindrops on the panes of glass in front of her. She opened the door to him, her shoulders shaking. She was sobbing uncontrollably.

Once inside the house he took her in his arms and held her close to him. He'd never before seen her quite so distressed.

'What on earth has happened? It's not Uncle Harry, is it?'

'No, it's not Harry. It's his younger sister, Eleanor. She collapsed at home earlier this afternoon. There was some sort of internal bleeding. She's been ill for weeks now – terrible stomach pains. Her doctor thought it might be some form of ulcer.'

'So what's happened? Has she gone to hospital?'

'Yes, to Dover, about an hour ago, Harry's with her now. He's dreadfully upset. It was only three months ago that Eleanor's husband was lost at sea. I'd be at the hospital, too. But Harry insisted that I wait for you to arrive. He told me that he'd telephone as soon as there was any news.'

He sat her down in the nearest armchair and wiped away her tears. Then he took off his greatcoat, stepped out of the room and brought in his valise from the front porch. By now she had started to compose herself, but remained very upset. She was still shaking.

By the time he arrived back with a glass of brandy, she had settled down and was re-touching her make-up. She rose from the chair, cupped his face in her hands, kissed him tenderly, and then stood back to look at him.

'I'm so sorry, Thomas. This is no way to spend the last two days of your leave.'

'Don't think like that. I can't imagine anywhere else I'd rather be. Now, let's…'

But he was interrupted by the telephone ringing in the hall. His aunt scurried out, returning a few minutes later.

'Yes,' she said, 'that was Harry. Eleanor's having an emergency operation. Harry is staying on at the hospital this evening.'

'Would you like me to call a taxi so that you can join him there?'

'No. He's insistent that I stay here with you. There's nothing I'd be able to do at the hospital anyway. Now, you put your things in your usual bedroom and make yourself comfortable. I know how tired you must be. I'm going to get on and cook the meal I'd planned for the three of us. Once we've eaten we'll probably hear from Harry again.' She raised her hand to stop him as he tried to speak, 'No arguments, Thomas. Do as you're told.'

Two hours later, flopped out on a chaise longue, he remembered his manners and did his best to stifle a yawn. He felt relaxed now, but realised just what an exhausting train journey he'd had that day. His aunt needed no further cues and ushered him up to his bed.

He fell asleep immediately, but was soon enduring a familiar recurring nightmare: The sudden explosion, a blast of hot air into the dugout, acrid fumes… and then the frenzied shouts of: "Stretcher bearers! Stretcher bearers!"

Then the chaotic dash along the trench and the realisation that the officer, with whom he'd been in conversation only ten minutes earlier, was almost certainly buried beneath several tons of earth, timber, iron and other debris of trench warfare – all of which, only seconds before, had formed another smaller dugout barely twenty paces away. Then next, the futile clawing at the mound of earth, and the anguish on the faces of the other men around him. All of them struggling in a desperate bid to uncover the officer.

Two minutes becoming five; five minutes becoming ten, until…at last! A hand, a sleeve, shoulders and then a head were painfully uncovered.

But it was all too late: the blue and open lips and a mouth choked with soil were incapable of ever drawing breath again. Within a short while the officer would have to be buried once more.

* * * *

Second Lieutenant Thomas Winson raised his head from the pillow and turned to look at the clock on the dressing room table. France now seemed a world away, and the trenches of the

Somme a distant fantasy. This was Folkestone, England. Albeit an England that was two and a half years into a ghastly world war, in which there seemed to be no means of ending a military stalemate which had confounded generals and politicians alike.

His eyes strayed across the room to a calendar and a circled date: *Saturday 20th February 1917.* One more day beyond that date and his leave would be over. He slowly got up out of bed and looked at himself in the dressing-table mirror. He earnestly searched his face for any signs of premature aging, or any after effects of the disturbing dream. Such dreams always seemed to be so much more graphic and focused when he was actually away from the battlefields. A little surprised at his image in the mirror, he concluded that there perhaps hadn't been too much deterioration in his features, and that he still bore reassuring resemblance to the vigorous twenty-five year old who had first gone off to war less than twelve months ago.

Tomorrow he would be crossing the English Channel again to rejoin his regiment and to be caught up in yet another "push" or "show" of the generals' deciding. But for the time being, at least, here he was in a comfortable bedroom in the small but elegant townhouse belonging to an aunt and uncle, who were always delighted and relieved to see Thomas whenever he was passing through the town.

A knock at the door signalled the arrival of his morning tea. His aunt entered the room, her face clearly troubled as she handed him the cup and saucer.

'I'm afraid that we had another telephone call earlier this morning. I hope it didn't wake you up. Apparently Eleanor's so poorly after the operation that the hospital has put her on the danger list. I'll have to go over there immediately, and it looks as though Harry and I may have to stay overnight again. I'm so sorry about this. It's such a pity when you have to embark only tomorrow.'

'Good heavens above, don't mind that,' said Thomas. 'I'm only sorry that Eleanor is in such a state. Can I help in some way? Would you like me to come over to Dover with you?'

'No, certainly not! If we can't be here, then at least we want you to relax and make the most of what little time you have left in England. Will you be alright looking after yourself on your own?'

Thomas beamed at his aunt, reached across and kissed her cheek: 'Of course I'll be alright, auntie - you spoil me! No, I'll be fine. There's some essential shopping I need to do this morning, then, if it's a decent day, I'll stroll along the Leas and generally relax. I can get some lunch out somewhere.'

'You're such an understanding chap, Tom. Harry and I will just have to make up for this the next time you get back on leave. Meanwhile, you lie-in as long as you wish to. You'll find a good cooked breakfast left in the oven for you.'

Once she had gone, he supped his tea, looked again at the clock and decided against risking any more nightmares. He washed, shaved and then pulled on his civilian clothes, perhaps for the last time in many months. He then had a leisurely breakfast, savouring the bacon, eggs and sauté potatoes waiting for him downstairs.

Half an hour later he stepped out of the front door and headed for the shops in Rendezvous Street. He needed to replenish shaving kit, socks, gloves and a brown scarf. After finding these and a number of other sundry items, he found himself browsing in a bookshop just off the High Street. Here, he reflected that books were a rare commodity in the trenches, and the conditions for enjoying them even rarer. Despite this, he was glad to purchase a couple of titles by Conan Doyle and hoped that, perhaps when billeted behind the lines, he would find some opportunity to satisfy his love of reading.

Then, as he stepped back into the street, he recoiled, first with surprise, and then with great pleasure, at recognising a face, which he knew so well, but had not expected to see in Folkestone.

He called out across the busy street, quite oblivious to the traffic and all the passers by: 'Amy! Amy Nicholls!'

The young woman who turned towards him, seeking out the caller, was an elegant figure in a dark green winter coat. She was tall, fair-haired and with brown eyes and a beautifully textured skin. She was distinguished by strong, high cheekbones and an assertive jawline. Finally, as she caught sight of Thomas' raised arm and broad smile, her own face showed the surprise and pleasure which she, too, felt at recognising an old friend in strange and unexpected circumstances.

As Thomas crossed the road towards her his memory was working overtime. It must have been two and a half years since he'd last seen Amy Nicholls, just after her wedding, in fact, at which he had been the best man. Her husband Edward, together with both Amy and Thomas had been schoolteachers together at an elementary school in Maidstone. Amy and Edward had married in the August of 1914. Soon afterwards the war had broken out and Edward had volunteered for the army almost immediately.

Thomas' fate, however, had taken a very different turn. While returning from a camping holiday in Wales that same month, he had crashed his Sunbeam motorcycle and suffered serious groin and abdominal injuries, which were to render him unfit for any military service for the next eighteen months.

By the time that he was finally declared fit for the army it was early in 1916. Several months later, following basic training, he joined his regiment, the Invictas, in France, but was mercifully spared during the slaughter of the Somme later that summer.

But Amy's husband had been much less fortunate. By the middle of that same year he had risen to the rank of captain, and was a company commander with a Military Cross to his credit.

However, on July 1st 1916, along with almost twenty thousand others, he died from wounds during one of the most abortive British attacks of the war.

Thomas had lost contact with both Edward and Amy long before that summer and, although he had subsequently seen Edward's name on the casualty lists, by then he was himself in France, behind the front near Albert. He had written a letter of condolence to Amy and had tried to visit her in Maidstone last autumn, but had found her house boarded up and unoccupied. Now, the initial pleasure at seeing her again was quickly giving way to feelings of intense sorrow and poignant memories.

'Amy, I was so dreadfully sorry to learn of Edward's death last year. I tried to visit you at your house last October, when I got my first leave. There was no one there, and I had no way of finding where you were in the short time I had.'

She put her hand on his shoulder, kissing him fondly on his cheek, and wiped a tear from her eye.

'It's alright, Thomas. I knew that you would have contacted me if you could. I was certainly glad to get your letter after Edward's death. At the time I couldn't bring myself to write back to you. You see…I lost my brother Fred on the Somme as well. It was a ghastly time, and left me badly depressed for several weeks. But the worst is over for me now. Eventually, I left the house in Maidstone and came down to this area to live with my parents for a time. Then, last November, I started teaching again. I've rented a cottage up the hill in Capel, quite near to the village school where I work. Life has to go on, doesn't it, Thomas? God knows there are so many other widows everywhere now.'

She had turned her head away for a moment. Her brow had suddenly furrowed and her eyes had taken on a desperately melancholy look. But the moment passed quickly, she looked at him closely, and soon she had fully recovered her fetching smile.

Thomas was pleased how quickly Amy had regained her composure. But he had always remembered her as a strong, spirited young woman, always apparently so positive in thought and action. He had clear memories of her determined nature and independent will. He also had keen memories of how very attractive he had always found her, and the difficulties he had experienced years earlier once it had become apparent that his friend Edward had won her affections first. He now tried, somewhat unsuccessfully, to dispel such thoughts from his mind. He returned her smile, and was reassured when she put her arm through his.

'Now, sir,' she asked, 'what brings you to Folkestone? Are you a soldier too?'

'Yes, they finally gave me the King's Shilling last spring. It

7

took me almost until then to fully heal from the motorbike crash. The army brought me back from France last October to train as an officer. Tomorrow afternoon I have to report to the harbour camp to go back to France. Which particular unit I'll end up with there will be in the lap of the gods.'

'So,' continued Amy, 'what are your plans for the rest of the weekend?'

'That's an interesting question, Amy,' he replied, smiling ruefully. 'Until a couple of hours ago I was expecting to be spending the time with my aunt and uncle who live a few streets from here. But they were suddenly summoned to Dover to help with a relative who is dangerously ill. So, I have another thirty-six hours or so in Folkestone – and having done a final bit of shopping, I'm footloose and fancy-free.'

'Well then, why don't we spend a bit of time together? I've no more need of the shops this morning, and it's turning out to be such a gorgeously sunny day. Tell you what – why don't we go through to the cliff-top and have a gentle stroll?'

By now her eyes seemed alight, and Thomas took much pleasure from seeing her looking again just as he'd remembered her before last year's tragedies. She continued, now sounding positively mischievous: 'Or does that sound too much like a route march to you, Captain?'

'Route marches certainly aren't on my agenda, Amy, and I'm sorry to disappoint you, but you are talking to a humble subaltern here. I did tell you that I've only just been commissioned.'

She chuckled and squeezed his arm. 'Yes, alright, Thomas, but I know only too well that that pompous note you've just sounded is only an act. I'd already worked out your rank. I referred to you as "Captain" simply as a tease. I was remembering your antics on that sailing boat you used to have in the old days. You loved being skipper and shouting orders at us, didn't you?'

'I suppose that I did, really. Not that you ever took much notice of me, of course.'

He smiled broadly at her: 'Actually, I always regarded you as a rather mutinous crewmember. I just hope that your behaviour has improved after all these years. If not, well… I suppose I'll have to practise some of my newly learnt platoon commander's skills on you.'

By now their stroll was well underway and the sun was displaying a noticeable warmth as they approached the cliff-top. They paused at the top of the hydraulically operated Victorian cable lift, and gazed with fascination as water gushed from a pump into the open reservoir, which served as one of the counter-weights to slowly and sedately propel passengers up and down between the upper and lower promenades.

As they continued to walk, Thomas remarked on how The Leas and the Folkestone seafront now appeared to be almost totally dominated by the military. There were troops everywhere, and the hotels and houses along the cliff-top all seemed to have been taken over for soldier accommodation.

'It's hardly surprising,' said Amy, 'almost every day up to eight or nine thousand soldiers pass through the town, going to or from France. It's difficult to imagine how this place can ever return to being the genteel holiday resort it used to be.'

'Whatever will be the same again,' remarked Thomas ruefully. 'The town may not be too much changed, if this wretched war ever finishes – but what about all the people? What about ordinary folk like you and I? What chance will there be for us to ever get back to being the people we once were?'

She stopped, turned to face him and took both of his arms in her hands, looking intensely into his eyes. 'We have to have faith in the future, Thomas. In the last seven months I've lost a husband and a brother. I've plumbed the very depths of despair. Now, I have to move on and try and make the best of my future. You must do the same – we must look forward and be positive, otherwise there's no hope left, is there?'

Thomas suddenly regretted the comments he'd made, and said as much to Amy. She was only too pleased to accept his apology, knowing that he had already seen action in France, and dismissed the matter with a kiss on his cheek. They interrupted their stroll again, this time to admire a beautiful stallion being exercised on the Leas by its rider, who was dressed in the uniform of a Canadian cavalry regiment.

'Where on earth do you think he has come from?' asked Thomas.

'Oh, we've got a whole community of Canadians in the town now,' Amy replied, 'they even have their own eye hospital here – well, just over there, in fact.'

'And very welcome the Canadians are, Amy, but as I shall be cheek by jowl with hundreds of other troops crossing the Channel tomorrow, then I really think that you must rescue me from all these uniforms. Isn't it time that you provided me with a diversion now?'

'Of course it is! What about us having some lunch back in town? There's a hotel in Dover Road that runs a really good restaurant, despite all the shortages. Will that be diversion enough for you?'

'You've won me over,' he chuckled, 'and I'm really hungry now after all this sea air. Consider our stroll to be over – march me to this restaurant.'

Twenty minutes later, having retraced their steps back, they paused before turning back into the town where Thomas looked at the latest detachment of soldiers passing by to begin their reluctant descent to the military camp and harbour area below.

Amy grinned at the sombre expression on Thomas' face. 'Now come on, don't pretend to me that you'd rather be with them and spending tonight in one of those awful army doss-houses down behind the sea-front.'

Thomas pretended not to have heard her and gazed fixedly down at the west side of the harbour area which had been converted into one huge military transit camp, with whole blocks of hotels and boarding houses commandeered to house troops shuttling to and fro between Folkestone and France.

But finally he turned, his face brightening as he spoke. 'No you're absolutely right. At this moment there's nowhere else that I'd prefer to be but here with you. Now, let's go and get that lunch we've promised ourselves.'

Chapter 2

Thomas was still trying to put the thought of tomorrow out of his mind as he walked with Amy through the entrance of the York Hotel. Having enjoyed the previous two hours so much, he now hated the thought of his reunion with Amy being cut so short. But he was quickly distracted, by the hotel manageress, who welcomed Amy as though she was a long-lost daughter. They were shown to a quiet corner table and left to peruse the restaurant's menu.

'It may not look very posh in here, but I can certainly vouch for the food,' said Amy, 'the manageress' husband is Italian. He seems to be able to work wonders with meat and two veg.'

'That sounds pretty good to me,' said Thomas, enthusiastically, 'and do you think that you can work your obvious influence here and persuade them to find us a bottle of wine? We really must celebrate our meeting up again after such a long time.'

Five minutes later they had already begun to demolish a bottle of Burgundy and were being served with steaming bowls of fresh vegetable soup.

'So, how does this compare with army food, Lieutenant?' asked Amy teasingly.

He didn't rise to the bait, but simply pointed out how relieved he had been to find that there had been no mention of bully beef and army issue biscuits on the menu.

She laughed, looking at him closely, realising gradually that the man before her now seemed to bear little resemblance to the person she remembered as her old colleague and friend of a few years ago. In truth she had always regarded Thomas as a little arrogant, flippant and, usually, too out-spoken. Now he certainly seemed to have changed and matured into someone very different. Perhaps he was right, she thought. The war itself *was* changing everyone.

'A penny for them, Thomas,' she asked, after he had fallen quiet for several minutes. 'You couldn't stop talking as we walked along the Leas. Now you seem to be miles away. Please come back.'

'I'm really sorry. I didn't mean to appear rude. It's just that sitting here now in such peaceful and agreeable surroundings, and with such pleasant company…well, it just brings it home to me how detached I've become from normal life. It's the same for everyone who has experienced life in the trenches.'

Amy reached over and took his hand. 'You don't need to apologise. I know exactly what you mean, and how it must be for you all over there. I used to be a soldier's wife, remember? So, enjoy this time with me. I'm certainly enjoying my time with you.'

He smiled broadly and squeezed her hand. 'No problems with that – this wine is beginning to go down a treat!'

* * * *

Two hours later they had both eaten well, had emptied their wine bottle, and Thomas was savouring a brandy and reflecting on how interesting Amy looked with a slight flush in her cheeks. His thoughts were then suddenly interrupted by the clock on the dining-room mantelpiece, striking three.

'So, you don't expect your aunt and uncle to be back at their place before tomorrow, then?' Amy asked.

'Unfortunately, no. Things sounded pretty desperate, according to the telephone message from Dover. And there was I, expecting to be shamefully spoilt by my auntie during the last night of my leave.'

'Then you must come back to Capel with me,' said Amy, looking at him earnestly. 'We'll spend the evening together. My cottage is warm and cosy – certainly an improvement on your aunt's empty house.'

'That's a wonderful idea!' said Thomas, already on his feet, and making no pretence of hiding his pleasure. 'And we certainly won't leg it up to Capel, or even bother to try and catch a 'bus. No, we'll do it in style – we'll get a taxi.'

Half an hour later Thomas was helping Amy out of the taxicab and then opening the gate of her cottage garden on the outskirts of the village above Folkestone. In the mid-afternoon sunlight he turned back to admire the fine views over the fields to the cliffs above the English Channel.

'You're some distance from the village centre, then.' he remarked.

'Good heavens, yes, it's the village school that I teach in, remember? It's best not to live right on top of the job.'

But suddenly he was not listening to her. His ear, well schooled in such matters, had detected a very different sound to Amy's voice. He tried to suspend disbelief for a moment - and it was only for a moment - then a mixture of experience and primitive fear instantly reminded him that the sound he was hearing was the unmistakeable pulsating roar of a rapidly approaching, large calibre, high velocity shell.

But nothing could have prepared them for what happened a split second later: the taxi that had fetched them up from the town, and which had barely started on its return journey, so that it was still only a hundred yard away from them, exploded suddenly with a blinding flash and a deafening roar.

Even as he recoiled, and instinctively dropped into a crouch position, pulling Amy down with him, Thomas looked up again, finding himself fascinated by the unmistakeable silhouette of the taxi's back axle spiralling upwards fifty feet or more above the skyline.

For a further few seconds the air space in the middle distance was filled with tangled fragments of metal, pieces of timber and

13

tattered remnants of the vehicle's upholstery. Once the debris had subsided, Thomas and Amy stood there, transfixed, looking across the field to what was now a huge shell crater and a rising plume of black smoke, darkening the afternoon sky. Together they both recoiled as a few isolated clods of earth and scattered stones thudded down into the garden around them.

Then, almost immediately, Thomas picked up the sound of another approaching shell. This time its noise was equally evident in both of his ears – a clear indication to him that the next missile was heading directly towards them.

His next reaction was unequivocally rapid, as his shock, fear and panic were overwhelmed by his instinct for survival. He grabbed Amy's arm and thrust her into the cottage's porch.

'Quickly, Amy, inside! Do you have a cellar?'

She gulped, almost choking as she tried to reply, but could not utter a sound.

Another deafening explosion, this time much closer than the first, shook the cottage around them, blowing in the glass of an adjacent window. This time he snatched at her shoulders, pulling her face towards him: 'Quickly!' he bellowed, 'There's no time to lose, or we're both goners. Do you have a cellar here, or don't you?'

'Y-y…yes,' she stammered, almost frozen with fear, 'through the door in the corner of the kitchen. For God's sake, Thomas, what's happening?'

He didn't hesitate, ignoring her question, but bundled her quickly through the narrow door in the kitchen. There, enveloped in darkness, he felt the handrail to a flight of stairs, and pulled Amy behind him as he descended the stairs into the cellar. Groping for the surfaces of the walls, he pushed her roughly into a corner as yet another explosion shook the walls of the cottage above.

If they were to die in the next shell-burst, Thomas didn't want it to be in pitch darkness. He felt that there was quite enough darkness, of a terminal nature, involved in burial itself. He fumbled in his jacket pocket for his cigarette lighter, and in the light of its flame saw an old oil-lamp on a nearby shelf. He lit the lamp and looked closely at the room around and above him. The cellar had solid chalk walls and a reassuringly sturdy set of roof beams supporting the cottage floor above them. He knew that, excepting for a shell hitting the cottage directly, they should be safe where they were.

Meanwhile, Amy was now beginning to regain some semblance of her earlier composure, but was still visibly shaking. 'In mercy's name,' she said, 'what is happening out there? Those terrible explosions – what is causing them?'

Before Thomas could answer her, two more enormous thumps shook the ceiling beams above them, with the accompanying sound of more breaking glass.

'We're being straddled by a salvo of high explosive shells,' he finally blurted out. 'Don't ask me how or why, but until it stops we must sit tight in here. This is the safest place to be, believe me.'

He pulled her towards him and sat her down on some old cushions piled in a corner of the cellar. She felt his arm around her shoulder, and she snuggled up closely to him, feeling amazed at how decisive and controlled his actions had been in the preceding minute.

'Is this what it's like for you and your comrades in the trenches, Thomas? How on earth can you bear it?' she asked, pressing her head firmly against his breast.

He grinned nervously, immediately thinking again of the recurring nightmare, which had disturbed his sleep again only earlier that morning. 'It can be far worse than this in the trenches, I'm afraid. We rarely have somewhere as secure as this cellar to shelter in.'

A few more minutes passed, and an awesome silence descended upon them. Then, Thomas' acute hearing picked up the sound of very distant and muffled gunfire, this time without any subsequent noise of shells' trajectories or any more local explosions. He waited for another full half hour, for most of which time they sat in almost total quiet. Finally satisfied that the incident was over, he got to his feet, gently pulling free of

15

Amy's hand, which was seemingly welded to the lapel of his jacket.

'Amy,' he said softly, 'the shelling seems to have stopped. The distant gunfire has stopped, too. I want you to stay here now, while I go back upstairs and try to see if it's safe outside.'

'No – please stay down here! You might be killed.'

'It's alright. I really think that the danger is past now,' he said soothingly. 'Believe me, if I think that I hear the merest whisper of another approaching shell, I'll dive straight back down here.'

Swiftly, and without giving her the opportunity to argue with him further, he disappeared up the cellar steps, through the kitchen and out into the cottage garden.

Now, through the fading afternoon light, and far away over the cliff-tops, out over the sea, he could make out the tiny flashes of what could only be naval ordnance. A distant rumbling and then some bigger flashes of light beyond the horizon suggested a ship possibly being struck by shellfire.

He turned away as a different sound took his attention. Two cars were driving slowly along the lane from the village, heading for the cottage. Inevitably they stopped just short of the crater where the taxi had been so comprehensively destroyed less than an hour earlier. Then, several uniformed policemen and two naval officers got out of the cars and began to make their way towards him over the field. He couldn't fail to notice that one of the policemen was carrying a rifle, and that both the naval officers wore holsters containing revolvers.

* * * *

'Who are you please, sir?' Asked the police sergeant.

'My name is Winson, Thomas Winson.'

'And what are you doing in the village, sir? Do you live in this cottage?'

'No, I'm visiting Mrs Nicholls. She lives in this cottage.'

'And where is Mrs Nicholls just now, sir?' said the sergeant looking about him.

'She's still sheltering in the cellar beneath the cottage. We both dived down there when the shelling started.'

By now one of the naval officers had just joined them, and asked Thomas if he was carrying any evidence of identification.

'As a matter of fact I am,' replied Thomas, 'I'm an army subaltern on leave. As it so happens I'm wearing my identity discs. If you'll permit me, I'll reach into my shirt and get them out for you.'

The sergeant nodded his assent and Thomas undid two of his shirt buttons, pulled out his two discs and showed them to the sergeant. One of the naval officers, a commander by rank, then stepped forward and examined the discs, too.

The commander looked closely at the discs and asked: 'What is your regiment?'

'Royal Invicta Regiment.'

'Where were you born?' asked the sergeant.

'Maidstone.'

'What was your mother's maiden name, sir?'

'Ingoldsby.'

The sergeant and the naval commander noted all these facts down. All the while they did so, Thomas was nervously watching the policeman carrying the rifle.

Finally the commander began to speak in a quiet, guarded manner: 'We're not sure exactly what's happened here, Lieutenant, but we think that the shelling must have come from some German raiding ships out in the Channel. Our own ships from the Dover Patrol are pursuing them now.'

'Well,' replied Thomas somewhat dismissively, ' the Germans were way off target if they were trying to attack the harbour.'

The second naval officer now joined the conversation: 'They were certainly off their target. But we don't believe they were firing at Folkestone. We suspect they were firing into Capel to try and knock out our airship sheds on the other side of the village.'

'Of course!' exclaimed Thomas, cursing his own stupidity. 'The airships! I'd forgotten that they were based near here. It didn't enter my head that the shells were being targeted on them.'

'Well, that's the theory we're working on so far,' said the commander. 'The Germans have long been aware that the airships provide us with our best means of spotting any enemy submarines in the seas either side of our blockade of the Dover Straits.'

They were then interrupted by the police sergeant, who still clearly regarded Thomas with very thinly veiled suspicion: 'So, are you on leave at the moment or what, sir?'

'Yes, I'm just at the end of a spell of leave now. I'm due to report to the harbour tomorrow. I'll probably be embarking for France by the evening.'

'That's as maybe, Lieutenant. Firstly, one of my men has gone back toward the village to find a telephone. We must check on your identity with the army authorities before you can leave here. In the meantime you were saying that there is a young lady in the cottage with you?'

'That's right. Mrs Nicholls is a teacher up at the village school. She's still sheltering in the cellar of the cottage. She must be wondering where I've got to, actually. Can we go in and reassure her?'

'One of my men will attend to that, sir,' said the sergeant, turning to another of his men and whispering instructions to him. 'Meanwhile I'd like you to remain here with me.'

By now the two naval officers had explained to the sergeant that they were going to walk up the lane to the village, and then on to the airship sheds. They moved off, while the sergeant instructed another police constable to go into the field and examine the nearest shell crater.

At this point Thomas realised that he had completely omitted to acquaint the sergeant with the fate of the taxi-driver: 'Sergeant, you need to know that Mrs Nicholls and I were brought up from Folkestone by a taxi earlier this afternoon. The taxi received a direct hit from the first shell, just after it had started its journey back to town. It was blown to pieces, and the driver with it. You'll find nothing of that poor devil's body that won't fit into a couple of sandbags. I'm sorry, but that's the way it is. I've had enough

18

first-hand experience of the effects of shell-fire to know what I'm talking about.'

The sergeant paused and searched Thomas' face long and hard, trying to discern the signs of acute distress, which he believed should be clearly evident.

Instead, all he felt that he could make out there was an impassive, war-weary familiarity with sudden and violent death. He concluded that the facial expression he was looking upon was common among veterans of the trench warfare in France. It was what made soldiers strangers to anyone who had never experienced such terrors, and who knew only of their own peacetime existences.

'Thank you for that information, sir. Alright, Constable, you heard what the Lieutenant said. You'd better get that field cordoned off. I'll send for more men presently, and we'll make a systematic search for the driver's remains.'

He turned again to Thomas, gesturing towards the cottage's open door: 'Come along then. Let's join Mrs Nicholls inside.'

Chapter 3

Thomas and the police sergeant entered the cottage to find that Amy had already emerged from the cellar and was busy lighting a fire in the kitchen range. However, before either she or Thomas could say anything to each other, the sergeant began to question her.

'May I ask your name, ma'am?'

Amy turned, looking quizzically at Thomas, who appeared discomforted, but who nodded reassuringly to her. His own experience with the sergeant outside had made it fairly clear to him that both he and Amy were under some suspicion for the fact that they had happened to be literally on the spot where the German shells had fallen. The sergeant was now bent on satisfying himself with regard to the full situation at the cottage. Until he had, Thomas and Amy would remain suspected as possible collaborators – as the means by which the enemy had targeted Capel village.

'My name is Nicholls, Amy Nicholls,' she replied. 'I live in this cottage and I teach at the school here in the village.'

'Do you live here alone, Mrs Nicholls?' said the sergeant, his eyes now resting on Amy's wedding ring finger.

'Yes I do. My husband was killed in France last year.'

'I'm very sorry to hear that Ma'am, and I regret having to ask you this, but will you show me your resident's permit, please? It is necessary for me to establish your identity and your right to be living in this village.'

Amy hesitated, and turned back toward Thomas, looking at him pleadingly.

'Amy, don't be alarmed,' said Thomas reassuringly, 'the sergeant here came up to the village with two naval officers. They think that the shellfire might have come from some German ships carrying out a surprise raid from across the Channel. It's possible that the shells were being aimed at the village to try and hit the airship base.'

'Well, if that's the case, then where in God's name was the Royal Navy?' snorted Amy angrily. 'I thought that our own patrol ships had made the English Channel safe by now.'

'I can't help but share your sentiments, Mrs Nicholls,' replied the sergeant. 'I'm sure that the Admiralty will be facing some very awkward questions by this evening. But the fact is that my own priority now is to satisfy my superiors regarding the general security up here in Capel. If you would cooperate with me, then, as soon as I'm satisfied that you are who you say you are, I can leave you and your friend in peace.'

'Of course, Sergeant,' she replied in a far more conciliatory tone, 'please bear with me for a moment.'

She turned away and opened a small drawer in a Welsh dresser just behind her. After a few seconds' searching, she turned back and handed her resident's permit to the sergeant. He examined the document closely then handed it back to her.

'That appears to be fine, Mrs Nicholls, thank you.'

'Incidentally, Sergeant, Lieutenant Winson here is a very old friend and colleague of mine. He used to work with my husband and me in Maidstone before the war.'

At last the sergeant's face softened, and he smiled kindly at them both.

'I'm very glad that Mr Winson was here with you during that shelling, Mrs Nicholls. It must have been terrifying for you. Sadly, the lieutenant's had more experience of such things, but I only wish he'd been spared such a shock on the last day of his leave. Let's hope he has a quieter time when he gets back to France. Now, in the meantime, I think that you good folk should have a strong cup of tea and a relaxing sit down. As for me – I'll make myself scarce.'

As the sergeant left the kitchen he paused briefly, then turned and shook Thomas' hand firmly. 'Good luck with your crossing tomorrow, sir. I'm sure that the Dover Straits will be quite safe again before this evening is over. The Royal Navy won't get caught napping like this again, I'll be bound.'

Thomas saw him as far as the garden gate and waved him off. By the time that he had got back into the cottage, Amy had two steaming mugs of tea on the kitchen table.

* * * *

She stood in front of him, looking pale and drained. Thomas took her in his arms, pulled her close and held her tightly against him.

'I'm not sure what upset me more, the shelling or the police sergeant's questions,' sobbed Amy gently, trying hard to smile through the tears, which he could feel dripping warmly on to his shirt.

'He had a difficult job to do,' said Thomas. 'The police and the navy have to convince themselves that the German ships had no help from within the village community.'

'I suppose you're right. Does this mean that the rest of the village will now be under suspicion?'

'Possibly, for a while, at least. The police will probably carry out further questioning, and make a particular check of any properties nearer the cliff-top. I suppose it's just possible that someone could have been signalling the Germans from near here.'

'That's a horrible thought,' said Amy, 'it's difficult to imagine there being a spy in Capel.'

'There almost certainly isn't,' said Thomas, smiling to reassure her, 'but better safe than sorry. Anyway, our own bona fides have been established. I can't imagine us being bothered by the police again this evening.'

Amy stepped back and then gently pushed him into an armchair. She shook her head, then knelt beside him, saying:

'Oh, dear, I'm so desperately sorry that I invited you back here. You should be back at your aunt's place and relaxing before your big day tomorrow.'

'Amy, Amy, don't be daft. The really important thing is the fact that we are both alive and well. None of those German shells had our names written on them. I'm just glad that I was here with you when it all happened. Had you been here alone, you might have run off in any random direction, which could have put you straight under another falling shell. To be shelled at any time is a terrifying experience. To be shelled for the first time is worst of all. Now, would you like me to stay here with you until morning? I'll gladly do that if it will put your mind more at ease. I'm not due to report to the harbour until late afternoon.'

'Oh, will you stay, please?' she said, beaming at him. 'I can't face the thought of being on my own here tonight. If you're sure that you can stay, I'd really appreciate it. So, if you can go and light a fire in the parlour, I'll make a start on getting some food for us. I don't know about you but, and despite that lunch today, I'm famished!'

Two more hours later found them both curled up in front of the parlour hearth, gazing into the flames of a log-fire.

'That supper was scrumptious, Amy. I had no idea that you were such a talented cook.'

'Flattery will get you everywhere, Lieutenant,' she replied with a chuckle, 'now, how would you like a glass of brandy as a night-cap?'

She quickly produced a bottle and glasses and poured them both a generous measure.

'Tell me, Thomas, do you have any idea where you'll be sent when you get to France tomorrow?'

'None whatsoever, and even if I did, well, I couldn't tell you, could I?'

'Oh I see,' she muttered, 'I'm being cast as the local spy again, am I?'

He laughed, and sipped his brandy before retorting:

'No, seriously, I've been away from the battlefields for some months now. I may even find myself posted to another regiment. The loss of officers since the Somme offensive started last summer has been so huge that replacement subalterns like me can be deployed almost anywhere. I'll just have to wait and see what my orders are when I reach Boulogne tomorrow.'

He suddenly saw that Amy's face had clouded over. He instantly regretted his reference to the Somme. He had clearly opened up old wounds for her.

'How awful it is for us all,' she said finally. 'You know this war horrifies me. I see so much wretchedness among the children at school. I don't think that there can be one family in the village that hasn't suffered some form of loss.'

He drained his glass, snuggled up closely to her and then whispered:

'Amy, I don't want to think about the war tonight, and I certainly don't want to talk about it. For me, this reunion is something really special that I want to lock into my memory and take with me when I leave here tomorrow.'

She didn't answer, but turned and looked him directly in the eyes. Slowly she touched his cheek with her fingers, and gently put her lips to his.

He was in sudden awe at the sense of relaxation he felt. He responded slowly but enthusiastically to her kiss. Then she recoiled slightly, and looked downwards.

He realised that the spell had been broken and quietly said:

'I'm sorry. You must think that I'm taking advantage of this situation. Your terror at that shelling, then the relief at being safe, then the police sergeant, now this brandy, and…and… I know how you must still be feeling. It's memories of Edward, isn't it? This is too soon; he's still too close to both of us. I'm sorry – forgive me, please.'

But even as he had been speaking, Amy had slowly got up from the settle, and when she spoke again there was a controlled, determined tone in her voice: 'No, you're mistaken, Thomas. This isn't remotely wrong. Edward isn't too close. I loved him dearly, but he's been gone these many, many months. What almost happened to us this afternoon makes me realise how precious life is. You and I both still have our lives, and God knows they've been brought together today in extraordinary circumstances. No, that kiss we shared wasn't remotely wrong. Any thoughts of conscience, or recrimination on your part, or mine, are misplaced – totally misplaced.

'Now,' she went on, 'there's just one thing I'm certain of: after today's events, neither you nor I can know what tomorrow might bring. I believe that you and I should grasp what little pleasure and comfort that we can from each other. To be honest and direct, I'm sure that we must do that without any further hesitation.'

She kissed him again on the cheek, then whispered in his ear: 'Frankly, I really think that we should go to bed. Give me five minutes, then come to my bedroom.' She turned and smiled at him with an engaging mischievousness: 'And, incidentally, don't bother to knock at my door.'

* * * *

He paused for several minutes after Amy had gone to her room. Despite her very clear and open invitation to join her, he found that his emotions were very mixed. Her husband Edward had been one of his closest friends. The fact that Thomas had been best man at Amy and Edward's wedding a few years earlier also made him somewhat ill at ease. But, nonetheless, fate had taken a decisive hand that day, and Amy's words about the sheer transience of life still echoed in his ears. As a new subaltern, his chances of survival in the trenches would be slender indeed. What future chance might he have to enjoy a little happiness – especially with such a desirable woman as the one waiting for him at that moment?

In all truth he knew that he really would soon join Amy in her bed. He felt spellbound by her single-mindedness of purpose. He was, after all, only flesh and blood. He saw no point in arguing the matter any further. So he turned to the hearth, raked over the embers of the now dying fire and then went into the kitchen.

Here he poured himself some hot water, quickly stripped to his underwear and washed hurriedly, at the same time managing to shed any further troublesome thoughts of misplaced moral uncertainties. Amy had left her bedroom door slightly ajar, and he entered the room quietly. The oil-lamp beside the bed had already been dimmed. Only Amy's face showed above the bedcovers. Thomas looked down momentarily before slipping gently into her bed. Neither of them made any attempt to speak. He reached across to her, rather falteringly, and instantly touched her naked body. He did his best to counter his nervousness: 'I'm afraid that you are improperly dressed, Ma'am.'

'Really, Lieutenant,' she replied winsomely, 'does this mean that you're going to put me on a charge?'

But before he could even begin to think how he might answer, he felt Amy's body suddenly pivot in the bed, her hands pushing his shoulders back as her thigh swung over his hip, so that he found himself straddled beneath her.

'This has been an unforgettable day, Thomas,' she whispered in his ear, as her breasts caressed his face, 'now I want us both to have a truly memorable night. As far as I'm concerned, the whole bloody German navy can come back and do its worst. I'm past caring about anything except keeping you in my arms and loving you as though there's absolutely no tomorrow.'

He didn't utter a word but, as Amy gazed down at him, she decided that the expression on his face reminded her of that once seen on the face of her parents' Siamese cat many years earlier, after it had crept into their kitchen and devoured half a pint of double cream.

Now Thomas's own lips made to stir again, but his utterances were instantly silenced as Amy smothered his face with a barrage of tender and long-sustained kisses.

Chapter 4

The next morning Thomas woke from a sleep that had been mercifully free of nightmares. His slumbers seemed to have obliterated all thoughts of the war from his mind. Astonishingly, even the trauma of the previous afternoon had not disturbed his rest.

But the night with Amy had been far from uneventful, and his mind roamed gently back over other details of their night together. They had wanted to leave the bedside lamp burning and, after the initial haste of the first lovemaking, they had later embarked on more measured and blissful episodes. He had made them both cups of tea just before dawn and, as the sun started to come up, they had spoken tender words before gently drifting back to sleep again.

Now Amy was beginning to stir, too. She lay, almost motionless, but with her toes softly caressing his leg. Her tongue traced patterns on his chest. She had realised that night that Thomas had displayed what she found to be intense sensual inclinations. She remembered how she had gasped, as his tongue had lapped at her breasts and thighs, and the acute pleasure she had experienced as his fingers etched patterns on her hips, arms and neck. Her mind raced, too, at the thought of his tongue sliding subtly into her ear, and she marvelled at the ecstasy she had experienced when his lips had pulsed over her nipples.

Then suddenly, she realised that he was slipping out of the bed and making towards the parlour.

'What time is it? Do we really have to get up just yet?' she asked, groaning gently.

'It's past nine o'clock. I heard voices outside in the lane. It could be the police again, I suppose. You stay where you are. I'll go outside and see what's going on.' He returned a few minutes later, sat down on the bed, bent down and kissed her once more. The expression on Amy's face spoke volumes.

'My god, Thomas, have you any idea how you made me feel last night?'

'Last night was wonderful for me, Amy. Perhaps I'll try and explain just how wonderful a little later on. But for the moment, I was right about the police - they're back, and they seem to be accompanied by a detachment of troops. They've probably brought them up here as a working party to fill in the shell craters and clear away the debris from yesterday. I imagine that both the police and the military authorities will want to restore normality to the village as quickly as possible. They'll need to reassure the locals, and close the incident as soon as possible. Now, I'd better get some clothes on in case we have any more callers.'

By ten o'clock Thomas had the kitchen range piping hot again and another good fire burning in the parlour. He'd washed and dressed and was just about to forage for some food in the kitchen larder, when he heard knocking at the front door.

He opened it to see the inquisitive looking face of a middle-aged man, who was wearing gumboots, corduroy trousers, a heavy brown overcoat and tweed cap. The stranger looked Thomas up and down, but did not have time to speak before Amy appeared in her dressing gown.

'Why, Mr Aston!' she said, not attempting to mask her surprise. 'I'm glad to see you safe and well – and your wife and family, too, I hope?'

'We're all safe and sound, thank you, Amy. Mercifully, there's no sign of any damage up in the village, and no reports of any other casualties. Everyone's shocked by the dreadful death of that poor taxi driver. It could so easily have been you, too.

Apparently, according to the police, all the shells fell close to your cottage.'

'Thomas,' said Amy, turning to him, 'I must introduce you. This is John Aston, our head teacher at the school. Mr Aston, this is an old friend of mine, Thomas Winson. We met up by chance down in Folkestone yesterday morning. It was the poor man who drove us up here who was killed yesterday. Thomas and I had only got out of the taxi a few moments earlier.'

'Yes, I know,' replied Aston, 'my wife and I were terrified for you when we heard all the explosions coming from this direction. I tried to get down here but was overtaken by a police car soon after setting out from the schoolhouse. Fortunately, within a short while one of the policemen came back up to the village to use our telephone. He explained that you were unharmed and that you had someone here with you.'

Aston then turned to address Thomas: 'I'm very glad to meet you. The policeman told me that you were a soldier. It was so lucky for Amy that you were here with her. It must have given her a great deal of reassurance. Now, is there anything I can do for the two of you?'

'We're both fine, thank you,' answered Amy, 'but I do have two small windows broken. It was the blast from the shells. Oh, yes, and a few cracks in the wall-plaster, but as far as we are concerned – not a scratch on either of us. We've been incredibly lucky. But I'm forgetting my manners. Won't you come in for a cup of tea?'

'Thank you, but no,' said Aston. 'The police and navy have taken over the school assembly room while they sort out yesterday's mess, and I really think that I should stay close at hand to them. On my way back I'll tell Cooper the builder about your broken windows. I'm sure he can do some sort of emergency repair for you today.' He turned to go, but then spoke again to Thomas: 'How long will you be staying here, Lieutenant?'

'That's a problem which I hadn't got around to thinking about yet,' said Thomas with a smile. 'I really have to be down at the harbour to report for embarkation by mid-afternoon. In the present circumstances I doubt that I'll be able to persuade another taxi-driver to come up here today and take me back into town.'

Aston paused for a few moments; then he took out his pocket watch, looking at it thoughtfully. 'I'm sure that I can help you with that,' he said finally. 'Unless the police up at the school raise any objection, I'll take you down to Folkestone in my car. I can be there and back again in an hour or so.' He looked once more at his watch. 'It's almost half ten now. Give me until noon and then walk up to the school house.'

'That's extremely kind,' said Thomas, and Amy was already beaming her approval.

As Aston began his walk back up the lane, Amy and Thomas went into the cottage, where she immediately began to fry some bacon and eggs for their breakfast.

They both ate heartily, but there seemed to be little scope for conversation. Both their minds were still too preoccupied by the heady events of the previous day and the after effects of their amorous adventures of only a few hours previously.

Certainly they seemed to share a tacit agreement that there should be no speculation regarding how or when they might see each other again. Less than an hour later, Thomas kissed Amy once more, pulled on his jacket, left the cottage and began the half-mile walk up to the village schoolhouse.

*   *   *   *

Aston was already waiting for him in the road outside the house. He was checking the oil and water levels in the open engine compartment of what Thomas instinctively recognised as an unusually handsome and very sporting looking motor-car.

'You approve of the transport, Lieutenant?' said Aston with a knowing smile, 'And I suppose you're wondering what right a humble village schoolmaster has to own such a splendid beast as this?'

Thomas was by now already walking around the motor, running his fingers admiringly over the gleaming red coachwork and green leather upholstery. 'None of my business, is it?' he said politely. 'Anyway, I'll be perfectly happy to have a ride in her. I never realised that Vauxhalls came as grand as this.'

'Neither did I until a couple of years ago when an old uncle of mine died suddenly. He'd made a fortune in the coal trade. I was surprised and delighted when his widow contacted me and explained that I'd been left the car in his will. Anyway, for your information, it's a 1913 Prince Henry sports car,' said Aston proudly. 'It has a four cylinder, four litre, water-cooled engine. There are four forward speeds, shaft drive, and the suspension boasts semi-elliptic springs at both front and rear.'

'And does it play "Rule Britannia", too?' said Thomas with a laugh.

'Not yet, but I live in hopes. Now, come on, jump in. There's no luggage for us to worry about, then?'

'No, I didn't expect to be spending last night up here. Come to that, I didn't expect Jerry's shells to be searching me out so far from the Somme.'

'It was a devil of a shock for all of us,' muttered Aston with a shake of his head. 'Mind you, in your case it was a very bitter irony that your leave should end as it did. Perhaps it means that you'll have a quieter time when you do get back to France.'

'I doubt that, somehow,' observed Thomas ruefully, as he climbed into the front passenger seat of the Prince Henry, 'but as far as today is concerned, I'm just hoping that the sea crossing is uneventful.'

'Are you worried that the German ships which shelled us might still be on the loose somewhere in the Straits?'

'Not really, I'm sure that our navy is taking all necessary precautions after yesterday. No, it just isn't much fun being on a crowded troopship.'

His companion nodded sympathetically, started the car's engine and drove away from the schoolhouse, heading for the Folkestone Road.

'Tell me,' he said, 'how did you come to know Amy?'

'It doesn't still show, then?' said Thomas with a broad grin.

'I'm another schoolteacher. I taught in the same school as Amy and her husband before the war.'

'Ah, I see,' replied Aston, 'damned shame about her husband. I never knew him, of course. Meeting you again yesterday must have been a bitter-sweet experience for Amy. I gather it was just a chance meeting, she said?'

'That's right. I'd no idea, even, that Amy had moved down to this area from Maidstone. I was actually finishing my leave with a weekend visit to some relatives in the town. I was doing some last minute shopping yesterday morning when I caught sight of her as I came out of a draper's shop. We had a very pleasant lunch together and then came back to Capel. No sooner had we turned our backs on the taxi, than the barrage started and the first shell fell directly on it. As I later said to Amy, clearly the shell didn't have our names on it.'

Ten minutes further driving brought them into the town, and presently Thomas found himself on the pavement outside his aunt's house. He shook Aston's hand: 'You've been more than kind. I really do appreciate this – and it was a special pleasure to ride in such style!'

'The pleasure was all mine. Good luck with your crossing this afternoon. Perhaps we'll see you again up in the village when you get your next leave. I hope so. Goodbye now.'

With a flourish of his gloved hand, and a roar from the car's exhaust, Aston drove off, leaving Thomas to open the door of his aunt's still empty villa.

Back inside the house he stripped his clothes off, washed and shaved, put on his officer's uniform and carefully packed his valise. Finally, he made himself a strong cup of tea and found some bread and cheese for a snack lunch. After this, and realising that what little time left of his leave was now rapidly ebbing away, he began to scribble an explanatory note for his aunt. No sooner had he put pencil to paper, than the telephone began to ring.

'Hello, Thomas?' He heard his aunt's voice.

'Yes, it's me. I'm still here, Auntie. How are things in Dover?'

'Very bleak, I'm afraid. The hospital has kept Eleanor on the danger list. The rest of the family is in a terrible state. Thomas, we've no choice but to stay over here. I'm so dreadfully sorry about the weekend, and that we won't be there to see you off this afternoon.'

'You really mustn't worry about me,' said Thomas soothingly. 'I'm all packed up and ready to go. You must stay on where you are most needed. I shall be sure to see you again when I get my next leave.'

There was a long pause, and then he heard her muffled sobbing at the other end of the line. Finally he heard her ring off.

He put the telephone down, slowly shaking his head. He screwed up his piece of notepaper and threw it into a wastepaper basket. Finally he placed the house key on the mantle piece, pulled on his greatcoat, picked up his valise and set off on his ten-minute walk down to the harbour.

Chapter 5

The air-cooled engines of the airship roared angrily as the craft accelerated into its ascent just north of the town.

Thomas paused for a moment and looked up at the airship clearing the cliff-top and heading out to sea, where it would soon begin its search for any other enemy shipping that dared to approach the Dover Straits in broad daylight.

As he continued his journey he pondered over yesterday's dramatic events and, in particular, how different things might have been had the German Navy's guns been more accurately ranged on the giant sheds which formed the airships' lair at Capel.

He knew only too well that in daylight hours the airships' main task, apart from observing surface-borne shipping, was to keep a special watch for the tell tale wakes left by the periscopes of German submarines.

Thomas, together with all his comrades in arms, was keenly aware that if the enemy submarines enjoyed freer rein of the Straits, then the British ability to maintain its armies in France and Belgium would quickly be compromised. He therefore took corresponding comfort from the flight of this first airship, and was even more reassured when a second one emerged from behind the cliff-tops and set off on another course in the direction of the Belgian coast.

Today, compared with his previous Channel crossings, he also noted that there appeared to be a much higher number of Dover

Patrol vessels manoeuvring off Folkestone. Apart from several Royal Navy destroyers, he could see two French torpedo boats scurrying to and fro just outside the harbour entrance. Clearly some hard lessons had been learned the previous day.

Increased military guard presence was also very evident as he approached the entrance to the harbour's transit camp. He later found himself stopped not once but three times as he joined queues of other officers and men all converging on the embarkation area of the camp.

At one point he was called out to one side and subjected to a body search, and later required to look on as his neatly packed valise was opened and emptied, and the contents comprehensively checked by a navy petty officer and two ratings standing behind a trestle table.

Then Thomas felt a hand on his shoulder. He turned and recognised the smiling face of one of the two naval officers who had been in the police car near Amy's cottage the previous afternoon.

'So, we meet again then, Lieutenant. You still have enough faith in His Majesty's Navy to take another sea trip this evening, then?'

Thomas grinned, and took the other's outstretched hand. 'I've little choice in the matter. But I hope that any confidence I have in the Navy won't be misplaced. It's certainly very obvious that both the army and the navy are very much on their toes today.'

'Exactly so, the airships are still flying, and the Dover Straits are like Piccadilly Circus. Also there are more allied ships on patrol today than you've had hot dinners.'

'Hot dinners are hard to come by in the trenches, Commander.'

'Touché, Lieutenant. I really must choose my phrases more carefully where you army types are concerned. But look, I'm due a short break here. Let's get a hot drink together before you have to find your boat.'

'Fine. A cup of tea and a sandwich may help my sea legs. I'm not the best of sailors when a troopship starts to roll.'

They were soon settled at a table in a nearby mess hall where a small army of women of all ages plied their customers with mugs of steaming tea, and piles of sandwiches and buns.

'My first name's Thomas, by the way.'

'Oh, I already know that. I had to do some further homework on you after my visit to Capel yesterday. You're newly gazetted as a subaltern, and freshly arrived from Crowborough Camp. Your home used to be in Maidstone and your mother's maiden name was Ingoldsby. Do I need to go on?'

He waved Thomas' attempted reply away with an engaging smile.

'I'm Lieutenant Commander Mockett. You can call me Simon.'

Thomas, although initially disarmed to hear his own brief biographic details trotted out, was glad to shake his new companion's hand for a second time. He also carried out a snap retaliatory assessment of the man facing him: Navy regular, age about thirty, mercurial personality, easy but decisive manner with strangers.

'Am I allowed to ask what else you discovered about yesterday's incident up in Capel?' Thomas said.

'Yes, you can ask. But to be perfectly honest there isn't much more I can tell you. The shelling was definitely carried out by six German warships, which had apparently launched a sudden raid of opportunity. They were undoubtedly after the airship hangars, but because of the undulating terrain behind the cliff tops, they were basically shooting blind. Our own destroyers pursued the raiders back across the Channel and we actually sank two of them. I very much doubt the Germans will try the same trick a second time. On our part, you can rest assured that there'll be no further complacency in the Channel.' He paused for a moment, before adding: 'Oh yes, and we are as satisfied as we can be that Jerry had received no help from anyone in the village itself. The police however are still investigating. I understand that there is going to be much more strenuous watch keeping from the coastal strip after yesterday's little shock. There are to be more cliff-top lookout posts set up, and extra aerial reconnaissance by aircraft flying from Walmer, just along the coast. You'll find, I think, that the navy's air service will now work more closely with the Royal Flying Corps. God knows, we're all fighting the same war.'

'So you think my friend Mrs. Nicholls can now feel safe in Capel?'

'I'm sure you needn't worry on that account. She's recovered from the shock, I hope?'

'Oh yes, she recovered very quickly, thanks.' He looked at his watch and stood up. 'Simon, I'm sorry, but I must make a move. I have to look in on the embarkation office, to find out what I have to do when I arrive in Boulogne this evening. I'm really glad that we met again today.'

They exchanged friendly salutes, and Thomas turned and hurried away to find out what his initial movements would be once he was back in France.

* * * *

The embarkation officer, a major wearing the Africa Star, looked intently at him and then down at a scribbled message on a notepad. 'I see you managed to get caught up in that business near the airship base yesterday. What exactly were you doing up there?'

'I was visiting an old friend of mine. We met by chance in Folkestone, earlier in the day.'

The major stroked his chin pensively. 'Well, it seems the pair of you had a very narrow escape. I'm glad you're unhurt, though. I hope your luck holds out in France.'

He shuffled some typed lists and ran his finger down one of the pages. 'Ah, yes…Winson, Thomas. Invictas. You're down to sail on a fast paddle steamer. I don't know if any other Invicta officers will be crossing with you, but there is a corporal and two sections of men from your regiment travelling on your ship. Which battalion were you with as an NCO, incidentally?'

'I was with the Seventh. But I've already assumed that once I'm in France I might be sent almost anywhere.'

'Yes, perhaps even a different regiment. You'll just have to wait and see. Anyway, the corporal and men I referred to are replacements for the Sixth Battalion Invictas. They should be on the dockside by now. You'd better move off. The boat sails in an hour. Number four Dock. When you get to Boulogne find the landings officer. He'll advise you on your next movement.'

Dusk was falling rapidly by the time he arrived at the dockside. From what he could see, the paddle steamer looked pathetically small, but he never underestimated transport officers' talents for cramming countless numbers of men onto such craft.

Eventually he spotted the familiar Invicta cap badges worn by a group of men who were by now moving slowly towards the steamer's forward gangplank. Having recognised no other familiar uniforms, he decided to introduce himself to the corporal who was accompanying the twenty or more infantrymen.

In the twelve months of his army service Thomas had developed a strong dislike of the social chasm that still stubbornly persisted between the British officer class and the army's rank and file.

He did not believe that for officers and men to be regarded as different species was functional to the successful waging of modern warfare. He realised, however, that the lines of social class had been so very rigidly drawn before 1914 that it would take superhuman efforts, coupled with appalling attrition levels in the trenches, to effect any real change.

For the moment, a mere glance at the replacement men in the corporal's charge brought it home to him just how fundamental the results of the attrition had been. "Men", in fact, was a misnomer. These new soldiers were boys: most of them looked to be still short of their nineteenth birthday – victims of the national conscription programme introduced the previous year, which had already resulted in many youngsters receiving call up papers on the very day they reached eighteen years of age.

But by now, the corporal had turned and noticed Thomas' own Invicta badge. He saluted and said: 'Welcome aboard, sir. I'm Corporal Jenkins. We're part of the Sixth Battalion.'

* * * *

By now the darkness was finally closing in, and the last of the vessel's mooring lines were released. Then, with a variety of noises, vibrations and finally some ironic cheers from a few of the men, the paddle steamer moved ponderously aft and, aided by two tugboats, slowly moved away from the quay to clear the harbour and begin the first leg of the cross-channel journey.

The ship's enormous engine-room took up so much space that there was little scope for any accommodation below deck. Not that many men, even if the opportunity had presented itself, would have risked leaving the vessel's topsides. The troops were very tightly packed onto the ship's upper decks, and their bulky lifejackets, together with all their military kit and weapons would have allowed for little mobility even if some circulation space had been available. These factors, coupled with the men's natural anxiety about possible further German infiltration of the Channel that night, meant that for almost all the soldiers onboard, the three hour crossing would be an uncomfortable and static affair, but a journey at least completed from a position where, if escape from the ship became necessary, it would still be possible. The sheltered bowels of the steamer, especially in the hours of darkness during which troop carriers crossed the Dover Straits, held no attraction for anyone, Thomas included.

By now Folkestone had disappeared. Everyone aboard the ship found themselves both mesmerised and comforted by the circling gleam of searchlights on accompanying destroyers, and the three French torpedo boats making up a small convoy for the crossing.

Thomas now found himself wedged in a standing position between the handrail of an open companionway on one side and Corporal Jenkins on the other. Several of the other men in Jenkins' group were sitting opposite them, huddled together on the raised edge of a closed deck hatch.

'I take it these men are all recent conscripts, Corporal?'

'That's right, sir. It's their first taste of active service. Most of them were called up last autumn. They finished training last week, had a few days leave and soon they'll be in the thick of it, replacing some of the poor sods we lost on the Somme.'

Thomas looked at the corporal's profile, which was now emerging as breaks in the cloud allowed some moonlight to illuminate a now increasingly choppy sea. He took the man to be about his own age. 'Not your first visit to France, of course.'

Jenkins shook his head whimsically, reflected for a moment and then turned to speak to him in an almost conspiratorial way, as though suggesting that he didn't want the younger men opposite to hear him. 'Far from it. I was one of the idealistic fools who actually volunteered for this mess in 1914. I'm a lot older and wiser now, and very cynical into the bargain.' He paused before adding: 'I'm sorry, sir. My disillusionment always peaks when I finish a leave and have to say goodbye to my wife and daughter again.'

'I think our conversation is sufficiently private for you to drop the "sir." So what were you doing in civilian life, before your idealism got the better of you?'

'I qualified in Art and Design. I was a junior lecturer at the art college in Rochester, and just beginning to get some commissions as a book illustrator.'

'I'm surprised you haven't taken a commission in the army yet.'

'Are you, now?' said Jenkins, with a bitter edge to his voice. 'Perhaps you aren't married with a young family. For myself, I decided early on in this war that the better chances of survival went with those who didn't go over the top of a trench in a collar and tie, with pips on their shoulders, a Sam Browne belt, and waving a pistol at an enemy who came out of thirty foot deep dugouts, carrying lots of heavy machine guns.' He turned away for a moment, quickly regained his composure and smiled again. 'I'm sorry. No offence intended.'

'None taken,' said Thomas good-naturedly, 'I was a corporal myself until last October. I can fully appreciate your point of view. Certainly I, too, weighed up the ifs and buts before agreeing to train as an officer. At the end of the day, and I don't want to seem arrogant, I was attracted by the challenge of leadership.' He looked across at the young soldiers in front of them. 'Don't you think these youngsters are worth leading – perhaps a little better than has been managed so far?'

Jenkins moved closer to him and lowered his voice still further: 'I'll be totally honest with you. My position hasn't been as simple as I've perhaps led you to think. It's perfectly true that I'm selfish enough to want to survive this war and get back to my family, who doesn't? But there's more to it than that. Two years ago, soon after I got my first stripe, and when we were in reserve behind the line, I found myself sitting in a tent with five other NCOs, all of them strangers to me. It was half an hour before dawn, and we'd been told to have our rifles with us.

'Then a captain came into the tent with a regimental sergeant major who told us that we were to make up the firing squad for the execution of a soldier who'd been tried and convicted of cowardice. He was to be shot that dawn.' Jenkins shook his head hopelessly and stared wildly, straight into Thomas' eyes.

'I'll never forget those next few minutes as the sun started to come up and we paraded in front of a high wall somewhere. The youngster they brought out to tie to the post was sobbing like a baby and begging us not to shoot him. His legs were shaking so much they had to bind him limb and torso to that post.' He sighed heavily, shaking his head again.

'I'll tell you this, Mr Winson: I've seen more death and mutilation since that day than I ever thought possible, but the one enduring image I can never get out of my mind is of that wretched, gibbering boy who we were forced to shoot like a dog. You asked me why I hadn't tried for a commission. Alright, let me tell you. If there ever was one defining moment when I decided that I never wanted to be an officer, then it was when the captain in charge of us that day walked round from behind us after we lowered our rifles, took out his pistol and put a final bullet in that poor lad's head.'

Thomas looked away, feeling that any reply he made now could only trivialise the moment. Instead, he looked quickly about him to make sure they were not observed, reached out discreetly with his left hand, and squeezed Jenkins right forearm. Then he turned away, seeking a lighter interlude with the conscripts a few feet opposite.

One of them, he noticed, was looking a little pale, and might benefit from a little conversational distraction.

'What's your name, soldier?' Thomas asked.

The youngster looked up, somewhat nervously. 'Hughes, sir.'

'How old are you?'

'Eighteen last August, sir.'

'Ever been to France before?'

'No, sir. I've never left the country before.'

'So, where's your home, Hughes?'

'Sheerness, sir - Bluetown. Near the dockyard.'

'Yes, I know it. I used to do some sailing on the Medway before the war. We would often moor up off Queenborough, if we were making a weekend of it. What did you do in Civvy Street, before the army grabbed you?'

'I was a driver, sir. Cars, lorries, sometimes charabancs.' Hughes suddenly smiled proudly. 'I got my driving licence when I was fourteen years old.'

Thomas smiled back at him, delighted to find that the lad was beginning to relax.

'Well, good for you. But I'm surprised they haven't sent you to a transport depot somewhere.'

'They've trained me as a Lewis gunner instead. I did well at gunnery school.'

'Well, you be sure to keep your head down once you get into those trenches, Hughes. Glad to have met you.'

'Yes, sir. Thank you, sir.'

Thomas turned away. By now the troop ship had been in transit for over two hours. He was feeling stiff and cold and decided that, despite the cramped conditions on deck, he would have to stretch his legs.

He managed to work his way through to a handrail on the port side, just aft of the steamer's paddle housing. The sea was very lumpy by now and the vessel was beginning to roll quite badly. One or two of the men near him were leaning over the rail and retching noisily, much to the discomfort of soldiers immediately downwind. Some coarse language was being exchanged, though good humour characterised much of it.

Then suddenly the steamer's throbbing engines began to slow down and Thomas realised that the ship was approaching the outer harbour at Boulogne. He looked up, trying to make out the shape of the cathedral tower on the hill at the top of the old town, but could make out no recognisable features, as the skyline was barely visible in the darkness.

Within half an hour the steamer was mooring in the inner harbour, and he could hear the shouted orders for the men to begin disembarkation. Feeling the mass of men beginning to stir behind him, he turned and thrust his way back to take his leave of Jenkins, whose transit orders out of the port would certainly be different from his own.

Finally, after a few steps down the gangplank, his boots touched French cobbles again. His war was about to resume.

Chapter 6

It took only a brief visit to the landings officer's headquarters to confirm what Thomas had already expected. He would have to spend that night in Boulogne and then continue his journey to the huge Base Camp at Etaples, from where he would eventually be despatched to whichever unit required him as a replacement officer.

He was advised to try and find himself a room at the Hotel Metropole, near to the railway station, and less than ten minutes walk from the docks.

As he began his short journey out of the harbour area, his attention focused on the enormous quantities of war materials dominating every available square yard of ground space about him.

There were stack upon stack of sandbags, endless rows of rolls of barbed wire, great piles of steel pickets, scores of limbers for machine guns and case upon case of ammunition. He had never ceased to be amazed by the sheer scale of provision necessary for modern, mechanised warfare, and was by now fully convinced that by the time the war did end, Britain, France and Germany would all be quite bankrupt, both in terms of men and money.

Then his thoughts were suddenly interrupted as he crossed the bridge over some lock gates. A group of youths passed him, one of them stopping and calling out: 'Hey, Tommy officer. You gig-a-gig my sister for some tins of bullee beef?'

He didn't even turn his head. He was only too accustomed to the realities of life in the French ports serving the British and colonial armies. The economics of the French people, even this far back from the battle-front, meant that basic wages were badly depressed, prices high, and ordinary folk tempted by the money which they were convinced filled the pockets of the soldiers who flooded their towns.

But as one of these soldiers, he knew this belief to be hopelessly ill informed. For the rank and file soldiers, at least, basic army wages meant that even the cheapest whores were usually beyond their means. This, coupled with a still well established code of sexual conduct within the officer class, made him wonder just who did make up the clientele for the world's oldest profession. Little did he realise, as he found and entered the hotel, that this question would soon require him to act as a sort of honest broker that very night.

*   *   *   *

The Hotel Metropole was a typical war weary French provincial hotel. It was situated on a busy main road and just a stone's throw from the railway station, which was itself a prime staging post for troop movements to and from the battle zones. The hotel had long since lost any claim to whatever class or glamour it might have once displayed in pre-war years.

The foyer was cold and cheerless and virtually empty. A porter seemed to be the only staff in evidence, and he was clearly irritated from trying to do several other hotel jobs as well as his own. Thomas looked mournfully at a clock on the wall. Half-past ten. Little hope of getting any food at this hour.

The porter stood behind the great mahogany reception desk, his face a study in jaded incredulity. A smartly dressed woman in her mid thirties stood facing him, persisting with arguments and explanations which had, so far, made no impact on the porter, who was now using quite desperate body gestures to reinforce his insistence that neither the hotel manager, nor any one else, was available to deal with arriving guests. He was not prepared to offer the woman a room.

The woman paused for a moment, looked down, and then turned and saw Thomas. The relief in her face was clear as she recognised his uniform.

'Thank heavens!' she said, dropping what he had assumed up to that point was native French speech. 'Will you please convince this man that I must have a room, and that I am not prepared to leave this hotel and try and find anywhere else at this late hour.'

She went on to introduce herself as Mrs Marion Brenchly, a new member of the Voluntary Aid Detachment, and en route for Etaples, where she was to start work as an administrator in one of the field hospitals at Camiers. She showed Thomas her passport, then went and sat some distance away in the hotel lounge, leaving him to negotiate with the porter.

His own grasp of French was nothing like as good as Mrs Brenchly's, but within a few minutes he had established that there were several vacant rooms left in the hotel, that he wished to take one for himself, and that he could vouch for the character of the lone English woman. It did not surprise him when the porter then lowered his voice, and in a conspiratorial manner leaned over the reception desk and explained that the hotel had an on-going problem with "Les femmes de la nuit…"

Thomas nodded knowingly. One of his most memorable experiences as a private soldier the previous year had occurred in the army base camp above Boulogne. When darkness fell, it took all of the platoon sergeants' ingenuity to keep local tarts from invading the men's tents. A few additional words of commiseration for all the difficulties the porter was suffering, an advance of several Francs, and Thomas was able to go and give Mrs Brenchly the good news that she at last had a room for the night. Then, as sensitively as he could, he explained the reason for the porter's reluctance to deal with an unaccompanied woman so late in the evening.

She laughed, and her brilliant blue eyes twinkled

mischievously. 'So, "Tis Pity She's a Whore," is it? Ironically, I've always wanted to see that play performed. Do you see me in it, Lieutenant?'

He chuckled at her unexpected flash of wit. It seemed that Marion Brenchly was a woman of the world, and not given to prudish reactions.

'I don't think the porter will give you any more trouble,' he said, 'but I imagine that you move on to Camiers tomorrow, anyway.'

'Yes, though I'm hoping to meet my husband briefly before then.'

'Your husband?'

'Oh, yes, he's here in France. Major Paul Brenchly. He's with Haig's staff at British HQ in Montreuil. Unfortunately, I think he regards my arrival in France as a major embarrassment. But I won't bore you with the details of that.' She looked away, and Thomas didn't ask what the nature of the embarrassment might be. It was clearly none of his business.

'Have you had any thing to eat this evening, Lieutenant?'

'No, the Channel crossing destroyed my appetite earlier. On reflection, the last bite I had was a rather tired ham sandwich this afternoon before leaving Folkestone.'

Marion Brenchly stood up and without any hesitation strode purposefully back into the hotel foyer. Thomas eavesdropped on another animated conversation between her and the porter, which ended with references to a sum of French Francs, two omelettes and a jug of coffee.

Twenty minutes later they were both seated at a corner table in the dining room and tucking into plates of hot food.

Initially, he had misgivings about joining the English woman for a meal, welcome as the food was. He knew that the army's strict code of behaviour decreed that officers were not supposed to socialise with VADs, whether on duty or off. However, the hotel seemed to be empty, and it was hardly likely that the porter had any interest in the perverse social mores that characterised the army's attitudes to the growing numbers of British women now providing a supporting role to the war in France.

Their conversation quickly revealed that Mrs Brenchly was newly recruited to the VAD at Etaples. Her skills as a proficient short hand typist and fluent French speaker being urgently needed to help cope with the complex medical logistics at the ever expanding base hospital there.

However, Thomas' suspicion that her background was rather more exotic than the initial facts suggested, quickly proved to be well founded.

'You don't come across to me as a run-of-the mill keyboard tapper,' he said somewhat cheekily.

'How perceptive of you,' she replied, her eyes beginning to come alive again. 'Actually, I was a professional actress until I married ten years ago. Not in the West End theatres, I'm afraid, but I enjoyed regular work in the provinces. Hence my reference to that play I mentioned after the hotel porter's comment about me. But my dramatic career ended when the major made an honest woman of me.' She looked away for a second, perhaps thinking of the reaction she might expect when she met her husband again the following morning.

'Then tell me,' said Thomas, 'how did a busy actress find the time to learn short hand typing? Or have you mastered those skills since leaving the theatre?'

She laughed again. 'My early years in the theatre required me to be a general dog's body. The actor-manager who ran our touring company originally employed me as a stagehand and then as an assistant stage manager. He was a very successful professional, but his business affairs were chaotic. In exchange for him bringing me on as an actress, I had to do secretarial training between our main repertory tours. And now here I am in France to do my bit for the war effort.'

'From what you said earlier, your husband is less enthusiastic about it, though?'

'Very much so, unfortunately. He's from a military family whose traditions seem to stretch back to the Wars of the Roses.

He came out of Sandhurst well before the Boer War. As far as he is concerned women should have no rights to either work or vote under any circumstances, least of all during war time.'

Thomas frowned. He was already creating a mental picture of Major Brenchly sitting astride a horse, proudly displaying his staff officer insignia and still wondering why the cavalry's fortunes were so much in decline. Thomas wondered further if the major had ever seen the inside of a front-line trench or had witnessed at first-hand the murderous capability of a modern machine gun. His thoughts were interrupted, however, by several raised voices coming from the hotel foyer. The loud dialogue was all in English, and it took both him and his new companion only moments to conclude that another group of army officers had arrived at the hotel.

She got up immediately, smiled at him and stretched out her hand. 'Goodbye then,' she said. 'It's best I go up to my room now. I mustn't embarrass you in front of your fellow officers. I'm well aware of army and VAD rules about this sort of thing. Many thanks again for your help with the porter earlier on. If I don't see you in the morning I hope that all goes well with you in France. God bless.'

He barely had time to mumble a reply before she was gone. By now he was very tired, and decided to turn in himself. He successfully evaded the new arrivals, collected his room key and went upstairs. He was asleep within moments, dreaming again of shell bursts and entombments in the trenches.

Chapter 7

He wriggled impatiently on the slatted hardwood seat as the train finally, after yet another hold-up, drew out of Boulogne en route for Etaples.

There was no-one else in his compartment; but the transport officer in Boulogne had informed him that the train was mainly occupied by Australian troops, who were known for their impromptu displays of "high spirited behaviour," if journeys were in any way delayed. This warning, if warning it was, had been lost on Thomas, who was still preoccupied with wondering which unit he would be attached to after an initial spell in the huge military transit and training camp to which he was now headed.

In normal peacetime circumstances the train journey down to Etaples would have taken well under an hour. However, he knew from bitter experience the previous summer and autumn, that military travel behind the front in France was invariably chaotic and totally unpredictable. He reached into his valise for a sandwich he'd managed to get in Boulogne and settled down on the unforgiving seat, pulling his greatcoat around him on what was another raw, overcast February day.

After less than ten minutes' bumpy travel the train slowed and then ground to a halt. He looked out of the windows on both sides of his compartment, but could see no signs of a station. He then heard a whole series of choice swear words from above, and loud thumps on the carriage roof. More shouting was then followed by what was obviously the sound of boots thudding on the roof of his carriage. Then the train jerked into motion again, accompanied by shrieks of laughter and even louder shouting from above.

The engine was now gathering real pace at last and the French countryside was beginning to open up. Looking out to the West he could see extensive pine forests and heath-like areas reminiscent of parts of Norfolk he'd visited as a boy. But the next moment, what had earlier been high jinks by the Aussie soldiers above him had clearly ended abruptly. A very different shouting could now be heard, suddenly followed by an anguished scream and desperate cries for help.

'Stop the bloody train…. for Chrissake stop it! Charlie's gone. He didn't duck soon enough at that last bridge. Someone get to the engine driver…quick! He's gone I tell yer.'

Now the sound of many pairs of boots echoed above him, all moving in one direction, towards the train's engine. Then there was silence for some moments, followed by the squealing of braking wheels as the train came to an abrupt stop.

He then realised that legs, several of them, were appearing and dangling down over the sides of his compartment. Khaki clad figures dropped rapidly onto the sides of the tracks and he could see Aussie troops running back along the railway line. He opened the carriage door, jumped down and followed the running figures. After about a quarter of a mile he found himself approaching a huddle of subdued men bending over a crumpled body whose head was a pulverised and bloody mess. He looked about him but could see no sign of any Australian officers. Then he turned and saw a sergeant approaching.

'Are there any officers with you on the train?' Thomas asked.

'No, mate,' replied the sergeant, either ignoring or being oblivious to Thomas's own subaltern's uniform. 'I'm taking a detachment of replacements down to Etaples. There are a couple of corporals with me, but I'm the only other NCO on the train.'

'Then you have a nasty problem, I'm afraid. One of your troops, Charlie they called him, was obviously knocked off the roof at the last bridge. There's nothing can be done for him. He must have been killed instantly.'

'Oh, bloody hell!' groaned the sergeant. 'I knew something like this would happen one day. Perhaps this'll finally teach those silly buggers a lesson. Snag is, I'll soon be parting company with these three stripes on my arm, won't I? There's no-one else to carry the can.' The sergeant hurried on, mouthing profanities at the group of his men now carrying the body of their dead comrade back towards the train.

Thomas turned and headed back for his compartment, doing his best en route to try and explain what had happened to an exasperated French railway guard. Eventually everyone was back on the train, the journey resumed and within another twenty minutes he found himself looking out towards the sand hills of the coast fringing the estuary of the River Canche on the outskirts of Etaples.

* * * *

The transport adjutant sighed resignedly, and tapped his pencil against his teeth. He looked war weary and made no effort to conceal his obvious boredom and disaffection with the job he was doing trying to coordinate military traffic in and out of the enormous military monster that Etaples had become.

'Well, Winson, these Australians are a law unto themselves, I'm afraid. They're damned good soldiers, but away from the Front they just don't know what discipline means.' He paused, stood up and walked across to look out of a window, giving Thomas a little longer to wonder just how much accountability would attach to himself as the only commissioned officer who had been on the train from which the Aussie soldier had fallen.

'There'll have to be some sort of enquiry, and an appropriate report made,' continued the adjutant, 'but I really don't see why it should detain you. I've listened to your account of what you heard. Any blame must rest with the sergeant who was charged to accompany those men to Etaples.'

'Perhaps I should have done something to stop things getting out of hand when I first heard them on the roof of the train, sir.'

The adjutant's face was now a picture of both disbelief and muted astonishment. He sat down again, examining Thomas's face for any suggestion of intended irony there.

'Do you seriously believe it would have made any difference if you had tried to do something to stop their fun and games? Who do you thing you are – some sort of Don Quixote figure? You would have probably ended up being de-bagged and thrown off the train yourself. No, there's no blame attached to you, Winson. Now you move off and report to base camp. I'll deal with this. Good luck.'

Thomas saluted, turned on his heel and stepped out of the adjutant's office. He found it difficult to believe that he hadn't even been given a severe reprimand. He was relieved that the adjutant had apparently treated him so lightly. He quickened his pace as heavy rain began to fall, heading away from the railway station towards the tented camp a short distance away.

It was an inauspicious arrival for him as he entered the enormous military complex. He was directed towards a group of bell tents and presently found himself dumping his valise on to a camp bed in one of them. Of the several other beds in the tent, only one had other belongings on it, but no one else was present. He looked at his watch: five-thirty. He felt sure there would be no requirement for him to attend to any formal duties at this late stage in the day, and he left the tent, picked his way through deepening puddles, and soon found a mess hall and a bowl of hot stew. He hoped his stay in such surroundings would not be too prolonged.

*   *   *   *

Over the next few days he underwent further training; the main preoccupation being with gas drills. These involved donning respirators and filing through a gas-shed half buried in the ground. He also took his turns on the firing ranges, particularly enjoying his success with the Lewis machine-gun, a weapon he'd come to respect very highly the previous year. He was also instructed in how, as a new platoon commander, he would be expected to supervise the range of routine maintenance work required in the trench systems to which he would eventually be posted. After a few days he was becoming restless, however, and with a welcome improvement in the weather, he was glad by the Thursday to finish his training stint for that day and head into the town to explore the riverside.

He ambled through the fish-market, stepping around piles of nets and heading towards the bridge, which carried the road over the river and towards the pine woods, which separated Etaples from the coastal resort of Paris Plage a few miles away.

Then, as he passed one of the now empty fish stalls, his ears picked up the sound of raised and animated English voices about twenty paces away.

'You stupid, stubborn woman,' a man's voice was saying, 'I told you not to come out here. I don't give a damn what work you think you're going to do at the Base Hospital. Your place is at home, keeping control of our house, the estate and what few staff we have there.'

Thomas immediately recognised the woman's voice that answered. It was that of Marion Brenchly, who had briefly been his companion at the hotel in Boulogne the previous Sunday evening.

'You arrogant bastard, Paul! Unless you've forgotten, this is nineteen seventeen, and we are all well into the third year of this ghastly war. Even our political masters understand that women's work can't be dispensed with now. Who the hell do you think make the munitions your troops have to depend on?'

'Spare me that factory girl tripe, Marion. I want you back in England looking after our family interests, not tapping a bloody typewriter, making out casualty lists which any Pitman trained clerk can do.'

By now Thomas had realised that the man arguing with Marion Brenchly could be no one else but her husband. He was wearing the uniform of a staff major, with red hatband, cavalry breeches and long, immaculately shiny brown leather boots. He was a tall man, fresh complexioned and sporting a neatly trimmed moustache. He had fallen silent for a moment, but his eyes now had a wild look about them, and his temper was barely in check. His wife, however, was clearly not minded to let this intimidate her.

'Thank you for that charming appraisal of my capabilities,' she replied quietly. 'I might have known that our four months separation since your last leave wouldn't have improved your attitude to what I'm trying to do out here. Aren't you in the least pleased to see me?'

'Not in these absurd circumstances, no I'm not!' he snapped. 'I'd feel much happier to hear that you were on the next available boat back to England.'

'That isn't going to happen, Paul. I can do far more out here than tap on a typewriter, as you put it. I'm a good organiser, I'm fluent in French and there's a huge need for skilled administrators in the Base hospitals, whether here in Etaples or elsewhere. That's precisely why I was recruited. And as for the family interests you seem to be so concerned about, well – the land's being efficiently farmed by tenants who are quite happy to be free of your interfering ways, and the house is being perfectly well cared for. The truth is, you are simply unable to accept that I am capable of doing more than just being your dutiful wife.'

Thomas suddenly noticed the major's face blacken and become etched with fury. He had finally lost control and seized his wife by both arms, holding her in such a menacing way that she was rendered speechless and ashen-faced, trembling and struggling to break free. Thomas immediately strode across to them, attempting to feign a relaxed and casual manner as he approached, just as though he was quite oblivious to their row.

'Why, it's Mrs Brenchly! What a surprise and a pleasure. I never dreamt our paths would cross again, certainly not quite so soon.'

It seemed an age before either of the Brenchlys appeared to notice his arrival on the scene. But eventually the spell was broken by the major, who finally turned his head towards him, his face a study in fury and disbelief.

'Who the bloody hell are you?'

Thomas continued with his pretence of knowing nothing of the row he'd interrupted. He saluted the major, and smiled as affably as he could manage.

'Winson. Thomas Winson. I met Mrs Brenchly at the Hotel in Boulogne last Sunday evening. She was having difficulty getting a room for the night. I managed to be of some help to her.'

'Really? Well now you can help us both by clearing off. My wife and I have things to discuss.'

Thomas stood his ground. He'd observed the basic courtesies and done his best to enable the Major to save face. He now turned to Mrs Brenchly, whose frightened eyes were now filling with tears.

'Are you all right, Mrs Brenchly? Can I assist in any way?'

'The only thing you'll be assisting with is making big trouble for yourself,' said the major with undisguised menace. He appeared now to be getting increasingly apoplectic. 'Make yourself scarce before I…'

'Don't try and bully me,' said Thomas, 'I made a polite approach here to spare your wife further abuse and to save you a little face. I suggest that you calm down a bit.'

'Calm down! Why you insolent…'

'Oh, stop this!' interrupted his wife. 'There's no need to insult this young man. What he said was true. He did help me when I arrived here at the weekend - I was very glad that he did, Paul - for God's sake don't make this scene any worse.'

By now Brenchly had released his grip on her shoulders. He turned to Thomas with a contemptuous sneer, then looked him closely in the eye and asked, threateningly: 'I don't suppose you care to tell me which unit you are attached to here?'

'Would that I could, Major, I'm in transit, as they say, and still waiting to be assigned to a unit. But I'm sure that very soon I'll be back in a trench system somewhere.' He paused for a moment, but then felt quite unable to stop his tendency for sarcasm getting the better of him. 'It's not likely that you will ever join me in a trench, is it?'

Brenchly ignored the jibe and turned back to his wife. 'I'm going back to Montreuil, Marion. Remember what I told you. For my part, I won't be satisfied until you are back in England where you belong.' With that he turned sharply on his heel and strode off, not giving either of them a backward glance.

Marion Brenchly looked at Thomas as she wiped a tear from her eye. 'I'm so dreadfully sorry about that, but you really shouldn't have intervened.'

'Well, I'm not so sure. He was being so aggressive that I got the distinct impression that he is unbalanced.'

'I've never seen him like that before. The war must have changed him. Our marriage has never been a particularly happy one, but he has never treated me like that. For a time I was very frightened.'

'So you should have been.'

'Well, it's over now. I'll give him a few days to cool off, and then I'll telephone him at his HQ. He'll have to come to terms with the situation eventually.' She paused before smiling again. 'Look, you've been quite the hero today. I'm living in a small house just a couple of streets away from here. Come back there and have some brandy with me. We both need something to steady our nerves.'

* * * *

Her house was what, in England, would have been described as an artisan's dwelling. It was a small, two up and two down, with tiny kitchen and an open yard at the rear of the building. The inside was dark and sparsely furnished. The pictures on the walls, and some other decorative items, were very French, and it looked as though the previous occupants had left in a bit of a hurry.

'It's not very grand, I know,' she said with a knowing smile, 'but it suits me far better than sharing hutted accommodation with the other women up at the hospital. In my actress days I was used to theatrical digs, so I quickly felt at home here. Do you take water with your brandy?'

'Not likely,' he chuckled. 'Army water has a nasty habit of being heavily chlorinated, especially any that comes in cans, so I never risk spoiling a decent drink with it.'

'How much longer do you have in Etaples, Thomas?'

'A day or two at most, I'd say.'

'Well here's to your good health, wherever they send you.'

They both sank two very large glasses of brandy before he looked at his watch and reluctantly got up. 'I must get back to camp. Even I might be missed eventually.'

She reached out for his hand and then leaned forward and kissed him warmly on the cheek. 'God bless you, then, and thank you for your help today. Now, remember. If you come back to Etaples, it mustn't be as a casualty. I don't want to walk into the hospital one day and find you taking up good bed space.' She opened the door on to the street and he walked off, hoping fervently that her wish would be granted.

Chapter 8

'So, Winson,' said the postings officer, 'I see that before being commissioned you had a spell in the Invictas.'

'Yes, sir. I was with the Seventh Battalion on The Somme.'

'Well, you're going to rejoin the regiment. But I'm sending you to the Sixth Battalion. They're currently in training south of Arras.' He looked up from his sheets of paper and noticed the surprise on Thomas' face. 'What's the matter, have I said something funny?'

'No, sir, it's just that I happened to share a paddle steamer with two sections of men from the Sixth Invictas last Sunday. I had a conversation with their corporal.'

'Really? Well you'll probably be conversing with the corporal again soon. Anyway, they had a new CO two or three months ago. Drummond's his name – a lieutenant colonel at the ripe old age of twenty-six. The adjutant is Captain Falcon; report to him when you get to Battalion HQ. There'll be someone to meet you in Arras railway station tomorrow evening. Now here's your travel permit.'

'Thank you, sir.'

'Oh incidentally, Winson. There is one other matter. I had a telephone conversation yesterday with Captain Jameson, the transport officer at the railway station here. You met him on Monday, I gather.'

'Yes, sir, there had been some trouble with...'

'Yes, I know all about the trouble. Well, I've been asked to tell you that that wretched business has been resolved. You won't be required to give any testimony regarding what happened to that Australian who killed himself.'

'I'm very relieved about that, sir.'

'All right then, off you go. And by the way, when you get to Arras, don't hang around during daylight. You'll find out why very soon enough.'

* * * *

He dozed fitfully, nervous that this next train journey might be as eventful as the last. But this time there were no Aussies on the train, though stops and delays were still a feature of the journey. The trip to Arras meandered through the river valleys of Picardy, past the old fortified town of Montreuil, criss-crossing marshes and forests near Hesdin and St. Pol, and then finally, as the afternoon light gave way to darkness, tracked the Scarpe river before turning south into Arras itself.

As the train drew to a halt and he got out, he realised that what he could see of the city was in almost total ruins. But he had barely started to walk along the platform when a sergeant approached him.

'Mr Winson, sir?'

Thomas nodded a reply.

'I'm Sergeant Parris, sir. The adjutant, Captain Falcon, sent me to collect you.'

'That's a relief. I had no idea how to make the rest of the journey. My god, this town's in a mess, isn't it?'

'You're almost in the front line here, sir. Jerry's got his forward trenches in the southeast suburbs of the town. It's only possible to move about this place after dark, when the shelling stops. A couple of weeks ago, before the battalion was moved out, my company was in a trench facing Jerry's forward trench, which was only twenty yards away.'

'Then I'm glad I arrived two weeks later, Sergeant.'

Parris laughed. 'Actually, sir, it must sound daft, but when trenches are that close together there's less to worry about. The fact is it means our artillery can't shell Jerry, for fear of hitting us, and it's the same for them. So basically, we just kept our heads down and they did the same. We used to call out to each other sometimes.'

By now the two of them had walked on out of the station. 'So exactly where is the battalion based now?' asked Thomas.

'We've got a training camp about ten miles west of the city. I think that they are getting us ready for another big push in the spring.'

Thomas groaned, 'Does this mean a long walk in the darkness, Sergeant?'

Parris chuckled. 'We can do better than that, Mr Winson. As it happens, I've got a lovely old London omnibus waiting for us just round the next corner. Now, give me your valise and follow me.'

The streets of Arras, considering the enemy proximity, were remarkably well lit, Thomas decided. There seemed to be noisy bustle all about him. Shops and bars had all come to life within the last hour as darkness had fallen. Troops were moving about at will and many civilian inhabitants were enjoying a freedom of movement that was denied them in daylight hours. 'So where on earth does everyone go when the daylight returns?' he asked. 'Jerry may not be shelling our forward trenches, but he seems to have scored hits on just about everywhere else in the city.'

'They go underground,' his new companion replied enthusiastically. 'The whole eastern half of this place is riddled with cellars, caves and sewers you could drive a lorry along. Our engineers have been extending the cellars and caves for years now. There's even a hospital and an enormous generating plant down there.'

'You'll be telling me there's a railway line down there, too, I suppose.'

'Yes, they've even got that. Funny old war, isn't it, sir?'

A moment later, just as the sergeant had promised, they were mingling with a small group of other Invicta men alongside a brown painted omnibus with its window apertures timbered over.

A young private soldier looked up from tending the acetylene headlamps of the omnibus, stared intently at Thomas with piercing blue eyes, and addressed him directly: 'Allo again, sir. Remember me?'

'Good lord, yes! We met on the paddle steamer last weekend, didn't we? It's Hughes, the Lewis gunner, isn't it?'

'That's right, sir,' replied Hughes, smiling bashfully. He was both surprised and embarrassed that his name had been remembered.

'So, I saw you adjusting that headlamp,' said Thomas, 'does that mean you'll be driving us back to camp?'

'That's right, sir, it's a temporary job in between field training. Seems they just can't find enough drivers who can manage these things.'

'And you can manage it, then?'

'If it's got an engine and gearbox, sir, then I can drive it, don't you worry.'

'Yes, all right, thank you, Hughes,' interrupted the sergeant, 'now, let Mr Winson get aboard. He wants his supper, just like the rest of us. Jump in, sir, if you will. We'll drop you off at the officers' club in Avesne-le-Comte. That's not far from the camp. You'll get a decent meal there, and I'll pick you up later and take you to Battalion HQ.'

* * * *

For the first time since landing back in France almost a week earlier, Thomas at last found himself in the convivial company of some other junior officers who he hoped to get to know better.

The officers' club in Avesnes-le-Compte was based in an elegant house with spacious rooms and comfortable furniture. He quickly found himself enjoying a glass of wine with two other subalterns, both of whom had also recently been deployed as replacement platoon commanders to the Sixth Invictas.

'I'm Armstrong, 'C' Company,' said the first, with a broad smile.

'And I'm Broadbent, 'B' Company,' said the other.

'I'm Winson, yet to be assigned. But please, call me Thomas. Now, what do your aunties call you?'

'I'm Jamie,' said Armstrong, smiling again, and clearly welcoming the informal approach.

'And I'm plain John,' said Broadbent.

'That's better,' beamed Thomas, turning and sinking into a fine leather armchair. 'Now let's have another glass of wine.'

Jamie Armstrong seemed a little uncomfortable as he asked: 'If you don't mind me saying so, Thomas, you seem a bit older than most new subalterns.'

'Steady on, Jamie,' Broadbent chipped in, 'we haven't all come here straight from public school, have we?'

'It's all right,' chuckled Thomas, 'no offence taken. Yes I am a bit older than both of you. 'I'm twenty-six to be exact.'

'That's interesting. It makes you the same age as the battalion's CO,' replied Armstrong.

'So I understand,' mused Thomas, 'he must be a truly remarkable man.'

'Fearless as they come, by all accounts,' said Broadbent enthusiastically, 'but not the easiest man to get along with, apparently. He can't suffer fools gladly, and he'll only accept the very best from his junior officers.'

'Thanks for the warning,' replied Thomas, doing his best to look earnest, 'I'll be sure to remember that advice.' He looked into his wine, wondering how his new companions could be so well informed, when they were both only a few months into their war. In normal circumstances both Armstrong and Broadbent would either be in only their second term at university, or a few months into training for some sort of professional career. Now, their future prospects on the Western Front were uncertain in the extreme. He wondered how both of them would cope with life in the trench systems, a far cry from the comfort of the officers' club.

His thoughts were then suddenly interrupted by a servant, whispering in his ear that Sergeant Parris was waiting outside to take him to the battalion's billets. He drained his glass, shook hands with his new companions, collected his greatcoat and valise and reluctantly took his leave of the seductive comfort of his armchair.

* * * *

The following morning found him nestling in clean sheets in his very own, and very French, 'grand lit' in a small bedroom somewhere in his new billet, wherever that might be.

The previous night had seen him whisked away from Avesnes-le-Compte by the sergeant and transported by pony and trap a mile or so along country lanes to a complex of farm buildings deep in the countryside. There he was shown his room inside a rambling old farmhouse. He had completely lost his bearings as they climbed a stone spiral staircase and traversed various landings and corridors to reach the bedroom where he had been left alone just before midnight.

Now it was eight in the morning and he could hear a whole range of sounds outside and below his window.

He left the warmth of the feather bed and drew back the curtains, revealing what he immediately decided reminded him of a modern day equivalent of a scene from a painting by Pieter Breughel.

Three floors below him was an enormous cobbled courtyard bustling with all sorts of activity. Two horses were being saddled, another, steaming in the cold morning air, was being rubbed down after its morning hack. A short distance away, a motorcycle's engine was puttering to a stop and its rider dismounting and handing over a dispatch pouch to a waiting officer. A further few yards away two soldiers, one of whom he recognised as Hughes the Lewis gunner, were dodging about grabbing chickens and immediately wringing the birds' necks. The two men then seemed to disappear in a storm of feathers as they raced to pluck the chickens before the warmth in the birds' bodies was lost to the raw morning air.

Further along was an open brazier, its fire burning fiercely as another soldier fed it with dry wood. Beyond this, Thomas looked to where one corner of the courtyard opened up into a wide gateway, through which he could see a motley collection of motor lorries, wagons and Lewis gun limbers - clearly the battalion transport. He shivered momentarily, realising that now a swirling flurry of snow had suddenly developed outside the window.

A loud knocking at the bedroom door suddenly interrupted his thoughts. 'Who is it?' he called, reaching for his greatcoat.

'It's Private Walters, Mr Winson. I've been assigned to you as servant. I've brought you some hot water for your wash and shave.'

Thomas opened the door to find himself looking at a fresh faced, balding man in his mid-thirties. He was short, stocky and neatly turned out, from his close cropped hair down to the diminutive boots he wore as he strode purposefully into the room.

'Captain Falcon, the adjutant, sends his compliments, sir. He'd be glad if you could look in on him in his office at about nine o'clock.'

Walters crossed the room to leave the jug of hot water on a small dressing table next to the window. 'Welcome to Beaufort Farm, sir. You'll find this is as snug a billet as you could wish to find this side of Blighty.'

'Thank you, Private Walters. I really appreciate the hot water, and I hope we'll get on well together.' He extended his hand and was pleased to find Walter's reaction apparently quite free of any embarrassment at the handshake. Walters smile seemed to be that of a mature, relaxed and confident man – not that of one conscious of a 'them and us' relationship between officers and men.

'While you're washing and shaving, sir, I'll press your shirt, breeches and tunic for you. The adjutant may want to introduce you to the colonel. The CO's a stickler for appearances once we're out of the line.' Within a moment he had gathered up the clothes and was gone, leaving his new master to rummage in his valise for soap, flannel and razor.

Half an hour later Thomas was deep in conversation with Bill Falcon, the battalion adjutant. He was a quiet, softly spoken man who, as Thomas responded to his various questions, made neat, pencilled notes in a small notebook.

'Now, Winson,' he murmured, 'I have a meeting with Colonel Drummond shortly. Hopefully, I'll be able to introduce you to him. A quiet word of warning, though. He's a man not usually given to a soft turn of phrase. He tends to call a spade a shovel. You might even find his manner a little provocative and intimidating. Nonetheless, he's a formidable leader of men, and greatly respected by superiors and subordinates alike.'

'Thank you for that, sir. I'll do my best to remember your advice.'

'Fine. I'm assigning you to 'B' Company as a platoon commander. The chap leading the company has only been out here for three or four months himself. The battalion's losses in November were massive, I'm afraid. We've had to reinforce with a great many newly gazetted officers since then. No disrespect to you, of course. Incidentally, I gather you saw some action on the Somme last summer.'

'That's right, sir. I was part of the Seventh's reserve force for the early part of the battle, and then went into Trones Wood later in July. We lost half the battalion in a forty-eight hour period, but we held on somehow. Many of us had to swap our rifles for Lewis guns by the second day. The regular Lewis teams were decimated. We had to learn to use the machine guns on the job, so to speak.'

'But you cleared Jerry out of the Wood.'

'Eventually, yes - but only because two other battalions came in to reinforce us. We'd never have been able to hold Trones Wood without the reinforcements.'

By now Falcon was making more notes in his little book. After a pause he spoke again: 'And you were promoted to corporal after that?'

'Yes,' Thomas continued, 'soon after we came out of Trones. But to be frank, Major, the battalion had lost so many officers and NCOs by then that there were stripes aplenty to be handed out.'

Falcon looked up from his notebook, studying Thomas's face intently. 'Your modesty becomes you. I'm sure that you merited your stripes. But I understand what you are saying. I suppose that most of us have become greater realists over these last six or seven months. But anyway, when did you leave the Somme?'

'By the end of July they'd moved the Seventh up to a quiet part of Flanders. I was there until the autumn, and then I decided to apply for a commission. I finished training at Crowborough Camp less than two weeks ago.'

Before Falcon could reply, there was a peremptory knock on the door, which opened immediately, revealing the colonel, immaculate in riding boots, jodhpurs and a loose-fitting riding jacket over his tunic.

Thomas jumped up, saluting smartly and standing rigidly to attention. Falcon rose languidly from his chair, smiling benignly. 'Good morning, sir, an enjoyable hack?'

'Not bad, not bad. Who's this?' he enquired, staring intensely at Thomas.

'Second Lieutenant Winson, sir. Newly gazetted. He arrived late last night. A replacement for 'B' Company.'

Colonel Drummond waved Falcon back into his chair, told Thomas to stand at ease, then he sidled behind the adjutant's chair, taking stock of the new arrival.

At the same time Thomas took the opportunity to size up the CO. 'Size up' being the operative term. The colonel was a big man, tall and very athletic looking He was strongly built, with broad shoulders, dark, impeccably trimmed hair and sporting an extremely neat moustache. His face was handsome, classically proportioned, with penetrating blue-green eyes, which, Thomas was convinced, were looking straight through him.

'So, Winson,' asked Drummond, after what seemed an eternity, 'what are you, then, a Cavalier, or a damned Roundhead?'

'sir?'

'The question was plain enough, damn it,' barked the colonel. 'Well, are you a royalist or a bloody parliamentarian?'

Thomas' eyes momentarily wandered nervously downwards until they met those of the adjutant, but he could see no hint of guidance there. Falcon's face remained benign, but gave no clue as to how Thomas might sensibly now respond.

'Are you wanting some sort of political response from me, sir?' Thomas finally asked in a faltering voice.

'Of course I am, dammit! I like to know where my junior officers' loyalties lie.'

'Then I think they lie on the side of Parliament, sir. I never had much time for the concept of the Divine Right of Kings.'

As soon as he had uttered these words, he felt that he had as much as shot himself in his own foot. He sensed the adjutant wincing and fumbling uncomfortably with his notebook. Thomas steeled himself for the next missive from the CO. He did not have long to wait.

'That's just the sort of clever answer I'd have expected from some smart-arsed varsity don, Winson, not from a new subaltern just out of training.'

'I'm sorry, sir, I intended no offence.'

Falcon rose decisively from his chair. 'Shall I take Winson along to meet Standish, his company commander, sir?'

'Yes, of course, good idea! Lieutenant Standish has done a fine job knocking 'B' Company into shape, Winson. I'll expect you to give him the best support, now that you've joined us.'

Thomas stood to attention again and saluted smartly. 'You can be assured of that, sir. I'll do my very best for you and the battalion, too.'

Drummond's face softened noticeably as he nodded and turned away to look out of the window, leaving Falcon and Thomas to make as dignified an exit as they could manage.

In the corridor outside, Falcon smiled at Winson. 'Don't worry yourself about the Roundhead and Cavalier nonsense, Winson. It's just the colonel's little private joke. He does that to all the new officers. In fact, I suppose you could call it the battalion's standing joke. Now, let's go and find your company commander.'

Chapter 9

Amy Nicholls smiled gratefully as the young boy finished rubbing the blackboard clean, picked up his cap and left her alone in the classroom. She shivered momentarily, realising that the open fire a few feet away had almost burnt out. She pulled a shawl around her shoulders and tried to concentrate on marking the pupils' arithmetic books in front of her.

But she had found that concentration had been difficult for her for more than a month now. Ever since the dramatic events in February, she had experienced problems with re-orientating to her comparatively uneventful life as a village schoolmistress.

She hadn't lost her nerve. She was still living in her cottage and, despite the residual memory of the shells bursting around her a few weeks previously, and the dreadfully violent death of the taxi driver, she had succeeded in recovering her confidence. Furthermore, she had convinced herself that she was far too sensible to dwell on what might have been, or to preoccupy herself with fears that the war might again loom large over the village, threatening it directly once more.

She wasn't sleeping badly; the occasional bad dream, even a nightmare or two, was only to be expected after what she had been through. Her teaching hadn't suffered, either. Indeed, she had been glad to get back to school the very next morning after that fateful weekend. Mr Aston and her other colleagues had been astounded by her resilience.

But now, life for her in the village simply didn't seem the same anymore. She shivered again, wishing now that she had fed the classroom fire with another measure of coal from the scuttle behind her. Perhaps, she thought, her state of mind was little connected to the shelling incident, and far more related to the effect her meeting with Thomas had had that weekend. She thought longingly of the burst of passion which they had shared that night, and wondered now to what extent the terrifying explosions of the shells had been the catalyst for their almost desperate love-making. Her own capacity for the unbridled pleasure they had shared that night had startled and confused her. She had felt ashamed to acknowledge that she had experienced emotions and physical sensations then, which, despite the experience of two years of marriage, had come completely new to her.

But, of course, Thomas had gone, just as suddenly as he had appeared that Saturday. Where he was now was anybody's guess. No, Amy was convinced that she was too mature and shrewd a young woman to even begin to think that she had fallen instantly in love that night. Thomas had met a need. He had satisfied a latent desire in her and distracted her from the trauma of the bombardment of shells. She, in turn, had given herself freely to him and if, as he stepped off British soil later that Sunday afternoon, he hadn't left with a residual glow of satisfaction in his loins, then it was hardly her fault.

She rose from her chair, grinning mischievously to herself, smugly satisfied at the ease with which she had rationalised things so neatly. Yes, of course she would be happy to see Thomas again, and to welcome him into her bed. But her bitter experience of such recent widowhood had set her mind against any further and sustained emotional involvement, at least while this bloody war was to continue. And as for the thought of Thomas' own feelings in this matter? Well, she was convinced that he, too, thought along the same lines as she. Yes, she'd been aware that at the time of her marriage only eighteen months previously, he had been disappointed not to be the groom himself. But that was all in the past. Now, he was a very different person. He must have calculated what sort of future life expectancy he might look forward to when he had applied for his army commission months previously. Once caught up in the next major military initiative, his existence as a new subaltern might endure for only two weeks or less. Certainly, as the two of them had taken their leave of each other on that Sunday morning, there had been tender embraces and kisses, but no pacts had been made regarding any possible future commitment to each other. She was staying in Capel, he was off to God knows where, and with poor prospects of a safe return. On this basis, things between them were ordered, tidy and uncomplicated. But why, then, Amy asked herself, was she feeling so unsettled…?

As the old clock on the classroom wall chimed half past four, she gathered her remaining unmarked exercise books into a bag, pulled on her coat and made for the door. Just as she turned into a short corridor she heard two male voices in the school entrance porch. One of them was that of John Aston, the head teacher. The other was quite unknown to her.

'Ah, here we are,' Aston said, 'here's Mrs Nicholls now. Amy, you have a visitor. It's Lieutenant Commander Mockett. He wishes to talk to you. Excuse me, if you both will, but I do have some business down in Folkestone.'

Amy found herself shaking hands with the stranger, and being impressed by all the gold braid on his sleeves.

'Mrs Nicholls,' he was saying, 'we haven't actually met before, but I was one of the first on the scene when you had that spot of bother outside your cottage last month.'

'Well, for obvious reasons, I didn't go outside, so you wouldn't have seen me.'

'No, of course not, I was with the police who came up from Folkestone that day. I understand that the police sergeant interviewed you later.'

'Yes he did,' said Amy with a smile. 'He needed to establish that my cottage didn't have a direct link to German High Command. I hope that I don't have to convince you of my innocence, too.'

'Certainly not,' he chuckled. 'Anyway, it was I who subsequently had to do some checking - on the visitor you had with you that day. I met Lieutenant Winson again the following afternoon, just before he had to board his troopship. We had a convivial cup of tea together.' He paused for a moment, seemingly unsure whether to continue speaking or not. 'We got on very well together, actually.'

'Oh, yes, Thomas can be very personable when he puts his mind to it,' replied Amy, with a contrived innocence, which surprised even her. 'Indeed I always used to think that his capacity for sarcastic humour was exceeded only by his charm. Anyway, I'm sure you haven't come all this way to see me just to discuss Thomas. What brings you up here again?'

'It's a courtesy visit, really. I'm based down in the harbour at Folkestone, but I had to make a liaison trip up to the village today.'

'Of course – the airship sheds, I suppose.'

'That's right. They were the reason, of course, why your cottage took a bit of a bashing last month. Actually, I think that the naval authorities would be prepared to offer you some compensation for any repair bills you faced after the incident.'

Amy looked at her visitor intently. Her suspicion being that his rank was perhaps a little too senior for him to be concerning himself now with the few minor repairs needed by her cottage. She broke this news to him ever so gently, but felt amused by the thought of what his reaction would be.

'Well...' he continued, but with little real conviction, 'I did say that I'd met your friend Thomas...so, it's only natural that I should want to meet you, isn't it?'

'Well, now you have, Commander.'

'Please, call me Simon.' He looked at his watch, clearly wanting to move the conversation on – and preferably to somewhere else. 'Please, my car's outside. Let me run you down to your cottage. I don't have to be back in my office at the harbour for another hour or so.'

* * * *

72

She sat back in her armchair looking pensively at Simon Mockett as he finished his cup of tea and a piece of her seed cake.

'Umm…lovely! There's something I find irresistible about caraway seed,' he said, 'my sister used to make cake exactly like this. Do you cook much, Mrs Nicholls?'

'No, I don't,' she replied, smiling pleasantly and continuing to study him. 'Incidentally, you may call me Amy.'

It had taken her about three quarters of an hour of subtle and devious questioning for her to be satisfied that she had not been spontaneously mentioned by Thomas during his brief meeting with Mockett on the Sunday of his departure. On that basis, and assuming that the commander's interest in her went someway beyond a concern for the fabric of the cottage in which they were now sitting, then it must have been the police sergeant who had sown the seeds of Mockett's interest in her.

If this was the case, then she felt flattered. Mockett was certainly a handsome man, and for the last hour, after he had overcome his initial embarrassment over the ease with which Amy seemed to have read his thoughts, he had proved to be interesting and stimulating company. But now he was on his feet again.

'Many thanks for the tea and cake, Amy,' he said - and then added very directly: 'I really do want to see you again. Will you agree to that?'

'I'd like that very much,' she replied in a firm voice.

He took a card from his tunic pocket. 'It would probably be a bit awkward for me to telephone you at the school. This is my office number at the harbour. Please, do contact me in two or three days' time. Perhaps we can have a meal together; next weekend if you can manage it.'

She saw him to the door and waved as he drove away up the lane, then returned to her sitting room. Looking out of the window towards the cliff tops she felt glad that the later sunsets were now sure proof that the spring equinox was not far away. She found her thoughts wandering again to her situation in the village and what might lie ahead for her. Perhaps Simon Mockett's visit was providing her with some sort of spur, to enable her to move her life on in a different direction. She resolved that she would try and use this opportunity to establish ways and means of influencing her future, whatever that might involve. Suddenly she had decided that the village school had become too much of a cloister for her.

The following Saturday as they sat facing each other across a dining table, she asked him directly: 'So, exactly what do you do in the harbour here, Simon?'

He smiled gently, looking straight back at her. 'Let's just say that I'm temporarily shore-based. I haven't always been. I had command of a minesweeper until quite late last year. Now I'm just part of the navy machine which helps the army to get its men and materials across the Channel. I don't want to sound evasive, but that's all I can tell you, I'm afraid.'

'I understand. It was stupid of me to ask.'

'That's all right. It was only natural that you should, especially after my brief involvement with your friend the subaltern. Have you heard from him since he left?'

'No I haven't. It had been over two years, in fact, since we'd last seen each other before we met again by chance in Folkestone last month. We'd lost contact with each other well before I was widowed last July.'

'So you don't have any plans to...'

' If you are asking me about Thomas, then, no, I don't have any plans. Really, Simon, can you stop this particular line of questioning, please?'

'Of course... I'm really sorry. I never meant to upset you. I just wasn't sure whether or not you...'

'It's all right, I'm not upset,' she said, moving on rapidly, 'I'll change the subject. Now, Simon, to be fair to you, I have to confess to having an ulterior motive for being here today.'

'You actually mean it wasn't just for the pleasure of my company?' he replied, feigning mild shock. 'Well, you've got me all intrigued now. What is this ulterior motive, then?'

'Well...that day when you called into school, I was very deep in thought about my personal situation. To be honest, I've felt very unsettled since that day Thomas and I were almost blown to pieces last month.'

'Hardly surprising, Amy, many men and women would still be recovering from the shock after an experience like that. You were both close to death that day, and you'd seen what had happened to the taxi driver. My god, it was horrendous.' He reached across the table and took her hand in his.

'No, you are very kind and understanding, Simon, but my state of mind goes beyond that,' she replied decisively. 'Actually, I think that I've recovered from the shock very well. When I say that I feel unsettled, I'm referring to my situation in the village… the job at the school, the life at the cottage, everything. Simon, I've decided that I must leave teaching and Capel. For the rest of the time that this wretched war has to be fought, I want to make a different sort of contribution. I think that you might be able to help me.'

He shifted nervously in his chair, his hand leaving hers and sliding slowly back across the table to his wine glass. 'Amy, I'm sorry, but they don't take women into the Royal Navy yet,' he finally said.

'I'm well aware of that, Simon. But I'm also well aware just to what extent women are now helping with the war effort in other ways. I think that I am quite well equipped to help, too. I'm physically strong and fit. I hold a driving licence, I've had some first-aid training, and I've more than a basic grasp of French.'

Mockett sat back in his chair, staring at her intently, obviously trying to read something in her face. 'Do I understand you correctly?' he asked in an even tone. 'Are you suggesting that you want to go overseas to help in the war effort?'

'Yes, if need be. But I'd be prepared to go wherever the powers that be wanted to send me.'

'Amy,' he went on, 'is this some misguided attempt to follow your subaltern again?'

'Oh, please credit me with more intelligence than that. The subaltern, as you refer to him, and I met just fleetingly again last month. He's now one of several million men fighting each other along a front, which stretches from the Belgian coast to Switzerland. If I really wanted to find him in those circumstances, what cat-in-hell's chance would I have?'

'I'm sorry, that was a cruel and stupid thing for me to ask.' Already his hand was holding hers again. 'Anyway,' he went on, 'if you've really set your mind on this idea, how can I be of any help? As I said earlier, the navy doesn't recruit women; nor does the army, come to that.'

'No, but I'm sure that you must have many other important contacts and spheres of influence. I'm sure that you can make some enquiries on my behalf.' She smiled at him mischievously, as she said: 'I'd be very, very grateful if you would, Simon.'

* * * *

She telephoned him again a few days later, the bit now firmly between her teeth. 'Well,' she asked demurely, 'what have you been able to find out for me?'

'Actually, I've been able to find out that there's an officers' dance at the naval drill hall on Saturday evening. I'll be expecting you to come.'

'Perhaps, Commander, perhaps. But, seriously now, what have you got to report to me regarding the other matter?'

There was a pause at the other end of the line, which, Amy decided, if followed by an admission from Mockett that he had nothing of substance to report, would have prompted an immediate and spirited riposte from her.

Actually, what he had to say next both pleased and surprised her: 'As it happens, I've arranged an interview for you.'

'An interview! With whom?'

'With a Mrs Brackley, she's a member of a sort of board of trustees, which deals with Voluntary Aid Detachments. I have occasional dealings with her regarding travel arrangements for certain VAD postings overseas. She'll be in my office next Saturday afternoon. I've explained your situation to her. She

76

seemed confident that she could refer you to one of her colleagues who actually deploys volunteers, both at home and overseas. She can see you at about three o'clock in the afternoon.'

'Simon, you're wonderful! I just don't know what to say.'

'That's easy, you just have to say that you'll stay on for the dance that same evening.'

'Done!'

The meeting with Mrs Brackley that following weekend was brief but helpful. Although it was made clear to Amy that the local branch of the VAD Board had no actual control over volunteers' subsequent recruitment and deployment, it was certainly made apparent to her that her offer of services was unlikely to be refused – assuming, of course, that she was able to measure up to the recruitment criteria.

A further meeting was also arranged for her one week later, when Amy would be introduced to a director of army hospital services.

In the meantime, she danced the Saturday night away in the arms of Simon.

'So, it looks as though you might be getting your way then,' he said, as he drove Amy back to Capel at the end of the evening.

'And what exactly do you mean by that?' she replied innocently.

'Why, Mrs Brackley, of course. She seems to know all the right strings to pull. By this time next week you could be about to change careers. I hope you know what you are doing, Mrs Nicholls. There's a big difference between being a village school mistress and being just another volunteer with immediate loss of all rights and privileges.'

'Yes, I've thought that through, Commander,' she said, echoing his playful tone, 'but I am a big girl now. I'm well aware of what I could be letting myself in for.'

By now the car had rolled to a stop outside her cottage.

'It's fortunate that you live in such a remote part of the village.' said Simon. 'I can just imagine all those wagging tongues now, if you lived further up the lane.'

'Are you more concerned about your reputation or mine, Commander?' she replied, trying unsuccessfully to suppress the twinkle in her eyes.

Simon leaned across, putting both arms around her in a warm embrace. 'At this moment, Amy,' he said, kissing her fully on her mouth, 'our reputations, good or bad, are furthest from my thoughts.'

Chapter 10

Thomas peered unenthusiastically at the remainder of his bread and stew, wondering when the battalion cooks, still huddled over their steaming dixies in the field kitchen a few yards away, might show a little more imagination in what they prepared for their comrades. He'd joined the other ranks for their midday meal today, occasionally doing this as his way of becoming better informed about the forty or so men he was now commanding.

So far the day, just like the meal, had been fairly predictable. For more than two weeks since he had joined them, the Sixth Invictas had been continuing with their field exercises well behind the lines, which lay twelve miles away to the east. The only reminders of the war were those of the rumble of distant artillery, and the occasional sighting of allied or enemy aircraft in the skies above.

The terrain not far from the base camp at Beaufort was reportedly similar to that of the proposed battle area for an allied spring offensive. Each day they marched to various outlying fields. Once in position, the men were being trained in strategies of infantry advance quite different from those employed so catastrophically on the Somme eight months previously.

Now, new battle formations and tactics were being practised. Instead of leaving trenches and moving forward in one unified line, walking slowly, and thus presenting the enemy machine gunners with optimum targets, the infantry was being trained to move forward quickly and more flexibly in small groups of men.

These groups would then gradually open out, using the terrain for whatever advantage was presented to them.

Company and platoon commanders were being trained to use their discretion during the advance, according to how battle conditions might vary. Orders to the men might range from "Take cover!" or "Open fire!" to "Advance!" This training activity was practised for two hours or so each morning and then, after a lunch break, again in the afternoon, when further advances would inevitably end with the successful capture of a dummy trench. This would then be followed by a debriefing from the colonel, and then a further march back to billets at the farm.

While Thomas didn't question the value of training as a general principle, he remained dubious about the extent to which such continued practice in dummy trench raids could adequately prepare troops for actual combat conditions. His own limited experience the previous year had graphically taught him that the chaos and confusion created by the terrors of enemy artillery and machine gun fire could so rapidly turn a planned, orderly advance into a noisy and bloody shambles.

Nonetheless, as the new commander of Seven Platoon, 'B' Company, he knew that he must, at all costs, keep such thoughts strictly to himself. He wanted to lead by example, and knew that any private fears he might have must be kept from the men he was now commanding.

And he was already identifying closely with the men of his platoon. Sergeant Jackson, the wily old campaigner with the Africa Star, and wearing two wound stripes on his tunic sleeve was a veritable tower of strength. Jenkins, the artist, who Thomas had met on the crossing from Folkestone, was one of the two platoon corporals. Hughes, the very young conscript, also on the paddle steamer, was one of the Lewis gun team. Together they were beginning to forge the bonds of teamwork and comradeship, which would be so crucial in the trials ahead.

'Mr Winson,' said Walters, his servant, suddenly bringing his reverie to and end, 'Lieutenant Standish wants to see all platoon commanders before the afternoon exercises.'

'Oh, Lord! Not another pep talk, I hope.'

'Probably is, sir. You can't expect the leopard to change his spots, can you?'

Thomas picked up his steel helmet and headed towards the group of officers already gathering beside a gun limber. Standish, the company commander, was checking some notes in a small green notebook. Looking up and seeing the platoon commanders all present, he began to rattle off a list of criticisms: 'I'm sorry, but the men's marching is still somewhat sloppy.' He turned to Thomas, addressing him directly: 'Seven Platoon has gone a bit slack. It was particularly noticeable this morning and the colonel spotted it. Please make sure there's an improvement once we leave the trenches this afternoon. I also want a full kit inspection for your platoon this evening. Now, everybody, please note this - during the advances this afternoon, I want to see much better teamwork between the Lewis gunners in all platoons. We need to ensure that the ammunition carriers keep pace with the gunners. I also want to see and hear you using your whistles to better effect when we are all moving forward. You really must give the groups sharper signals, and give the men clearer instructions on how and when to vary their positions.' He paused for a moment before continuing: 'Finally, I can now tell you that these training exercises are fast drawing to a close. We'll soon be leaving our base camp and moving up to an assembly area behind the lines. I can't tell you any more just now, but for the time being we must maintain tight field discipline, and keep the men on their toes.'

Thomas returned to his platoon's position, smarting from the criticism that had clearly been levelled at him as a new platoon leader. He saw Walters give him a knowing wink as he climbed down into the trench.

'Bad as you thought, the pep talk, sir?'

'Pretty much.' The two of them were sufficiently alone to enable Thomas to attempt some confidential information gathering: 'Tell me, why is Mr Standish such a stickler for drill, and doing everything by the book?'

'I think, to be honest, sir,' Walters replied in careful, measured tones, 'He's not had a lot of choice. 'B' Company had got into some very slack habits a few months back. It was common knowledge that the previous company commander wasn't up to the job, and that the colonel as much as sacked him. We needed pulling up by our bootstraps afterwards. Mr Standish was made up to lieutenant, and given the job of sorting us all out. He's certainly restored discipline. The men didn't like all the extra marching and drill they were put through, but it seems to have worked.'

Thomas nodded gratefully, picked up his binoculars and looked along the trench at the men who were all checking their own equipment in readiness for the afternoon's exercise. He found Sergeant Jackson and familiarised him with Standish's demands for platoon improvements.

The sergeant listened carefully. 'They're fair points, Mr Winson. I'd already decided to crack the whip myself when we head back to camp at the end of the afternoon. Bear in mind, though, we've a lot of new conscripts in this platoon now. They didn't get caught up in all the extra marching drill which Mr Standish ordered, when he took over the company a couple of months back. He's quite right about the Lewis gun teams, of course. We've got a crack shot in young Hughes, but he'll only be able to do his job if he's properly fed with the ammunition. I'll see that they buck their ideas up this afternoon, don't worry.'

A Verey pistol flare suddenly shot up into the sky above them, giving a minute's warning of the start of the afternoon advance. Thomas allowed the sergeant enough time to give the men their final reminders, then checked his watch and waited for Standish's final signal, before blowing his own whistle and leading the platoon over the parapet, out of the trench and into the fields ahead.

* * * *

The required kit inspection passed successfully that evening, and Sergeant Jackson later convinced Thomas that Standish had acknowledged immediate improvements in the platoon's afternoon performance, both in the field, and on the march back to camp. Thomas thanked him for the reassurance, and then turned to the next task before him, which involved censoring the men's mail before it was sent home the following day.

During his own time in the other ranks the previous year, he had always felt a little aggrieved at having to hand over his own private letters to an officer. Now the shoe was on the other foot, and he had the job of deciding what should, or should not, be obliterated from the many letters in front of him.

With several of the thirty or so letters, the task was relatively easy. Experienced Tommies had a clear working idea of what information would not get by their officer. But he was finding that things were far less straightforward with the young conscripts' mail, which now constituted a fair proportion of the letters before him.

Very young soldiers, many of them abroad for the first time in their lives, and with no previous combat experience, had a tendency to wax enthusiastically about where they were, and what they were doing behind the allied lines.

He scanned such letters for any clues, direct or indirect, which might reveal the battalion's position in France, the training tactics being used, or any information about the army's weapons systems.

In more than one letter, he found words or phrases suggesting that the writer was employing some elementary form of coded message – possibly one prearranged with the relatives at home. Where he was satisfied that this was happening, he carefully expunged the offending words, phrases or acronyms.

Far more difficult for him, though, was to try and remain detached and dispassionate about letters where the writer was obviously troubled and distressed about the state of affairs for his family and friends at home. Several of the older men were concerned over issues of the health of various family members, one or two others by the suspected infidelity of a wife or sweetheart.

The fact that such outpourings of the men's innermost thoughts had little bearing on military matters did nothing to make his work more palatable. He took no pleasure at all in being privy to such intimate details of the men's hearts and minds, and he was thankful that after a three-hour, highly concentrated censoring session, he could put his pen down and give his own innermost thoughts some attention.

Before he could do this there was a knock on his door, which heralded a visit from Bill Falcon, the adjutant, who now had the job of doing a further check on Thomas' first censoring efforts. Falcon smiled sympathetically as he collected up the wad of unsealed letters. 'You've been on the receiving end of this yourself, Winson,' he said affably. 'I'm sure that I'll only have to give these a cursory check-over. Just in case you have missed anything that could be important. You do understand?'

'Of course,' replied Thomas, 'I'd expect you to find one or two things which I've missed. I won't pretend that I found the task an easy one. I only hope that I haven't been too hard on some of the men.'

'Don't worry. I'm sure that you have done your very best. Believe me, you'll be able to do this job in your sleep within a few weeks.'

After Falcon had gone, Thomas wrote a brief letter to his aunt and uncle in Folkestone, but he decided against writing to Amy. He had resolved, rightly or wrongly, that he wouldn't send her any letters from France. He also felt a little troubled at the realisation that he had found himself brooding more about Marion Brenchly than about Amy. He'd experienced a strong feeling of attraction toward Mrs Brenchly, even after only two short meetings with her. He wondered if she had managed to effect any change in her husband's attitude towards her. Thomas felt somewhat disturbed at his own preference that the Brenchlys wouldn't have resolved their differences. For the time being though, he realised that his being totally caught up in the relentless workings of the military machine, rendered his personal feelings somewhat irrelevant. He couldn't reasonably expect any home leave for the next six months or so, possibly a year, and must therefore concentrate on his new role as an officer. For the moment, then, what he needed was some light relief and distraction.

This was found in the shape of John Broadbent, the other replacement subaltern in the company.

Broadbent, too, had been censoring letters, but under the close tutelage of Bill Falcon. As an eighteen year old, only a few months out of his cloistered public school existence, the youngster had required careful instructions in dealing with the challenges of censorship. Particularly those aspects of family life of which he could not be expected to have informed knowledge. He was refreshingly candid about the problems he had faced during the task, and smiled broadly at Thomas as he said: 'Have you got your own men's letters finished, then? I've just had a three hour session with the adjutant and, if nothing else, it's made me realise what a sheltered life I've led up until now.'

'Well, perhaps we could do with a decent bottle of wine,' said Thomas. 'Do you fancy a trip to the Officers' Club?'

'I was certainly hoping you'd suggest that. From what Standish was hinting at today, we might not have too many more opportunities.'

'Exactly,' replied Thomas, pulling on his tunic, 'Let's make hay while the sun shines, shall we?'

Broadbent's smile had faded by now, as he asked: 'Where do you think the battalion will be headed after we leave here?'

'I've really no idea. But I'm sure that we will know soon enough. Now come on, let's get to that bottle of wine, before 'A' Company's officers drink the place dry.'

The officers' club was extremely lively that night, and was a hive of speculation about the battalion's imminent movements, once manoeuvres had finished. Everybody seemed bent on making the most of the rapidly decreasing opportunity for enjoyment. Mercifully, as far as Thomas could read things, even the more senior officers appeared to be letting their hair down, and generally encouraging the subalterns' desire for escapism.

This trend certainly extended to Lieutenant Standish who, together with his usually quiet and enigmatic confidant, Gerry Porter, another platoon commander, actually asked Thomas and

Broadbent to join them at a table they were occupying in a corner of the dining room.

'Yes, please share another bottle of wine with us,' said Standish. 'I wanted to say a special word of thanks for responding so promptly and effectively to my criticisms earlier today. The CO keeps a very close eye on our company. He sacked my predecessor for incompetence, and made no secret of the fact that I'd go the same way, if I couldn't restore some better discipline among our men.'

'It wasn't a problem,' said Thomas with a knowing smile, 'he clearly has you marked out as a Cavalier. When I first met him, I fell into the trap of professing some sympathy with the Roundheads.'

Broadbent looked on quizzically as his three companions chuckled. 'I don't understand what you two are talking about,' he said finally. 'What is all this about Cavaliers and Roundheads?'

'I really don't think it sensible for any of us to enlighten you,' said Porter, 'after all, why should you be spared?'

'Quite so,' agreed Standish, feigning a heavy frown, 'better we leave the CO himself to initiate you.'

The conversation quickly moved on as the wine flowed freely, and Thomas did his best to learn some more about the qualities of leadership which Drummond, the CO had recognised in such a young and untried officer as Standish. Mortality rates among young subalterns had undoubtedly reached an unprecedented level in the last six months of the previous year, but it was surely rare for a nineteen year old, as Standish was, to be promoted to company commander. Drummond himself had a well-established reputation for unflinching bravery, which apparently extended to an almost total disregard for his own safety during combat. Had he recognised Standish as a 'like soul'? Also of interest to Thomas was the apparently subservient role which Porter, seven years Standish's senior, and a wounded veteran of the Somme, had adopted on returning to the battalion a few weeks earlier than when Thomas had arrived.

In the final analysis, however, none of this really mattered.

What was crucial, Thomas concluded, was how well Standish could lead the company once training ended and the real war resumed. How would they all react once the unreal nature of the field exercises was eclipsed by the terrifying chaos of flying shrapnel and the lethal chatter of machine gun fire? They would know soon enough.

As midnight approached, he felt the need for some fresh air. He made his excuses, left the table and decided to take a short stroll through the streets outside.

The bars in the town had long since shut up for the night. But there were a lot of rank and file soldiers milling about in the streets, many of them still consuming cheap wine from bottles bought earlier on.

Then, as he turned into a darker side street, he pulled up sharply at the sight twenty or so yards in front of him.

There was a huddle of men, and the muted growling and snarling of many voices, all of them with Australian accents.

The Aussies, their invective rising and falling in the cold night air, were directing all their attention to a man, clad only in his breeches and boots, who was bound up with rope, his back facing outwards, and secured in a reversed cruciform position to the wheel of a cart.

In the poor light from two or three storm lanterns carried by members of the group around the cart, Thomas could make out the vivid and bloody pattern of whiplash stripes on the victim's naked back.

'Go on, Frank, give the bastard another dozen,' called out a voice.

Thomas went to draw a little closer to the group, but then felt a hand firmly gripping his shoulder from behind.

'Don't make the mistake of trying to interfere with what's going on here, Mr Winson. The subaltern's pip on your shoulder won't cut any ice with these men. They're busy administering some rough justice here, and from what I've been told, it's more than deserved.'

Thomas turned and his face met that of Corporal Jenkins.

'What the hell is going on here, Corporal? Who is the man getting the whipping?' he demanded angrily.

By now Jenkins had led him back around the corner and out of the side street.

'The man getting the whipping is a company sergeant major from the Royal Fusiliers. At least that's what some of the Aussies told me. Apparently, they found out that two weeks ago, one of the fusiliers in the CSM's company was a day late returning from leave. The sergeant ordered that he should have twelve hours number one field punishment. The man was tied to a gun limber for the whole of a freezing cold night in just his shirt and breeches. The next day the man got pneumonia. He's since died.

'The sergeant wasn't disciplined in anyway – at least, until tonight,' continued Jenkins. 'The Australians got wind of the story from another group of fusiliers they met in a bar. They decided to administer some justice of their own.'

'We can't just stand by and do…' began Thomas.

'Nothing, were you going to say, Mr Winson? That's exactly what we must do, sir, you especially,' insisted Jenkins. 'When the Aussies have finished with the sergeant, he'll have had his back laid open, but he'll still be alive and kicking. The poor bastard who died of pneumonia won't get another chance, will he? Now, please, Mr Winson, you take my advice and make yourself scarce. Those men round the corner are bent on finishing what they started. If you try and interfere, they're just as likely to turn on you. We don't want that, do we?'

Thomas nodded reluctantly, but he knew that Jenkins was right. He remembered the dismissive comments of the transport officer back in Etaples, after the tragic incident on the train when the Aussie soldier had been killed. Those words rang in his ears again now: "Who do you think you are, some sort of Don Quixote…?"

He turned away, without another word to Jenkins, and strode unhesitatingly back to the officers' club.

Chapter 11

Amy listened patiently as Mrs. Williams, the chairwoman of the local Voluntary Aid Detachment recruitment panel continued:

'The plain fact of the matter is, Mrs Nicholls, that we need volunteers more now than ever before. What I'm about to say here, you won't read in any newspaper, but it's true, nonetheless. Last year saw the army medical services being completely overwhelmed by the sheer scale of casualties on the battlefields. It all came to a head last summer and autumn on the Somme. To be quite blunt, we've reached a stage now where the army's nursing service can no longer function without the VAD support it gets, both in the hospitals at home and, increasingly, in France and elsewhere abroad.

'What we believe to be inevitable is that the Government, now that we are halfway through a third year of the war, will have to create some sort of new national military force of women, in the way it has organised the munitions production.'

'You mean a sort of women's army corps?' asked Amy.

'Perhaps, yes. But that's some way off yet and, of course, it would require parliamentary legislation. In the meantime, the VAD has to do its best to support the existing services.'

'I'm sure that I can help you in that', said Amy confidently.

'Perhaps you can Mrs Nicholls,' replied the chairwoman. 'Your VAD application is a valued one. But our panel today must be sure that you have thought your action through carefully.'

'How exactly do you mean?'

Mrs. Williams shuffled nervously in her seat. 'I'll be candid with you, Mrs. Nicholls. You are a well-qualified young woman and professionally certificated as a teacher. The problem is, if you enter the VAD, you may quickly find that such success won't count for much with some of the people you'll be trying to help.'

Amy looked quizzically at each of the Panel members in turn, hoping for someone to illuminate what was being put to her.

An elderly lady to the left of Mrs Williams came to her aid: 'What you have to appreciate, Mrs Nicholls, and I'm referring here to hospital based VAD work, is that the army's nursing service, as far as women are involved, has only really been developing since the days of Florence Nightingale.

'But,' she went on, 'as Mrs. Williams has explained, that service has been overwhelmed by the huge scale of military casualties. Despite this, some of the regular nurses in the army's service do sometimes resent the voluntary help on which they now have to so desperately depend. You see, many of those career nurses feel that their own professional status is being compromised. A resulting problem is that there have, in many hospital wards, been clashes of personality between army nursing staff and some of the VAD recruits.'

The chairwoman now smiled gently at Amy and continued the explanation. 'What my colleague is saying, is that some of our volunteers from the higher social classes, and the professions, have found it difficult to cope with sometimes being spoken to, or treated, as though they were a housemaid.'

'I can perfectly understand what you are saying,' replied Amy, smiling knowingly. 'But, frankly, I'm from a very modest home. I've not been used to having servants at my beck and call. If an army nurse required me to undertake a servile task, then I'd get on with it. Furthermore, I can make no claim to having more than basic medical first-aid knowledge, so I would think it part of a natural order of things to take instruction from qualified army nurses. If I were sent to a hospital ward somewhere, I wouldn't be afraid to get down on my knees and scrub a floor, or get my hands dirty in other ways. All I would expect is that, in time, the nurses would respect me enough to make proper use of the other skills I could offer them.'

'Well said, ma'am,' chipped in the third member of the interview panel, thumping his hand down on the table, startling both his two colleagues with his interruption. 'That's the spirit! You've got exactly the right attitude for making a go of VAD work. Be prepared to do the dirty work, and take some hard knocks. You'll soon command the respect of your peers with that approach, whether it's an army nurse, or some poor devil who's had half his body blown away.'

Mrs. Williams shuffled uncomfortably in her seat. 'Alderman Prentice is one of our pillars of local industry, Mrs. Nicholls. He has wide experience of life on the factory floor.'

'Thank you for that, Madam chairwoman,' replied the alderman crisply, 'but remember that I've had experience of army life, too, and I know how it feels to be on the receiving end in a military hospital. That's why I am here today.'

'Yes, indeed,' said the chairwoman. 'The alderman fought in South Africa before setting up his factory in Folkestone, Mrs. Nicholls.'

'That's right,' said Prentice, relishing his words, 'which means I've fair knowledge of both barrack room lawyers and trades union militants. Mind you, I'm not sure I'd be able to handle a suffragette.' He peered suspiciously at Amy, 'You're not one of th….'

'Yes, we won't dwell on that,' interjected Mrs Williams quickly. 'Now, Mrs. Nicholls, You have certainly given us a robust account of yourself. We greatly appreciate your candour. I don't think that we need take up any more time interviewing you. I have just one more question to ask you: Tell us, how do you react to the sight of blood? Lots of it, mind?'

* * * *

Only half an hour later Amy found herself in the ante-room of the operating theatre in the hospital where her VAD interview had just taken place.

She had been provided with a surgical gown and shown by a theatre nurse how to scrub up before what was now clearly a practical test to see whether or not she was too squeamish to be considered for auxiliary nursing of seriously wounded men from a battlefield.

Suddenly, the theatre door opened and another nurse came out. 'Mrs Nicholls?'

'Yes, that's me,' said Amy, rising quickly from her chair.

'Good. The surgeon here is about to carry out a partial amputation of a man's arm. There was a very serious accident down in the harbour this morning. One of the dockworkers got one of his hands caught in a winch. The hand and lower arm were badly mangled. The surgeon has decided that he will have to amputate below the man's elbow. You are being invited into the operating theatre to observe. If you feel up to it, that is.'

'Yes, I'm sure that I do,' replied Amy unhesitatingly, 'I won't cause you any embarrassment.'

'Very good.' The theatre nurse looked at her watch. 'The doctor administering the anaesthetic will have put the patient under by now. Follow me into the theatre and stand a good step behind me. Don't get too close to me, mind – my hands will be kept very busy, and I don't want to find you getting under my feet. Now, one last thing - if you do feel faint or sick at all, get straight back into this ante-room. Mr. Crisp, the surgeon can't abide mess on his theatre floor.'

The nurse turned abruptly and went through the swing doors into the theatre. Amy followed closely, then she dutifully stood a yard back from the nurse. She looked at the unconscious patient on the operating table. The man's right arm was exposed below the elbow, revealing ghastly mutilation. The surgeon was carefully examining the wound with a probe and forceps. He turned to the doctor who had administered the anaesthetic, speaking quietly:

'There's so much damage to the hand and wrist that they can't possibly be saved. The partial amputation has to be proceeded with. I wonder how much blood he lost before they got him here?'

'Apparently he was extremely lucky in that respect,' replied the theatre sister. 'A replacement army medical detachment was just waiting to board a ship for France, immediately next to the loading winch that caused the accident. One of the medical orderlies kept pressure on the artery immediately above the wound. He then accompanied the patient, holding his fingers on the artery, until they got the poor soul up here to the hospital.'

'Then, hopefully, he won't have been too weakened by loss of blood,' continued the surgeon. 'Alright, then, let's get straight on with it. I'll make the incision about three inches above the wrist line. At the end we'll close the wound with square skin flaps.'

Amy didn't avert her gaze from the operation for one second. She watched in awe as the flesh and bone above the patient's wrist was skilfully cut through by the surgeon, and as the theatre sister assisted with clearing blood away and then helping with the ligatures to stem any more blood loss. The nurse in front of Amy turned once, just momentarily, to check that all was well behind her before resuming her own role in the operation.

A little more than twenty minutes later it was all over, with two hospital porters arriving to wheel the amputee away to one of the hospital wards. The surgeon, the theatre sister and the doctor who had anaesthetised the patient had disappeared, leaving just Amy and the second nurse alone in the theatre. The nurse unceremoniously tipped the surgical basin containing the remains of the patient's hand and lower wrist onto a folded square of muslin and tied it all up as a parcel. She then turned, proffering the parcel to Amy in one pointed and deliberate action. Amy didn't hesitate and took the parcel, betraying no emotion in her facial expression.

'What would you like me to do with this, nurse?' she said equably.

'Just outside you'll see a bin marked "Incinerator Only". Put it in there, please. Then when you come back in, I'd like you to give

this theatre floor a thorough mop with hot water and disinfectant.'
She looked hard at Amy. 'No objection to that, I hope?'

'Certainly not, I'm pleased to be useful. My name's Amy, by the way.'

'And I'm Nurse Mary Waite. As soon as we've cleared up, Amy, I'll take you for a strong cup of tea. Incidentally, well done. Mrs. Williams will be delighted to hear that you've passed muster.'

Three days later Amy received official notification that her services had been accepted for VAD auxiliary nursing duties. Her orders were to report to the Royal Victoria Military Hospital at Netley, near Southampton on March 25th. The news came as no surprise to her head teacher, John Aston, who had been aware of her intentions from the outset.

'Of course we'll all miss you in Capel, Amy. But we understand how you feel. Hopefully, when this war finally does come to an end, we'll see you back in your classroom here.'

The next two weeks seemed to fly by. She arranged for her cottage to be sub-let to her replacement teacher, another widow, who was moving into the village from Canterbury, put her local business in order, and packed two bags of clothing and belongings for the journey to Hampshire. Only one other thing remained to be done – to take her leave of Simon Mockett.

To avoid complications she had arranged for this to be done at the railway station on the day of her departure from Folkestone. Amy was feeling a little guilty at leaving the area so rapidly after Simon had set up her initial meeting with Mrs Williams. He quickly disabused her of her feelings: 'Not a bit of it, Amy. I really admire you for what you are doing. To be honest, meeting you has given me a bit of a kick-start. I've put in for a transfer from my post in the harbour. It really is time for me to get back to sea again. I've applied for a posting back to minesweepers. That's where most of the navy action is these days, and they're boats where I've had experience of command. With luck, I'll be leaving here soon, too.'

She leaned forward and kissed him tenderly: 'Goodbye, Simon. Thanks for being so understanding. I really am glad that you came up to my village to check on those airship sheds last month.'

'Well…. Perhaps I did have ulterior motives,' he replied with a chuckle, embracing her again. 'Bon voyage, Amy. God bless you.'

* * * *

Her travel instructions had been quite explicit: "Leave the Southampton train at St. Denys, one stop before the city's main station. Change to the Fareham and Portsmouth line and take a train, passing through Bitterne, Woolston and Sholing, to Netley Station, which is only half a mile from the military hospital itself."

As the main part of her journey drew to its close, she looked out on what she had realised from a glance at her Bartholomew's map must be the River Itchen. The river, hardly noticeable a moment ago, was widening rapidly now, as it snaked past the eastern side of the city, but then disappeared in a flash, displaced by the busy roads and tightly packed terraced housing of St. Denys.

She changed platforms for the Portsmouth line, noticing the station master in conversation with a porter a few steps away.

'Excuse me,' she asked, 'can you tell me when the next train for Netley is due?'

He looked at his watch. 'There's one due in about twenty minutes. But tell me, are you heading just for the village, or might you be wanting the military hospital?'

'I'm going to the hospital to join the Voluntary Aid Detachment there.'

'Then you face a problem, ma'am. Our next train will get you to Netley Station alright, but when you get there you'll find that the hospital gates will be closed to all civilians for some time.'

'Closed? What for?'

He looked again at his watch, adjusting his hat slightly, before continuing. 'They're loading up an ambulance train for Netley, down at the docks. Once it's loaded, it's due to follow on after the train that you are just about to catch here. The snag is, just before an ambulance train is due to arrive at the hospital station, and for some time until after it's fully unloaded, they shut and guard all the hospital gates.'

'For military security, I suppose,' said Amy.

'That's right, ma'am. But those ambulance trains are also distressing sights to see. The hospital authorities prefer all civilians out of the way when they are moving patients out of the carriages and into the hospital. It would be very upsetting for any relatives or other visitors to see the casualties until the medical staff has made them comfortable inside the hospital. Some of the poor devils that we see on those trains are still in filthy, mud-covered uniforms, and barely out of their trenches. I take it you're a new nurse?'

'Well…a nursing auxiliary, really, I'll have a lot to learn.'

He smiled kindly at her. 'I'm sure that you will be much appreciated there. That hospital is enormous now. It's spread all over the fields behind the main buildings. There are huts everywhere, tents as well. But I'm sure that you won't end up in one of those,' he added hurriedly.

'So, what exactly do you think that I should do when I get to Netley Station?' she asked.

'Well, what you might try is leaving your luggage at the station, and walking to one of the hospital gates – it's not far. The guards there might admit you. It's not as if you are a civilian visitor or any other Tom, Dick or Harry. They might let you in before the ambulance train has finished unloading. I'd give it a try.'

'Thanks. You've been very helpful.'

Within the hour she found herself strolling from the station at Netley and heading down through the village. It was a beautiful, sunny, crisp spring day and she soon found the coastal road, which, according to her map, would quickly bring her to the edge of the hospital grounds.

A gap between some houses and trees suddenly revealed a

view over Southampton Water, and she gasped momentarily at the sheer density of shipping spread out in front of her, against a backdrop of forest and heath beyond the distant shore.

Amy had grown used to seeing lots of ships plying in and out of Folkestone during her time near there, but the scale of what she saw now astounded her. She could see ships with great red crosses painted on their hulls, Royal Navy warships of every shape and size, tugboats and lighters scurrying to and fro, and sailing barges tacking near the far shore. It was a stirring sight, but one she found disturbing. She felt it could only mean that the war machine had now become so monstrous as to be almost uncontrollable. She reflected briefly on the thought that part of the wretched human cargo from one of the hospital ships was now making its own way to the same destination as hers.

A few more minutes walking brought her to within sight of what she realised must be fencing enclosing the military hospital. Through gaps between several very handsome Scots pine trees, she caught her first glimpse of the enormous complex of buildings ahead of her. She marvelled at the expanses of brick and facing stone, arched windows, pillared entrances, towers and cupolas, which seemed to stretch obliquely into the far distance.

At last she came to a gate guarded by three armed soldiers, with a civilian police constable accompanying them.

'Hospital and grounds are closed until further notice, madam,' said the constable. 'Ambulance train due to arrive here shortly.'

'Yes, I know. It was explained to me when I changed trains at St. Denys. But I was hoping that you would be able to let me in. You see I'm due to start work here. I've been attached to the VAD at the hospital. Here is my letter of notification and travel directions.'

The constable perused the papers, then handed them to the army sergeant nearby. The sergeant looked at Amy's letter. 'It looks genuine enough, missus, but our guards aren't supposed to admit anyone whose arrival hasn't been notified in advance. Can't you wait a few hours and come back this evening?'

'But I left Folkestone first thing this morning,' pleaded Amy, 'it's been a long journey. I'm tired and I'm hungry. Please, isn't there something you can do?'

The sergeant paused and scratched his chin. 'Normally we'd use our telephone in the hut here to check with the hospital office, but when a train's due we should only use that in an emergency. Look, Missus, tell you what we'll do. I'm on my rounds at the moment. I was just about to walk back to the main building. I'll take you with me and we'll see if we can find the superintendent of nurses. Hang on, though. Where's your luggage?'

'It's at Netley station. I thought that it could be collected later.'

'I see. Perhaps we can help with that later on – assuming HRH lets you stay now.'

'Sorry, HRH?'

'Her Royal Highness! It's what we tend to call the superintendent of nurses. Only when she's out of earshot, mind.' He winked, adding, 'Follow me then.'

* * * *

'Thank you, Sergeant, I'm grateful that you used your initiative,' said Miss Ransome, the nursing superintendent, smiling graciously. 'It wouldn't have done for Mrs. Nicholls to be left wandering about Netley for the next two or three hours. We were told to expect her sometime today. Clearly the message didn't get through to the officer of the guard on this occasion. My apologies.'

'That's no trouble at all, Ma'am. And certainly, the young lady didn't look at all like a saboteur,' he replied, grinning broadly and turning away down the corridor.

'What did he mean, saboteur?' said Amy, instantly thinking back to the German shelling of Capel, and the initial attitude of the policeman there.

'That was just his little joke, my dear. You mustn't let it worry you. But, actually, and you must understand this straightaway, we all have to take security matters extremely seriously here, both in the hospital itself and beyond its immediate bounds.

'You see,' she went on, 'quite apart from the safety of all the hundreds of sick and wounded allied soldiers we have here, there are also significant numbers of wounded German prisoners of war, too. On occasion, one or two of them make an attempt at escaping from here. When you next catch a train back to Southampton or London, you'll see more army guards at Sholing station. That's because two Germans once got all the way up to Waterloo before the army caught them.'

Amy shook her head and smiled whimsically. 'I've clearly led a sheltered life in my village school back in Kent.'

'Yes, that's right, a schoolteacher. We don't get too many of those in the VAD here.'

'I think that's because so many male teachers are off at the front, that the females are desperately needed to plug the gaps in the schools.'

'But they could spare you?'

'Yes. They've simply replaced one widowed teacher with another widowed teacher. We've become pretty thick on the ground these last three years, Superintendent.'

Miss Ransome didn't reply. She was preoccupied with a file containing Amy's details lying on the desk in front of her. Eventually, she rose from her chair and moved over to a window, clearly deep in thought, perhaps considering what to say next. At last she turned again to face Amy. 'Mrs Nicholls, when you learned that you were being sent here, did you assume that you would be helping us to treat wounded men?'

'Well, naturally I did. This is a military hospital, and the VAD panel who interviewed me in Folkestone made it abundantly clear how desperate the army was for auxiliary nursing help.'

'They were quite right, and, as it happens, you have been sent to the main military hospital in the country.'

'Then, and with the greatest respect, why are you now asking me whether or not I expected to be working with the wounded men here?'

'Mrs Nicholls, I'm going to be very direct with you. This is a huge medical enterprise here. Over these last six to eight months we've seen more than a hundred and fifty ambulance trains unload casualties from the hospital ships docking at Southampton. Every kind of physical injury can be seen in our surgical wards. But a growing difficulty is… well, not all of our casualties are suffering from physical damage as such.'

She went on. 'An increasing number of soldiers arriving here haven't made the journey back to England because of shells or bullets blowing holes in their bodies, or because they have been choked or blinded by gas. They've been so mentally damaged by battle conditions that they simply can't take any more. We have to tend to them, too. I want you to help us with those men, Mrs. Nicholls. Tell me, will you do that? Will you try and help us mend some broken minds and spirits?'

* * * *

She had slept deeply for more than twelve hours. Only waking after the other nurses sharing her dormitory had long since risen to begin another long day in the wards.

Amy sat up in bed, peered through a net curtain and found herself looking at the expanse of grass and shrub which she had walked over with the guards' sergeant the previous afternoon. It was another bright day, and already she could see much movement outside. Some of the patients were already being exercised – some through their own volition, albeit with the aid of sticks or crutches. Others were being transported in wheelchairs, some on trolleys. Porters, orderlies, nurses and other staff were criss-crossing the network of gravelled paths around and in front of the complex of buildings. Inside she could hear a myriad of sounds - voices in the corridor outside the dormitory, crockery and pots and pans on the move, distant bells ringing and the persistent opening and closing of doors.

She lay back on her pillow and glanced at her watch – nearly nine o'clock! She leapt out of bed, just before there was a knock at the door, followed by the appearance of a nursing sister carrying a spare VAD nurse's uniform over her arm.

'Mrs Nicholls? Yes? Well, VAD nurse Nicholls from now on.' The visitor walked in briskly before continuing. 'I'm staff nurse Jefferies. Welcome to Netley. Miss Ransome has asked me to get you started today. I've got your luggage outside. It was collected from Netley Station yesterday evening, so you'll be able to have a wash and brush up before you get into this uniform. Now, there's a night nurses' room just down the corridor. You'll find a bite of breakfast there.' She looked at her watch. 'I'll be back here at nine-thirty sharp. Please be ready for me.'

'Of course! Incidentally, thanks for letting me sleep on. I was very tired last night.'

'That's alright, Superintendent wanted you to be fresh and rested this morning. I have to take you across to 'D' Block.'

Amy was glad of the woollen cape she had been given as part of her new uniform. It turned out to be a long walk to the separate buildings, destined to be her place of work.

She found herself walking out behind the main hospital complex, crossing a branch railway line with the hospital train terminus to her left, and then passing a signpost to "Piccadilly."

'So what, precisely is this?' queried Amy, pausing at the signpost.

Her companion grinned. 'Piccadilly is the main thoroughfare for the hutted hospital we have here. There are scores of wards in huts, and hundreds more patients beyond the original ones in the main hospital. You'll keep fit just walking to and fro.'

Another few minutes found them approaching a relatively new neo-Georgian building.

'This is 'D' Block. I'm going to take you in to meet Captain Danvers. He is expecting you.'

Nurse Jefferies rang a bell to a heavy oak door. There was some delay before this opened, and the two of them were ushered in to a well-lit entrance hall. Amy was surprised and pleased to see a bright display of spring flowers in a large vase, and prints of soft impressionist paintings on several walls. She could also hear the muted sound of music being played on a gramophone somewhere off one of the corridors. The nurse who had let them in, having disappeared momentarily, now returned with a casually dressed, middle-aged man.

'Thanks for bringing Mrs. Nicholls over, nurse. Can we offer you a cup of tea? No?'

Jefferies shook her head, and smiling, made her exit and began her walk back to the main building.

'I'm Captain Danvers, Royal Army Medical Corps. Welcome to 'D' Block. Come into my office and have a pew.'

Amy was even more impressed by Danver's office than she had been by the entrance hall. Again, there were bright flowers on display, interesting photographs on the walls, several comfortable chairs, and shelves on one wall with a wide variety of ornaments, souvenirs and mementos spaced along them. Hanging on the back of a door was an army captain's uniform. Amy instantly recognised a Military Cross on it. She had one exactly the same – posthumously awarded to her husband the previous year.

Danvers himself, although in the casual civilian clothes, looked smart and urbane. His brown corduroy jacket and cavalry twill trousers and soft suede shoes gave his lean frame an artistic appearance. His hair was blond and thick and slightly ruffled. His tie-pin, apparently silver, bore the initials "RD." Amy decided that he had a sensitive face, with rather tired looking eyes. He certainly didn't have the air of a stiff and starchy officer about him. She liked what she saw.

'I hope that Miss Ransome has explained to you the nature of the work we do over here,' said Danvers, smiling at her earnestly, and taking a packet of Woodbine cigarettes from his jacket pocket.

'She made it clear to me that your patients here are suffering from mental disturbance. I've heard of soldiers suffering from shell shock. Are they the sort of patients you have here?'

'Shell shock isn't a term we tend to use here. The army doesn't like the description, and it can be very misleading.' Danvers got up to go to the window, revealing a slight limp and a dragging effect of his left leg, as he moved across the room. 'It's certainly true that most physical wounds in this war are caused by artillery weapons.' He turned and looked at her, with a new light in his eyes. 'The casualties we get here in 'D' Block are certainly traumatised by war, but not just through shellfire. For many men, the sort of horrific experiences in the battles they've been fighting for two and a half years now, have simply tested their bodies and minds to breaking point.

'Nurse Nicholls,' he went on, resuming his seat, 'I'm a clinical psychologist. I was transferred to the RAMC after losing part of a leg at Ypres in 1915.'

Amy smiled at him. 'If that's your uniform hanging on the door, Captain Danvers, then I'd already worked out that the Military Cross on the tunic wasn't awarded to you for your psychological work.'

He chuckled. 'Your sense of irony impresses me, Nurse. But I'm no longer a combatant now. I'm a psychologist, but one with a soldier's memories of the Western Front still fresh enough to understand what these men have been through, and I want to help them as much as is humanly possible.'

'Well,' said Amy standing up, 'if I'm going to work for you, then isn't it about time that you showed me around 'D' Block and introduced me to some of your patients?'

Danvers didn't answer her, but his face displayed the pleasure and satisfaction that he took from Amy's unhesitating reply.

Chapter 12

The battalion was on the move. It was the 25th of March. The weeks of manoeuvres in the fields around Beaufort were finally over, and the enjoyable distractions of the officers' club in Avesnes-le-Compte would soon be but a distant memory.

Thomas paused for a moment, letting his platoon of forty-six men move on briefly into the hamlet of Warlus, about halfway on their journey to Arras, which they were scheduled to reach later that evening.

Just as he'd anticipated, the eight hundred or so Invictas making up the Sixth Battalion were almost immediately given the order to stop and fall out for a twenty- minute rest. Within moments, the men were enjoying cigarettes and chocolate and were engaged in animated conversation as they removed their weapons, haversacks and gas helmet bags, to make the most of their brief respite. They hadn't decamped from Beaufort until early afternoon, after a busy morning completing the marshalling and packing of all the battalion's supplies and equipment. A tea wagon had been sent on ahead of them, however, and steaming mugs of tea were now rapidly appearing among the soldiers.

Thomas looked at his watch: four-thirty exactly. At this rate they would be arriving in central Arras well after dark and, hopefully, after the end of any German artillery fire on the city for the day. Apparently, they would then descend into the labyrinth of cellars below the city where they would be briefly billeted, before going into the front line just east of the city.

His thoughts were suddenly interrupted by John Broadbent, who had wandered over to keep him company.

'No blisters yet, I hope, Thomas.'

'Not so far, but then we've only strolled about nine miles. I might let you bathe my feet this evening, though.'

'It might cost you a bottle of wine – if they let us out of our billets.'

Thomas smiled. 'Certainly, it's at night when the city comes to life again. Apparently, it's a pretty dangerous place in daylight hours. That's precisely why we can't march the battalion in until after dark.'

'Have you been to Arras before?'

'It's where I detrained after the journey from base camp at Etaples, a few weeks back, when I joined the rest of you. It's pretty much a ruin, really.'

'Winson, over here, please.'

They both turned to see Lieutenant Standish, the company commander beckoning from the other side of the road. They walked across, and were also joined by Gerry Porter.

'Winson', said Standish, 'orders from the adjutant. It seems that a Jerry aircraft has crashed a mile or so north of here. A local farmer and his lad dashed into the village and bearded our colonel about it before he even had time to get off his horse. It's a genuine report – the farmer brought the pilot's Luger pistol back with him. He says the pilot's badly injured, especially about the face. They left him with the aircraft. Major Falcon has ordered me to send a detachment to the crash site; I'd like you to take a party from your platoon.'

'How do I find this aircraft, and who shall I take with me, sir?'

'The farmer's son will be with you in a moment or two. He'll act as guide for you. You'd better take a corporal and four other men. No – make it six. We'll have to leave a guard at the crash site after you get the pilot out; at least until a Royal Flying Corps vehicle gets to you. The adjutant is trying to telephone RFC now.

If the RFC are delayed, then leave two sentries there while the rest of you fetch the pilot back here.'

'Do you mean the battalion is to stay here until we do bring him back?'

'Definitely not, the rest of us have to get into Arras before too late into evening. I'm afraid that Colonel Drummond won't spare you a motor vehicle for this job either, and there isn't a civilian car in this place. Take an empty Lewis gun handcart with you in case you need it for the pilot,' replied Standish curtly, already walking away. 'But don't worry. I'll see that there's some motor transport to get you away from here and into the city later tonight. If the pilot is still alive, he might have vital information for Divisional HQ. Now sort your party out, and leave the rest of the platoon in the tender care of your sergeant.'

They'd been walking along a minor road for about twenty minutes, and had reached a high point with clear views to the north and east, when the lad grabbed his arm and pointed excitedly to a farm track a half mile away:

'…C'est là, monsieur! L'avion allemand!'

Thomas peered through his field glasses towards a hedgerow just off the farm track. The German aircraft, its fuselage painted a bright yellow colour, was inclined at a steep angle, its nose partly buried in the hedgerow. The blue tail-plane had a large black cross, painted on it.

'Any sign of life, sir?' said Corporal Jenkins, joining him.

'No, but I think that I can make out the pilot's head and shoulders…and perhaps an arm dangling over the side of the cockpit. We'd better hurry on down.'

Ten minutes later found them approaching the wrecked machine. Thomas instructed the men to separate and approach the aircraft cautiously, just in case the pilot was feigning unconsciousness, and might have another weapon. But their precautions were unnecessary. The figure in the cockpit was motionless, and around his flying goggles the rest of the pilot's face was a horrific red colour.

Smithers, one of the men in their party had by now clambered onto the wreckage of one the aircraft's wings and had taken a closer look at the apparently lifeless form of the pilot.

'His face looks badly scalded to me, Mister Winson. Just as though he's copped a load of boiling water over it.'

Thomas turned to the remaining men. 'Turner and Williams, take up guard positions about twenty yards away from both sides of this hedge. Keep your eyes skinned on the sky. It could be that some of this man's comrades might try and fly back to find him. We're miles from anywhere, and this field might permit Jerry to land a 'plane and try a rescue attempt. It's been done before, and if they try it today we don't want to be strafed first. Hughes, get up and see if you can help Smithers pull the pilot out of the aircraft. Be as gentle as you can.'

He stood back with Jenkins and Walters, his servant, who was also a stretcher-bearer and had had the foresight to bring a rolled up stretcher with them.

'Jenkins', said Thomas, 'do you have a sketch book with you?'

Jenkins smiled. 'It's my stock in trade, Mister Winson. I'm never without it.'

'Excellent! Get sketching the aircraft, then. And make them technical sketches, please. Note down any names or numbers of equipment on and in the aircraft.'

By now, Smithers had confirmed that the pilot was still breathing, but unconscious. Walters scrambled up to help the others lift him down from the cockpit. They laid him on the stretcher and Walters examined the pilot's body and clothes with his practised eye. 'No apparent bullet holes in him, sir. No blood, either. But his face is horribly scalded. Smithers was right.'

Thomas went over to the remains of the aircraft where Hughes was pointing out bullet holes on the top of the fuselage just in front of the cockpit.

'The engine's not an air-cooled one, sir. The cylinders are inline and water-cooled. See these reddish brown streaks on the fuselage: they're rusty water stains. The bullets must have punctured the engine's radiator and coolant pipes. That's how the pilot was scalded.'

Thomas turned back to Walters, scratching his head.

'Will he survive, do you think?'

'Difficult to say, sir. Apart from the shock of the crash, and the burns, we've no idea whether there are any internal injuries from the crash. He may have been knocked unconscious if his head hit the front of the cockpit, or those two machine guns in front of him. But he's still breathing, and there's quite a strong pulse, too…'

He was interrupted by a sudden groaning from the pilot, whose eyes were now just visibly beginning to open behind the misty glass of his flying goggles. The groaning was soon followed by movement, as the flyer attempted to raise one of his hands towards his face.

'Steady on now, old chap, you mustn't touch that face of yours.' Walters looked up at Thomas: 'At least he's regaining consciousness. But he'll be in agony if I don't give him an ampoule of morphine.'

'Go ahead - and can you put some sort of dressing over the scalded flesh?'

'I'll do what I can. But he badly needs a hospital. Let's hope the RFC transport gets here soon.'

By now, Jenkins had had a closer look at the aircraft and called across to them:

'The aircraft's called an Albatros – a 'D 111', according to an identification plate inside the cockpit….' He got no further, as a sudden shout came from Turner on the other side of the hedge.

'Mister Winson! Two more aircraft! See, approaching from the north. They've just turned towards us. I can't tell if they're German or ours.'

In a flash Thomas's binoculars were up and being tracked onto the planes. As the two aircraft banked and began another turn, he instantly spotted the black crosses on the aircrafts' side fuselage and tail fins.

'Take cover!' he bellowed at the top of his voice. 'Get into the ditch under the hedge – quick as you can. Have your rifles cocked and ready.'

'What about the prisoner, sir?' called Walters, anxiously.

'Leave him there, on the stretcher and out in the open. If they are aircraft from his squadron, the pilots might spot their pal on the stretcher and realise what's gone on. His leather flying coat and helmet make him pretty distinctive.'

By now the two planes were down to a hundred feet and roaring over the top of them. Jenkins pointed up excitedly.

'They're the same as the crashed aircraft – two more Albatrosses.'

'Open fire on them!' screamed Thomas, and there was a fusillade of shots as the men with rifles instantly fired off several rounds from their Lee Enfields. The aircraft banked sharply and flew off north. Within seconds all was quiet again. Thomas kept the men under cover for another minute, or two, until it was certain that the skies were again empty.

They pulled themselves out of the hedge, including the farmer's lad, who was now shaking uncontrollably. Thomas put his arm around the boy's shoulder.

'C'est tout. C'est fini.'

'Vehicle approaching, sir.' Hughes was pointing. 'Coming from the direction of the village we left.'

* * * *

By six o'clock that evening they were back in Warlus, sitting around a table in the farmer's kitchen eating fried eggs and chips, and doorsteps of well-buttered bread. The farmer's lad plied them with glasses of beer as he recounted his adventures to his parents, and used his hands and realistic sound effects to describe how the German aircraft had swooped over them, and how the soldiers with him had fired off their rifles at the enemy. Thomas and Jenkins, who also had a fair grasp of French, translated for the others.

''Course, pity was, sir, that we only had an empty gun handcart with us out there,' said Hughes, with a twinkle in his eye. 'Now if only I'd had the Lewis gun with me, I'd certainly have brought one of the other Jerries down, too.'

'Quite right,' echoed Williams, but then I'm pretty sure that at least three of my rifle bullets hit their mark.'

'What?' scoffed Turner, 'you can't hit a barn door at twenty yards. If anyone hit his mark on one of those aircraft it would have been me. Didn't you know I got top marks for rifle practice last...'

But the good-natured banter was then interrupted, by a knocking at the kitchen door. An army driver from Arras was outside to transport them into the city. Thomas thanked the family for their hospitality, shook the hand of the farmer's lad and led his men outside. They piled into the back of the truck and started the five or six mile drive into Arras.

Thomas was rapidly deep in thought. Had he been right, ordering his men to open fire on the enemy aircraft? What if the German pilots had retaliated and machine-gunned the hedgerow? What if he had lost the lives of his men in his very first experience of combat leadership, however unusual, almost surreal, the circumstances had been?

Should they have waited – in the hope that one of the other Albatrosses might have landed, thus perhaps enabling them to capture another airman, and an undamaged aircraft? No – the presence of the Lewis gun cart and his men's scattered other kit on the ground would have given that game away. He quickly convinced himself that the sudden orders he had barked out back at the crash site had been the correct ones in those circumstances. There had been enemy aircraft just overhead. Whatever the odds had been on one or two shots finding their mark on the swooping aircraft, he and his men were at war, and his act of defiance in ordering the men to shoot now seemed to hold some sort of symbolic potency for him.

Certainly the British Royal Flying Corps officer and his men who had arrived at the crash scene shortly afterwards had seemed impressed by what had been reported to them. They had been delighted to find a downed Albatros, confessing to Thomas that the German flyers were dominating the skies over the battlefields on the other side of Arras, and shooting down inferior allied aircraft at a disturbing rate. They admitted that the damaged radiator on the crashed Albatros had probably been inflicted by ground-fire, rather than as a result of aerial combat.

Thomas had taken little comfort from the informed assessment of current allied airpower which he'd had to listen to, and was glad to be told that all his party could leave the site to two aircraftsmen sentries, pending clearance of the crashed aircraft by the RFC later. The wounded German airman, meanwhile, had been spirited away to hospital in Arras.

His thoughts were suddenly broken by Corporal Jenkins: 'A penny for them, Mr Winson.'

'Oh, it's nothing… I was just wondering…' But he didn't finish, as his attention was instantly caught by the open sketchbook on Jenkins' knee.

'Good Lord, these drawings are really impressive. You've captured the scene perfectly. Your eye for detail is remarkable.'

'Thank you, sir, I did specialise in technical illustrations for many of my commissions before the war.'

'I can well understand that. Nonetheless your portrayal of the men you've included here is excellent, too. You've even succeeded in making Williams look normal!'

'Not an easy task,' laughed Jenkins, pointing at the victim of their joke, who was now fast asleep in the back of the truck and oblivious to the sound of his name.

By now, darkness had fallen. The truck was slowing down, and it shortly stopped at the first of several army checkpoints they would have to negotiate as they now made the last part of their journey through the western suburbs of Arras.

They had now entered the chaotic world of a medieval city caught up in the terrifying technology of modern warfare. For much of the last two and a half years the city had, quite literally, been part of the Western Front. The German army had been entrenched only yards from Arras' eastern edges. The city's buildings had been pulverised by enemy artillery, leaving a hopeless tangle of demolished brickwork, collapsed roofs, shattered timbers and broken glass.

But, as Thomas and his group were soon to experience, the supreme irony was that both civilian and military life in Arras still flourished – not in the ruins of the buildings above ground level, but in the extensive cavities below the ground from beneath which the chalk had been hewn for building much of the original city itself. The citizens of Arras, together with thousands of allied soldiers, had now colonised this vast network of cellars and caves beneath what remained of the streets, and had there eked out a sort of troglodyte existence, safe from the far-reaching shells of German heavy artillery.

Now, within a few minutes of alighting from their transport, Thomas and his comrades were being guided through the city's main square, the Grande Place, then around the remains of two more street corners, through a doorway and down some stairs. They had entered a labyrinth. The first cellar they went into had been connected to another, this to another. Holes knocked through other cellar walls had created a network of inter-linked subterranean rooms. Turning another corner they heard a babble of voices, and then came upon the familiar sight of several men sitting about the floor, with kitbags, haversacks, blankets and weaponry neatly arranged around the room.

'Rough lot in here, sir,' joked Smithers, 'it's 'A' Company.'

Thomas turned to a corporal who had stood to salute him. 'Where's 'B' Company billeted?'

'Just through here, sir. I'll show you the way.'

Two more large cellars later and they found the familiar figure of Broadbent, rummaging through his valise.

'Good to see you, Thomas, everything all well?'

'Yes, thanks, I'll give you all the details later. For now, I'd better report straight to Standish. Is he nearby?'

'Just around the next corner. Company commanders are with the colonel and the adjutant now. Rumour has it that we are only down here for one night. We might be going into the Line tomorrow.'

As he turned the corner, a door opposite him opened and the battalion's four company commanders came out. Standish's face lit up as he recognised Thomas' face in the dim lighting.

'Well done, Winson. Are you all back safely?'

'We are, sir. The RFC brought enough men out to the crash site to leave their own sentries there. We've just arrived – many thanks for the transport back from Warlus.'

'No problem at all. Incidentally, have you and the men had anything to eat since we left you?'

'Yes, thanks, sir. The farmer's wife did us all proud once we got back to the village – best eggs and chips I've had since leaving Folkestone.'

'Fine. I'll let the adjutant know that you are back. He might want to see you – oh, and he's got the CO with him, so be as cavalier as you can manage.' Standish winked, turned and knocked on the door. After a brief pause he beckoned to Thomas and ushered him into another cellar, which had effectively become the temporary battalion headquarters.

Colonel Drummond reclined casually in his chair as Thomas saluted him, then drew a deep breath and tut-tutted loudly, before bringing the flat of his hand down on the table top in front of him.

'Well, Second Lieutenant Winson....' He paused dramatically before continuing. 'German High Command isn't very pleased with you.'

'Sir?' replied Thomas, very weakly.

'It seems that this afternoon your men opened fire on two of their aircraft.'

'It seemed the appropriate thing to do at the time, sir.'

'That's as may be, now, personally, I couldn't give a tinker's cuss for what the Germans might be thinking. What annoys me, however, is not that the men opened fire on those aircraft. No, what annoys me is that none of you managed to shoot either of them down. What have you got to say for yourself?'

'Well, sir... I... I'm sure that the men did their level best....
We only had a few seconds, and...and....'

He stopped what he was saying, realising by now that the
adjutant was desperately trying to stifle a titter, and that the
colonel's face was opening up into a huge grin.

'Alright, Winson, just my little joke. Stand easy. We've had
a report from the RFC liaison officer, so we know what went on
this afternoon. You put up a good show. Let's hope one or two of
your men's bullets found their mark.' He turned to the adjutant.
'I'll leave you to take Winson's own report, Major.' The colonel
then lifted his tall and powerful frame from his chair and breezed
out of the room.

Major Falcon closed the door and beckoned Thomas into a
chair.

'The colonel finds it difficult to avoid displaying a mischievous
sense of humour, Winson, but you'll soon get used to it. The
problems come if you think he's being funny, when in fact he's
being deadly earnest. Now, you can forget that I just said that.
Understand?'

'Of course, Major.'

'Anyway, I can tell you now that the German officer recovered
from the wrecked aircraft is already in the underground hospital
here. Apparently, he was flying out of the aerodrome at Douai. Initial
reports suggest that he might live, but with a terribly disfigured
face. Anyway, your part in his recovery is now over. As the colonel
said, you put up a good show. Now, it's best you get back to where
your company is bedding down. The whole battalion stays put here
overnight. Tomorrow night we go into the forward and support
trenches outside the city, so be sure to sleep well. Your report of the
afternoon's events can wait for a day or two.'

* * * *

Ten o'clock the following night, and Standish and the company
sergeant major carried out a meticulous inspection of the four
platoons of 'B' Company.

114

The assembled men were in full fighting order and equipped for winter warfare in the open: leather jerkins were being worn, greatcoats had been rolled up, feet had been rubbed with anti-frostbite grease, and spare socks were stowed in haversacks. The men had donned trench gloves and steel helmets, and they carried their rifles and, in their bandoliers, the statutory one hundred and twenty rounds of ammunition per man.

Some of the men were also acting as ration parties, carrying two sandbags full of rations, and petrol cans full of chlorinated water. Added to all this was the additional loading of haversacks, gas helmet bags, waterproof capes-cum-groundsheets, and bags full of Mills bombs.

Thomas and the other platoon commanders had dispensed with their distinctive officers' uniforms and were wearing the same tunics as the other ranks. This had become accepted practice for many officers in the trenches, thus making it less easy for the German infantry, snipers especially, to pick them off first during any attacks made on the enemy trenches. Walters had considerately sewn a subaltern's shoulder pip onto the back of Thomas' tunic.

Eventually they were all ready to move, and on Standish's order they began the circuitous journey through the cellars, and then the climb back up to street level.

The men were all subdued as they emerged into the street, where the remainder of their equipment was waiting for them. The men said little as Jackson, the platoon sergeant, organised the hauling of the handcarts of blankets, Lewis gun and ammunition, trenching tools, food and basic cooking gear.

Finally, they moved off, through the ruined streets, heading for the city's eastern suburbs. The skies were black, the inky darkness above only punctuated by the eerie light of an occasional distant flare, or the sporadic flashes of far-off artillery.

Twenty minutes later, and the chaos of destroyed buildings, and the barely recognised road surfaces, seemed to have placed them into a nightmarish wasteland. The men gingerly picked their way through piles of brick-rubble and shards of roof tiles, trying to avoid tripping and stumbling and, if they failed in this, their profanities cut the cold night air.

Then a muffled order for silent movement came down the column. They were about to enter the system of communication trenches that would eventually lead them to their allotted places in the forward and support trenches. The next half an hour or so marked by far the most dangerous part of their journey. If the enemy artillery got wind of the mass movement of men and material through the congested trench systems, then all hell and fury would be unleashed on them. Darkness and quiet movement were now the Invictas' best allies, and the men had to embrace them unfailingly.

Silently they trudged on. By now their handcarts had been left behind them, all their equipment now being worn, carried or shouldered. Thomas shuddered momentarily as the assorted smells of the trench system began the inevitable assault on his nostrils: foul and stagnant water, damp and slimy sandbags, wet and rusting metal, spent cordite, the stench of latrines, men's sweat, creosote and chloride of lime.

Another brief pause, and then the men they were about to relieve from their stint in the trenches began to slowly trudge past them, their faces etched with the strain of their time facing the enemy. No words were exchanged, and a short while later the muffled footsteps of the other troops had faded away.

Chapter 13

Amy approached the bed at the end of the ward as quietly and as unobtrusively as she could.

She could see a pair of twitching feet on the floor, poking out from beneath the end of the bed. Blankets and sheets had been hurriedly and chaotically pulled about and over the bed, as though a hasty attempt had been made to convert it into some sort of child's shelter or camp. It reminded her of her younger brother's "secret place" from their infant days, in a bedroom of their house more than twenty years earlier.

Another patient, Lieutenant Ripley, approached her from the other side of the ward. He looked genuinely embarrassed as he stammered: 'I'm sorry, Nurse Nicholls. It's all my fault. I was tidying my bedside locker and…and… and I dropped my cigarette case. It fell with a bit of a bang. I didn't mean it, Nurse…it wasn't deliberate…honestly it wasn't.'

'Of course it wasn't,' said Amy gently. 'Don't worry yourself. I'll soon sort this out. You finish your tidying. I'm really pleased that you made the effort. It's a sure sign that you really are getting back to your old self. Leave this to me now.'

She turned back to the bed and the incessantly twitching feet. 'Captain Peters, are you in there? Can I have a word, please?' No answer.

'Captain Peters, it's Nurse Nicholls. Please answer me.'

Only a low moaning sound came from beneath the bed. She

slowly bent down and gingerly lifted a corner of a blanket a few inches off the floor.

'No! No! Don't show a light…they'll snipe us for sure. Drop that cover, or they'll get us, just as they got the sergeant. Drop that fucking cover!'

'Please don't swear like that, Captain Peters. It's quite unnecessary, and very offensive. There are no snipers here. There are no guns or enemy soldiers within a hundred miles of us. I've told you that many times before, haven't I?'

'What was that bloody bang, then?'

'That was simply Mr Ripley's cigarette case falling to the floor. You can come out now. It really is quite safe. Please believe me.'

She went around the bed, pulling up all the blankets and sheets. Captain Peters' face peeped out, displaying a tic like movement beneath his left eye, but he was reluctant to emerge any further.

'Please, Captain. The staff nurse is due to do her round of the ward very soon. You don't want to get me into trouble, do you? Now come along. Come out and help me tidy up this bed of yours.'

He slithered slowly out from his hiding place, looking nervously around him and clutching at the front of his trousers, across which a large stain had now spread. 'I've had an accident, nurse… I'm sorry.'

'Never mind. Let's get you to the washroom and get those trousers off you.'

She related the incident to Danvers as they made their way towards the hospital's railway station, partly by way of apology for being a little late and somewhat out of breath.

'Yes, I'm afraid that we've made rather slow progress with Captain Peters since he came out of the Neurological Section,' Danvers remarked ruefully. 'He's still hypersensitive to any sort of banging noise. We've a long way to go before we can overcome that problem.'

'Do we know what happened to make him like that?'

'No we don't know too much at all, yet. He was suffering from total amnesia when he arrived here, and was completely mute for quite a while. He also displayed extreme spasmodic movements, but the worst of that seems to be over. It's mainly occasional twitching now, and that persistent tic beneath his eye.'

By now they had reached the railway platform and Danvers glanced at his watch. 'This train due has a lot more customers for us, and they will all be heading for 'D' Block. I've had to arrange for some extra beds in two of our wards.'

Amy pointed, as the hospital train rounded an area of woodland and then began to slow as it approached the platform. Once it drew to a halt, a small army of hospital orderlies and nurses moved forward and began opening the train's doors to start the unloading of stretchers onto the platform.

Danvers waited patiently until it became clear which carriage contained the casualties whose wounds were mental rather than physical. Slowly, walking figures began to emerge from the rearmost carriage. Several men, some apparently stupefied, half stepped, half stumbled from the train. Their movements were rhythmic and spasmodic in several cases, and some of the men were only prevented from falling by the prompt and efficient attention of their accompanying nurse and orderlies.

Some of the casualties for 'D' Block were stretcher-bound, still suffering from transient paraplegia and nervous shock so great that they had no real control over their limbs. Even some of the walking wounded had grotesquely bent backs. Others were partially blind. Most of the men were trembling and clearly confused. Every face Amy counted seemed to be a mask of abject misery.

'I've counted twenty-six cases in all, Captain Danvers,' she said, as she saw the last of the stretcher cases carried off the platform.

'Good. Less than I expected, actually. But God help us if Haig orders a spring offensive next month. Now, I'm going to collect what medical records have come with these casualties. I'll see you back in 'D' Block in half an hour.'

* * * *

119

Late that night, Amy tucked in the last of her new patients, left the ward and went along to Danvers' office. She tapped gently on his door.

'Come,' a quiet voice summoned.

She went in to find him busily writing case notes on the new arrivals.

'It's time that you got back to your wife and family in Hamble, sir,' she said gently but firmly.

He looked at his watch, closed his folder and leaned back in his chair. 'Got the last of them into bed, then?' he queried.

'We have – just. But I suspect it won't be a very quiet or peaceful night. There are some very disturbed cases among this lot. Several of them will need the Neurological Unit in the main hospital, surely?'

'You may well be right. But they'll all be with us here for two to three weeks' probationary treatment first. Remember, we're first and foremost a clearing hospital for this type of casualty, and the work always begins here in 'D' Block. Anyway, you've met your first hospital train now. How do you feel about the experience?'

'To be absolutely frank, it's left me rather emotionally drained. I simply wasn't prepared for the pathetic state of those men as they stepped off the train and onto the platform. This shell shock – sorry! Neurasthenia, as we now have to call it, is it a phenomenon unique to this particular war?'

'No it isn't,' he replied, gesturing for her to sit down. 'In truth, this sort of trauma has probably been around as long as wars themselves. Certainly, there's documentary evidence of it being recognised centuries ago.' He tapped out the bowl of his pipe before continuing: 'Medically speaking, though, the problem really came to the fore fifty years ago in the American Civil War. That was almost certainly because the new rifles and ammunition developed then proved to be such efficient killers. Later, of course, our thoughtful friend Mr Maxim invented his machine gun. Now add to that the terrifying variety of heavy artillery being used on the Western Front, and it's hardly surprising that we are seeing so many traumatised men. What is unique to this war, though, is the sheer scale of it. I'm not just talking about the weaponry now. The conditions in the trenches are horrendous. Men on both sides are being dehumanised on an absolutely massive scale. Their bodies and minds can only take so much. In 'D' Block here, we see the ones whose spirits have broken. Their systems have collapsed. They've been so overwhelmed by anxiety, that they can no longer cope physically. Put bluntly, their nervous systems have been shattered.'

'And we have to pick up the pieces?'

'Exactly – and though you haven't been with us very long Nurse Nicholls, I think that you are doing a damn fine job. Now, you get off to your bed, and I'll take your advice and get back to my family.'

She could only toss and turn in her bed that night. Her tiredness taking poor second place to the impact on her mind of the pathetic figures she'd watched staggering from the hospital train that afternoon. Normal, peaceful sleep proved not to be an option for her. She found it quite impossible to get some of the men's tortured faces out of her mind, and in the few brief periods of fitful sleep which she did get, she found herself imagining first her dead husband, then Thomas, then Simon Mockett, slowly parading in front of her, all displaying the same overt symptoms of the neurasthenia she had witnessed earlier that day.

Finally, her alarm clock sounded her personal reveille, and she realised that within the hour she must steel herself to start a new shift in 'D' Block, and confront the task of trying to help in the painful and frustrating process of rehabilitation of the new patients – all of them newly arrived from the apocalypse known as the Western Front.

Danvers was already back on duty as she entered the ward where she was normally based. He had no time to notice her initially, however, as, together with a staff nurse, he was trying to comfort a patient who was sitting hunched up on a chair and sobbing uncontrollably, his shoulders shaking and tears pouring off his face onto the shiny floor.

'D-d-don't put me back to bed, please! I can't sleep…I don't want to sleep…I can't bear the nightmares I have…I…'

Danvers pulled up another chair and sat beside the patient, putting his arm around the man's heaving shoulders. 'Nobody is going to try and put you back into bed; that I can promise you. Now, if you can manage it, we'd like you to try and eat a little breakfast. Then, as it's such a fine day, we'll introduce you to Nurse Nicholls ...' He turned, catching sight of Amy, just behind him. 'Ah, here she is. Nurse Nicholls will take you into the garden later. You can enjoy some sunshine.'

'That sounds a splendid idea to me,' chipped in Amy cheerfully. 'Perhaps you can help me pick some daffodils. The captain here likes to keep our ward looking spring-like.'

While the staff nurse began to persuade the patient to wipe his eyes and face, Danvers ushered Amy to one side. 'I've just introduced you to Colonel Wilkins. He's a South African. He was CO of an infantry battalion that was pretty well wiped out in Delville Wood on the Somme last year. He was still holding things together until two weeks ago, when he suffered a total physical and mental collapse. He blacked out without any warning and was unconscious for eight days. When he finally came round, he couldn't even remember his name. According to his records he was regarded as one of the bravest, most inspirational battalion commanders the South Africans have got.'

'Until two weeks ago,' Amy added.

'Exactly. That's when he finally cracked. And, according to his case notes from the Base Hospital at Boulogne, without any apparent previous trouble during the previous six months.'

Amy looked across at the colonel, who was now seated at a table, staring impassively at a plate of toast that had been put in front of him. 'It's taken six months, then, since losing his battalion for his breakdown to happen,' she said. 'How long will it take for his recovery to materialise?'

Danvers looked her straight in the eye before answering: 'Maybe within the year, maybe next year, perhaps never. That's the terrifying aspect of what we have to deal with here. We can only do our best.'

The next day was her day off. She had borrowed a bicycle and was slowly pedalling along the lane that led through the woods and out of the hospital grounds towards Hamble village, barely two miles away. Smoke rising from some trees a short way off from the side of the lane indicated part of the woods being coppiced, or tidied. Or, she speculated, perhaps marked one of the occasional Hindu cremations, which took place after the death of an Indian patient from the main hospital. If so, the ashes of the deceased would later be fed into one of the streams, which led from the grounds down to Southampton Water. She reflected that it all seemed a far cry from the preferred River Ganges…

Eventually she emerged from the woods not far from a path which led to the hospital cemetery, climbed a grass rise to some meadows, and began to walk the bicycle to where she could connect with the road which led down to the waterfront at the bottom of the village.

Here she found a patch of grass, unpacked her sandwiches and sat to relax and enjoy the view across the river to Warsash and beyond. Slowly the tensions of the previous day began to ease as she watched the ferryman plying his trade to and fro across the river. Soon, she dozed off – waking with a start a few minutes or so later, to find a group of swans pecking at the ground around her, scavenging for the crusts she had dropped earlier.

Getting up, and brushing the crumbs from her skirt, and relishing her newly found feeling of relaxation, she remounted her bicycle to start the journey back to Netley, and to the harsh reality of the war in which she had now become personally involved.

Later that evening, an orderly came across from the main hospital with a message from Miss Ransome, the superintendent of nurses. It asked for her to be in the superintendent's office at eight o'clock sharp the following morning.

The next day Amy knocked on Miss Ransome's door with considerable trepidation. She had convinced herself that she was to receive some sort of reprimand - but why? What misdemeanour had she committed? Had she been too strict with her patients –

or perhaps too liberal? Was she to be told that she wasn't cut out for 'D' Block, and would be better deployed elsewhere in the hospital?

She finally entered Miss Ransome's office, finding her already deep in conversation with Danvers and an RAMC colonel she'd not met before.

'Ah, Nurse Nicholls,' asked Miss Ransome, 'How are you after your first two weeks in 'D' Block?'

'I'm surviving, I think, Miss Ransome. Of course, I find the work very demanding, but immensely satisfying. I do hope that my efforts have been satisfactory, so far.'

Miss Ransome smiled benignly at her. 'We've no reservations on that front. Quite the contrary, in fact. You're here this morning on Captain Danvers' personal recommendation.'

'Recommendation for what, Miss Ransome?' Amy asked.

The superintendent shifted awkwardly in her seat and turned to the colonel, who quickly responded to his cue.

'Mrs Nicholls,' he began, 'I'm Colonel Fenwick. Like Captain Danvers here, I work with neurasthenia victims.' He paused for a moment before continuing: 'Let me explain to you why I'm here. Since the beginning of this war, but particularly so since the Somme Battle last year, the minds of the army medical authorities have been sorely concentrated by the huge increase in the numbers of men who have been so seriously mentally traumatised while on active service. As you already know, this hospital at Netley is where they are first brought from abroad.

'Unfortunately, many of the casualties who arrive in 'D' Block here have faced a long delay since their condition was first diagnosed. What this means is that there has also been a long delay in providing initial treatment. Such delays often compound the problems. It can mean that subsequent treatment is not as effective as we would wish.'

At this point, Danvers turned to Amy: 'The colonel and I have been campaigning for some time to persuade the army medical service to provide some sort of reception and first aid treatment for neurasthenic victims much nearer to the actual battlefronts.'

'And at last the powers that be have accepted our arguments,' said Fenwick excitedly. 'They've agreed to the setting up of a trial field hospital in France, exclusively for the kind of casualty who often has to wait for too long before being taken to some sort of mental ward at a base hospital, or being brought back here to Netley.'

'Why are you telling me all this?' asked Amy.

'Mrs Nicholls, I've managed to recruit – well, press-gang, actually, a select team of army nurses to help me run this first field hospital. But I also need some VAD support, too. The people I'm looking for need to be able to offer me a great deal. They need to be very special.'

Miss Ransome looked directly at Amy: 'Mrs Nicholls,' she coaxed gently, 'we are all aware that you have only been here a few short weeks. But Captain Danvers has convinced us that you have particular talents for the job Colonel Fenwick has outlined. I won't spare your blushes. He has spoken very highly of your ability looking after the patients in 'D' Block. Furthermore, he doesn't want to lose you. But the colonel's brief is an exciting one; for the first time we have the opportunity of helping these poor neurasthenia victims with some prompt primary care in the field. I support the scheme unreservedly.'

'I agree with all that, Mrs Nicholls,' said Danvers. 'Of course we'd like to keep you in 'D' Block, but I can't stand in the colonel's way. He desperately needs one or two VAD people who are free to travel, can speak some French or German, can drive a motor vehicle, and who are robust and independent.'

'So, will you join our team, please?' implored the Colonel.

Amy looked from Danvers to Miss Ransome: 'Do I have any choice in this matter?'

'Of course you do, my dear,' said Miss Ransome, 'if you wish to stay in 'D' Block, then so be it. We will be only too glad to continue to have your help and support.'

'I second that, of course,' said Danvers.

'Do I have to give my answer here and now?' asked Amy, turning back to Colonel Fenwick.

The colonel smiled. 'I can give you a little time to reflect on your decision. But in seventy-two hours time my team leaves Southampton Docks for France. I'd really need your decision by tomorrow evening.'

'You'll have it by tomorrow morning, I promise you.'

'Thank you, Mrs Nicholls,' said Miss Ransome, smiling graciously, 'but remember, whatever you decide will be a right decision as far as Captain Danvers and I are concerned. And now I think that we have kept you long enough. We don't want your patients complaining to us that we have delayed your return to the ward.'

Amy shook hands with the colonel, nodded to Danvers and left the superintendent's office.

Ten minutes later she was trying to find Captain Peters under his bedclothes again.

*　*　*　*

Later that afternoon she was helping Lieutenant Ripley to pack his things. He was moving on to another hospital in Surrey.

'You're so much better now,' Amy said. 'I suspect that within another few weeks they'll let you go home to get acclimatised to civilian life again. Where do you live, incidentally?'

'Just outside Shrewsbury, it's a beautiful part of the country. I can't wait to see it again.'

'It might be two of us on the move this week,' mused Amy.

'What?' Ripley smiled. 'Don't tell me that they are going to let me take you with me to the new place in Surrey.'

Amy's chuckle vibrated around the ward. 'No, I'm afraid not. But it's a lovely thought. More importantly, do you realise what has just happened here? You're starting to get your sense of humour back? I'm so pleased about that.'

'So where are you going then?'

'Well, it hasn't been completely settled yet; but they want me to go to France – to help in a sort of field hospital. The only snag is, it would mean working with more people like you out there.'

She smiled mischievously, so that Ripley would be sure that she was joking, too.

He sat down on his bed, looking intently at her. 'Do you really mean it? A sort of ward like this behind the lines?'

'That's what they've told me.'

'I can understand why they want you to go. I'm sure that one of my reasons for improving here is because of what you've done for me. If there is such a thing as a talking cure, then I think you are it.'

'Do I really talk that much, then?' said Amy, feigning shock.

'Of course not, but you certainly have a knack of making people feel better about themselves. That's exactly what is needed in the casualty clearing stations in France and Belgium. When poor devils break down, and suddenly become useless, and can't look anyone in the eye… well, someone like you could make a world of difference, believe me.'

She didn't answer. Ripley's bag was packed, and she was needed elsewhere. She smiled at him and squeezed his arm. As she left the ward, she realised that an important decision had been made for her.

Danvers got to his feet, smiling as Amy entered his office. 'Well, then, you have some news for me, Nurse Nicholls?'

'Yes, I do have. I've decided to join the colonel's new unit.'

He reached out and shook her hand. 'I'm really pleased for Fenwick; not so pleased for 'D' Block, of course, but I'm sure that you'll be a great asset in France.'

'Do I need to contact the colonel myself?' Asked Amy.

'No. Leave that to me. I'll telephone him in Southampton, straightaway. Now, you will be required to embark from the docks the day after tomorrow, so you are excused any further duties here. Sort your things out; I'll get someone else to cover your next shift. Fenwick's a fine doctor, by the way. You won't regret deciding to work with him.'

'I hope that I won't regret giving up my work here. You've been an inspiration, actually.'

Danvers blushed, but gave her a beaming smile. 'Good luck,

Amy, I hope we'll see you back at Netley sometime. I'll look out for you every time a train arrives.'

By late the following afternoon she had managed to make a return shopping trip to Southampton, launder and press some clothes, complete most of her packing, and write several explanatory letters to relatives and friends. As she sipped a cup of tea in the nurses' rest room, the door suddenly burst open, and a staff nurse beckoned her, excitedly: 'Quickly, you're wanted down on the pier!'

'Wanted on the pier? What on earth do you mean?'

'I'm serious. There's a naval officer asking for you. He says his name's Mockett. His destroyer is anchored in Southampton Water. He definitely wants to see you. I explained that you were off duty now, and that I'd try and find you.'

Amy gave a hurried explanation and set off down the path to the pier.

Simon was waiting with a military policeman, who started back to the hospital as soon as Amy appeared.

'Simon, what on earth brings you here?'

'You, of course, Silly! Look, that's my ship out there. Isn't she beautiful? I thought I'd get a minesweeper, but they've given me a new destroyer. Anyway, aren't you pleased to see me?'

'Of course I am! But it's such a surprise. You must have pulled rank to even be allowed to land on this pier.'

'Of course I pulled rank, but enough of that. Now, what's this nonsense about you going off to France?'

'I suppose the staff nurse told you that. Well, it's no secret now. I leave tomorrow.'

'In that case I shall probably be leaving with you, then.'

'What on earth do you mean?'

'The navy certainly doesn't let young women swan off overseas unless they are properly looked after, you know. My ship might well be part of your escort tomorrow. If so, you'll be in good hands.'

She looked intently into his eyes: 'I'm not so sure of that, Commander.'

Chapter 14

The flare rose languorously upwards, bathing the night sky in a lurid green colour. No sound accompanied it and, as the ghostly light faded away, the silhouettes of sandbags and barbed wire above the parapet of the trench soon disappeared.

Private Walters, Thomas' servant, pulled back the blanket from the dugout's entrance then, having entered and carefully re-positioned it, he lit an oil lamp and turned to where Thomas was lying on a crude wooden cot.

'It's six a.m., Mr Winson. You wanted me to give you a shake well before stand–to.'

Thomas grunted a thank you, and then turned onto his side, grimacing as a large rat scuttled away over the earthen floor of the dugout and out into the night.

'Your rat control tactics don't seem to be very effective, Walters. I think that little bugger's had my last bit of chocolate.'

Walters grinned and pointed down at another sleeping figure on the other side of the dugout. 'Are you casting nasturtiums on poor Mr Broadbent here, sir?'

'That's another platoon commander you're referring to and, lucky for you, he's still fast asleep. No, I can't blame him for chewing this hole in my pocket.'

Walters peered down at what remained of the side pocket of Thomas' tunic. 'Well…. if you will leave titbits there, sir, what do you expect? Good job it wasn't your best dress uniform, that's all I can say.'

Thomas stretched, yawned and then reached out for his helmet, respirator and electric torch. 'Let Mr Broadbent sleep on, Walters. He was out on a wiring party for several hours. I want to go and do my rounds before stand-to.'

He moved out into the trench, carefully masking his torch with his other hand, and began quietly picking his way along the duckboards. He soon came upon Private Turner guarding part of the parapet. 'All quiet, here?' Thomas whispered.

'Like a graveyard, sir. Well... I suppose it is a graveyard of a sort here, isn't it, sir?'

Thomas edged past, nodding. He was impressed by Turner's display of black humour, but didn't comment on it. He paused at the junction with a communication trench that led back to the support trenches a hundred yards or so behind them, and still he marvelled at the hundreds of telephone cables snaking past him.

'Halt – who goes there?' said a quiet but alert figure further along in the gloom.

'It's Mr Winson. Just doing my rounds.'

'Advance, Mr Winson, it's Corporal Jenkins.'

Thomas hadn't been robbed of all his chocolate, and he handed a few squares of it to Jenkins, who smiled his pleasure as he took it and slipped it piece by piece into his mouth.

'So,' said Thomas, 'how are our new men coping with their first spell in a front line trench?'

'The ones in my section seem to be doing alright. It certainly doesn't seem to have interfered with their sleep much. Not so far, anyway.'

'I'm glad of that. Let them enjoy it while they can.'

'Sergeant Jackson keeps them busy enough when they are working but, generally, things have been pretty quiet for us up until now.'

Thomas continued his brief tour of his platoon's position, finishing up by crawling along a short trench, or sap, which led about fifteen yards out into No Man's Land to a shell crater. The sap was no more than thirty inches deep, and he slithered painstakingly along it to avoid offering any part of himself as a target to any nocturnal German sniper, who might be lurking out there in another crater or other hide.

He finally slithered down into the shell crater, where Privates Hughes and Smithers were on lookout duty.

'Morning, sir,' said Hughes, turning away from the sand bags lining the front edge of the crater.

'I was awake, too, Mr Winson,' chipped in Smithers.

'So, how did you know I wasn't a Jerry, then?' Thomas asked. 'I could have crept across no Man's Land and got round behind you.'

Smithers shook his head: 'No, sir. We'd have got wind of all that stale Jerry sweat and wet leather from a mile away. Now, you smell as sweet as…'

'Yes, alright, Smithers.' Thomas paused after speaking, and then gingerly moved a small piece of blanket, which was acting as a shroud covering a small gap between the sand bags just above their heads. He peered out of the gap, first checking that there was no light source from behind him to silhouette his head. 'Nothing to report, then?' he queried.

'We've neither seen nor heard a dicky bird, sir,' said Hughes. 'It must be almost stand-to time, mustn't it?'

Thomas looked down at his watch, jealously guarding the light from his torch. 'Yes, another ten minutes or so. I'll make sure that you are relieved soon after; then you can get back and…' He didn't get the chance to finish the sentence, as the sudden roar of an approaching heavy calibre shell compelled them all to dive down into the bottom of the crater.

The enemy shrapnel shell exploded immediately above the front line trench, about forty yards away from their own position. They could hear pandemonium breaking out behind them.

Thomas hissed an order for his two companions to remain at their post in the crater, then he rapidly crawled back along the sap to the main trench, where the sound of men's screams was splitting the cold night air.

His platoon sergeant, together with Walters and another stretcher-bearer, almost collided with him as he tumbled out of the sap.

'I think the shell must have exploded directly above number Nine Platoon's position, Mr Winson,' gasped the sergeant. 'I think our own platoon's alright. Corporal Jenkins had a narrow escape; a shell splinter almost broke his rifle in two. He's unharmed, though.'

'Thank God for that,' mumbled Thomas. 'Let's get along to Nine Platoon's position and see what we can do – quick about it!'

He felt his heart pounding and his legs shaking as they scurried along the duckboards to the part of the trench that had taken the full force of the overhead explosion.

By now they were officially into the thirty-minute 'stand-to' period immediately before dawn breaking. The scene they would normally have expected to see would have been one where all men would methodically be taking up station, weapons at the ready, in their preparedness to fight off any possible enemy attack at first light.

Instead, as they turned into Nine Platoon's trench section, the sights that met their eyes were nothing short of being apocalyptic.

The bottom of the trench, for several yards, was a ghastly stew of blood and water, full of the debris of human parts, timber from duckboards, pieces of blanket, fragments of hessian from sandbags, and assorted items of men's battle-order equipment.

Three men had been killed outright. One, a sentry, had been cleft in two from shoulder to pelvis. Another had been decapitated, and the third had been so dissected by a hailstorm of shrapnel that only a few recognisable parts of him could be seen in the chaos before them.

Thomas fought back against his immediate inclination to start retching, and tried to look beyond the immediate carnage in front of him. Several other men had been badly wounded and were in shock, their anguished faces now gradually being illuminated by the early dawn light. Other stretcher-bearers were now arriving and looking to see how best they could help their stricken comrades, before starting to get them away to the first-aid post further back in the reserve trenches.

By now, two otherwise unharmed men were vomiting, one of

them shaking and sobbing uncontrollably, as he saw the terrifying sight of the mutilated bodies nearby.

Standish, the company commander, had now arrived on the scene. Ashen-faced, but apparently calm, he found Thomas and Sergeant Jackson already trying to steady the other men, several of whom needed to be distracted with prompt and necessary activity to maintain the integrity of the trench's defensive systems.

'Where's Mr Armstrong, then?' asked Standish.

'We haven't been able to locate the platoon commander yet, sir,' replied the platoon sergeant.

'Mr Armstrong left his dugout about an hour ago, sir,' said another man. 'He was out on his rounds.'

One of Nine Platoon's corporals approached them. Together with a stretcher-bearer, he'd been helping with the grisly task of collecting body parts: 'Excuse me, Mr Standish. I think you should see these.'

Standish looked down at two items being shown to him. One was an officer's silver whistle, the other a gold wristwatch. He reached out and took the watch, turning it over. He showed it to Thomas. 'There are initials engraved on the back: "J.A."'

'It's Armstrong's watch,' said Thomas, trying desperately to control the tremor in his knees, and the quaver in his voice.

* * * *

By the end of that morning all the obvious effects of the shell burst had been cleared away. The surviving casualties from Nine Platoon, six in number, had been taken down to the underground hospital in Arras, the remains of the three dead carried away for subsequent burial, and essential repairs carried out to the area of trench which had borne the brunt of the overhead explosion of the shrapnel shell.

Thomas had returned to his own platoon in the neighbouring section of trench, where he had found several of his men numbed by the dawn experience, though none of them actually wounded. Astonishingly, some of the men who had been off-duty and asleep at the moment the shell exploded, had no recall of the incident.

Corporal Jenkins appeared calm and unruffled, though he had escaped certain death by just a matter of inches. The shell splinter, which had impacted four-square on his rifle stock and barrel, completely wrecking the weapon, had caused its owner no more than some bruised right ribs.

'My God, you were damned lucky,' observed Thomas, as he looked at the shattered Lee Enfield rifle still propped up against the trench wall.

'Well, that particular splinter clearly didn't have my name on it. It's a rotten shame about young Mr Armstrong, though. He didn't last long with us, did he?'

'It was sheer bad luck,' said Thomas.

'Yes, it so often is. One isolated shell: nothing coming before it, nothing afterwards. Not this morning, at any rate. Poor Mr Armstrong just happened to be in the wrong spot at the wrong moment.'

'Anyway,' Thomas continued, 'no one else in our platoon hit by any of the shrapnel?'

'Nobody at all. A few men felt some spent bits falling around their funk holes, that's all.'

Thomas pointed at Jenkins ribs: 'Are you sure that you don't want to get those checked by a medical orderly?'

'I don't think so, thank you, sir. I've had far worse on the rugger pitch before now. If they seem to be more than bruised, I'll get them looked at once we're out of the trenches. That can't be long from now – a few days at the most, I'd think.'

They both turned to see the adjutant, Major Falcon, approaching.

'Morning, Winson, Corporal Jenkins.' Like Thomas before him he looked down at the remains of Jenkins' rifle. 'Nine Platoon's sergeant told me about your close call, Corporal. I'm very glad that you are alright. Winson, a word with you in the dugout, please. Your servant has kindly brewed us some tea.'

Falcon sat down on the end of the cot in the dugout, sipping his tea and making copious notes as he spoke: 'We've done all we can for the casualties in Nine Platoon. As it happens, our battalion is due to leave these trenches tomorrow and go back into the city. We'll sort out young Armstrong's replacement from there.' He paused and looked up at Thomas: 'Did you get to know him well?'

'As well as one can during a few weeks of manoeuvres, sir. We had some convivial evenings at the officers' club, but he was barely out of school, of course.'

'Yes, I know that you are that much older and more experienced in life than he was.' Falcon paused as his brow furrowed: 'I must write to the lad's parents later today. The sergeant handed me his two effects found after the shelling.

'Actually, Winson,' he continued, 'if I hadn't had to come up to this trench today I was going to get a message up here to get you down to Battalion HQ. We have another job for you.'

'Really? What's that then, sir?'

'Well, as I'm sure you must be aware, the number of Lewis guns the army now uses has grown very significantly. Our battalion has sixteen of them, and the word is that the numbers of them may be set to double this year.'

'That has to be good news, sir. The Lewis is such a versatile weapon. Its mobility makes it so valuable – if we ever get out of the trenches for long enough to be truly mobile, that is.'

'You've hit the nail on the head there. And that is what the generals are hoping for, and sooner rather than later. Now, as part of this strategy of dramatically increasing numbers of light machine guns, all battalions are required to nominate one of their officers as Lewis gun officer. We'd like you to do the job for our battalion.'

'What exactly does it entail, sir?'

'Initially a week's training at the machine-gun school at Etaples. You'll be schooled in all the technicalities of the weapon, do a lot of range practice, and basically become a bit of an expert in the Lewis and its best use.'

Thomas thought for a moment before replying: 'Why an officer, sir? The battalion has plenty of trained Lewis gunners among the rank and file.'

'I won't deny it, Winson. But that's why there's the new

thinking among the generals. This war is getting more and more specialised. High Command is recognising that we need some specialism at leadership level, too.'

'As a matter of interest then, sir, what made you think of me?'

Falcon held up his notebook, tapping it with a finger of his other hand.

'I consulted this, and it helped me to remember that you'd told me how last year you had had to learn to use a Lewis gun in Trones Wood. You therefore already have some experience in the weapon. Added to which, you told me about your motorcycle exploits and how you used to keep the machine roadworthy. I concluded that you could already use a screwdriver and spanner if it became necessary in the field. Not too many of your fellow officers share those skills.'

Falcon, smiled kindly at him. 'So will you take the new job on, Winson? For a start, it gets you a week in Etaples. You won't be machine-gunning all that time. And the firing range is close to Paris Plage, on the coast, remember.'

'The prospect is too good to refuse, sir. When will I have to go?'

'Tonight. Our men will be in billets in the city for a week or more from tomorrow night onwards. As soon as your Lewis training is over, then you come straight back and join us there. Now, I'll see you at the Battalion HQ an hour after stand-to this evening. I'll have your travel warrant ready for you.'

* * * *

The train taking him back to the coast that evening was crammed with other officers and men, most of them going on short leave only. It seemed to be an almost open secret that April, now just a day away, would be the chosen time for the next major allied offensive on the Western Front.

Before he was fully settled down, however, he suddenly realised that, physically, he felt far from normal. He was experiencing strange sensations all over his body. His arms and shoulders seemed leaden and aching, and he found it extremely difficult to keep his eyes open. He felt totally disorientated and seemingly overwhelmed with the feelings of deep exhaustion. He tried to look about him, but the faces of the other men in his compartment seemed to merge into one blurred image, devoid of any real interest or meaning for him. The forces bearing on him seemed too powerful to resist. He fell into a deep and dreamless sleep, which, it transpired, lasted several hours. When he finally awoke, it was bright daylight and strong hands were pumping at his shoulders.

'Now come on', a firm voice was saying, 'this is the station where we all have to get off. You do want Etaples, don't you?'

Thomas found himself staring up into the face of a medical corps major. It was a clearly concerned face, whose practised eyes were looking closely down at him.

'If you weren't drinking heavily last night', said the major quietly, 'then I'd say that you'd either got a touch of trench fever, or that you were a trifle shell shocked.'

Thomas, already realising that he felt quite normal again, quickly got to his feet.

'I'm perfectly alright thank you, sir. I was just very tired.'

'More like totally exhausted, I'd say. Have you had a particularly bad time?'

'We had a nasty shell-burst directly above our trench outside Arras at dawn yesterday. Several of a neighbouring platoon were killed. The platoon commander was blown to pieces. He was an eighteen year old, just out of school.'

'Pretty traumatic stuff; your own body was clearly telling you something last night. Do you want me to get you looked over at Base Camp?'

Thomas turned away, nervously. 'It's a very kind thought, sir, but I really am feeling normal. That sleep worked wonders for me. I'm sure that I don't need to trouble you further.' He stepped briskly from the train and, without looking over his shoulder, headed toward the station exit.

*   *   *   *

The next morning found him seated with twenty other officers, all of them subalterns, in a lecture hut in the grounds of the army's Machine Gun School, just back from the sand dunes on the coast at Paris Plage. A young major strode into the hut, smiled broadly and addressed those gathered in front of him: 'Gentlemen. Welcome to the officers' Lewis gun course. You've all been selected specially to help lead the army's expansion of numbers of Lewis guns. Now, how better than to begin, but by paying proper homage to a great American military engineer and weapons genius: Isaac Newton Lewis. Lewis was a brilliant inventor, ignored by his own countrymen, but who came to Europe and rightly convinced the Belgians, and then ourselves, of the true merits of the light machine gun bearing his name.'

The major paused momentarily, before walking over to a trestle table and picking up a Lewis gun. He held the weapon in front of him: 'Now, if you haven't yet fired one of these, then very soon you will have the opportunity to do so. Over the next five days you'll also learn to strip and reassemble it blindfolded. You'll learn to master every skill your number one Lewis gunners can already boast back in your own units. By the time you leave here you will all be Lewis apostles and, if I get my way, crack shots into the bargain. For the moment, please answer the sergeant here as he calls out your name and unit...'

The rest of the day seemed to slip effortlessly away. Thomas revelled in the classroom tasks set for him and his fellow students and particularly enjoyed the afternoon shooting session out on the ranges behind the dunes. He found that the skills he had had no choice but to learn rapidly in Trones Wood eight months earlier seemed to have been autonomised in his psyche. The other students around him expressed their astonishment at his apparent natural ability with the light machine gun, and did not hold back their praises for him. Finally, as the late afternoon sun began to set, they were all dismissed for the day and hopped on to the London omnibus for the journey back to Etaples.

Thomas had declined all offers for a night out on the town with the other subalterns. His mind was set firmly on one thing: another visit to the small terraced house where Marion Brenchly lived.

Chapter 15

He waited patiently in the bar across the street from her little house. The end of the afternoon rapidly became evening. By seven o'clock he wondered if she would come at all.

Eventually he spotted her slim figure and graceful step approaching her front door. He quickly paid his dues at the bar and scurried across the road. She looked up from her bag, not recognising him in the dimly gas-lit street.

'Don't be alarmed, Mrs Brenchly,' he ventured. 'It's only me, Thomas Winson.'

'Good heavens, so it is. What on earth are you doing back here so soon, Thomas? I hope you haven't deserted, or something else dramatic.'

'No I'm here quite legitimately,' he said, rather pompously. 'My battalion felt that Etaples needed me more than they did. I'm back for another week's training over at Paris Plage.'

She smiled knowingly. 'Would I be far off the mark if I said "Rat-tat-tat...." '

'Not far, but I've finished my first day there. I hope you don't mind me looking you up again.'

'Not at all, and now that you have, you must come inside so that I can see you properly.'

She lit the gas-lamps in the living room, revealing just how she had made her mark on the house in the few weeks since his last visit. There were new curtains, and a rich red throw over a chaise longue. Several posters of past theatrical productions decorated various areas of the walls. A vase of daffodils brightened the crude wooden table beneath the front window.

'Please sit down,' she said. 'I'll open a bottle of wine for us. Do you have time for a glass of wine, or do you have to report back to the camp soon?'

'No, I'm not required for anything else today. As long I get back to Paris Plage in the morning, then the army seems satisfied. But tell me, was this a bad time to call on you?' He braced himself for an unfavourable reply.

She smiled broadly. 'No, I'm pleased to see you again. I never expected that our paths would cross again. And, of course, I'm delighted that you followed my advice and kept away from the hospitals here.'

'How's your administrative job going there, Mrs Brenchly?'

'Please… you can dispense with the formalities. You must call me Marion. And the job…well, I've just finished a particularly frustrating day. So let's talk about something else, shall we?'

He nodded politely, taking the glass of wine offered to him. 'Of course, no shop talk this evening. But you seem very settled in this little house of yours. Do you still live here alone?' He quickly went on, 'I'm sorry, I wasn't fishing for news about Mr Brenchly, I….'

'It's perfectly alright, you haven't offended me. Yes, I do live here alone. I'm afraid that Paul, my husband, has refused to accept that I'm determined to continue the job I came out here to do. I had only one other visit from him; the week after that scene of ours that you witnessed near the fish market. We haven't spoken to each other since. I did try to contact him by telephone at the staff HQ at Montreuil. On both occasions I failed to get past the switchboard there.'

'There may be sound military reasons for that,' said Thomas. 'It's an open secret that we're all going to be caught up in a major allied offensive next month. As a staff officer your husband could have been sent anywhere along the front lines to gather intelligence. It's hardly surprising that you have found it difficult to contact him.'

'That's a very charitable thought, Thomas. But I doubt that he would have found it too difficult to contact me if he'd really wanted to. But we won't dwell on it.' She looked at her watch. 'Good Lord, it's eight o'clock, and I'm ravenous. Would you like something to eat?'

'I certainly would, but you've obviously had a long day. Can't we both go out and have a bite to eat in a restaurant somewhere?'

She pondered for a moment. 'Would that be wise? Aren't there some rather silly army rules about that sort of thing? I mean, you fraternising with lesser mortals such as me?'

'Well, that's it isn't it? They are silly rules - but it's not as if you are a VAD nurse. That might be a problem for us. No, I don't think the work you do should stop us from having a bite to eat together. Anyway.... I'll be gone again by the weekend. Life's too short to worry about a brief interlude in a restaurant.'

She turned and looked at herself in the mirror before replying: 'Very well, you've convinced me. But do I look a bit of a wreck? Should I change?'

'Definitely not,' he replied. 'Let's just go as we are. And anyway....'

'Yes?' she asked.

'You look fine just as you are.'

* * * *

The restaurant was eerily quiet. They were shown to a small table in a candle-lit corner. There were no other army uniforms to be seen. The few civilians at other tables appeared to be middle-aged couples, quite smartly dressed.

'This place is mainly patronised by the business community of the town,' said Marion. 'I was introduced to it by one of the locals who supplies goods to the hospital. For some reason it's not popular with your officer colleagues.'

Thomas looked closely at her. He could easily understand why he had so much wanted to see her again. Her bright blue eyes darted about the room before settling again on him. Unless her husband's behaviour on the one occasion that Thomas had met him was totally out of character, he wondered how on earth she had married someone as apparently disagreeable as Paul Brenchly in the first place.

He decided to take the direct approach to satisfy his curiosity: 'Tell me, Marion…do you love your husband?'

Her gaze didn't falter. Perhaps her theatrical training had taken over. She looked him directly in the eye, pausing only very briefly before replying: 'Yes, I love my husband. The question you are probably trying to ask is *"Am I still in love with him?"* I should be telling you to mind your own business, Thomas.'

'So, are you in love with him?' he persisted.

'No. I'm not. I know very well the difference between loving someone and actually being in love. I don't believe that Paul and I were ever truly in love. Does that satisfy you?'

'Perhaps. It's just that, well… that first time we met at the hotel in Boulogne… you seemed so vivacious and in control. But your husband, apart from behaving so crassly towards you, at least when I saw him, just didn't strike me as the type you would have chosen for a soul mate.'

'Why are you asking me such intimate questions, Thomas? More to the point, why on earth am I answering you so candidly?'

He smiled, 'Perhaps I'm becoming a closet psychologist, Marion. I have to censor my men's letters home, remember. And in quieter and more private moments they sometimes seem to want me to offer them some counsel about their private lives.'

She laughed, and reached across the table to touch his arm. 'Well, this may be quiet and reasonably private where we are now, but please spare me the inquisition regarding my marriage. It's no concern of someone of such tender years as you. Ah! here's our cassoulet. Now, concentrate on your food if you please.'

He had the good grace to accept her mild admonitions, but was secretly pleased that she had been so forthright with him about her relationship with the Major. He remembered how offensive he'd found Brenchly's behaviour that day near the river, and how he had retaliated then with the ill-chosen remark about the distance of staff officers from the battle fronts.

But then suddenly and without warning, he found his mind beginning to wander inexorably back to the horrendous scene in the trenches less than three days ago, and the cruel way in which the life of young Armstrong had been so instantly and brutally terminated. In another few days he would be returning to other trenches, and the next big "push" – so what on earth was the point of not trying to make the very most of what opportunities for pleasure that life might yet hold for him?

'Hello, sir! Are you still with me?' she said. 'You seemed to be in another world then. A penny for them, please – your thoughts that is. And, incidentally, it is pudding time. I can recommend the crème brulee.'

'Please forgive me – I'm so sorry. I didn't intend to be rude. Yes, I was miles away for the moment. It won't happen again.'

'Thomas, you have big tears in your eyes. What in god's name were you just thinking about? What's wrong?'

'Well... I'm afraid that I left Arras in a bit of a hurry at the weekend. For a few moments then, my mind wandered back to a ghastly incident we'd had just before I left the trenches. We lost several men, including an eighteen year-old subaltern, to a shrapnel-burst. He was literally blown to pieces. The horror of it all just flooded back.'

'My god! You poor boy! Perhaps we should leave now. I could make you a strong cup of coffee back at the house. It's probably delayed shock setting in. You were sensible to talk about it, though. Now that you have, you must try and put it behind you. It'll be for the best.'

She took his arm as they turned out of the restaurant and headed back towards where she lived. She could feel his arm trembling as they walked silently. Neither of them spoke. Eventually they turned into the street, which led to her house. But then his steps faltered as they reached a small, unlit cul-de-sac just short of her front door. He turned into it, pulling her towards him. She felt his arms encircle her, and then his lips were on hers.

She made no effort to resist him, but after a second kiss, she gently pulled her head back.

'Thomas, I don't think this is a good idea – really I don't.'

'At this moment it feels like a very good idea to me.'

He tried to kiss her again, but she raised her hand and gently held his chin: 'If it seems like a good idea, then it's almost certainly because you still feel upset and fragile. That's not surprising after what you've just been through at the Front.'

He ignored what she said, and kissed her again. She responded, with no apparent lack of enthusiasm. But then continued: 'Is this why you were asking me all those questions about my relationship with Paul? Are you using what I said just to take unfair advantage? Did you call on me today just to set out to seduce me this evening? Thomas, I hope you didn't feign your upset back in the restaurant.'

He stepped back from her and gently pulled her out of the cul-de-sac to where they could clearly see each other's face beneath the gentle hiss of a street lamp.

'You have every right to question me like this, Marion.' he said in a steady voice. 'But no – I certainly wasn't pretending to be upset back there. I simply couldn't control the emotions I was feeling then. To be honest, I had a bad time travelling back here on the train. An army doctor was all for taking me into sickbay. He suspected shell shock. He knew damn well that I wasn't myself. I thought I'd pulled myself together again. But seeing you tonight… it's just made me a bit emotional, I suppose. We have to suppress all these things in the trenches. The stiff upper lip is our only option – unless things really fall apart. I haven't got to that stage yet, God willing.'

Half an hour later, and after some strong coffee, they sat in her parlour looking at each other. Thomas wasn't sure what he should say next. She was deep in thought, but eventually broke the silence.

'I've never been unfaithful to Paul. And, despite his recent behaviour, I couldn't just take up a casual relationship with someone else – especially someone I've hardly known – and ten years younger than me, I should add. But I have to say that I feel very disorientated by this last hour or so. On balance it's a pity for both of us that you came here this evening. I don't want to seem cruel, Thomas, but that's how I feel at this moment. Now tell me truthfully – exactly why did you come back here again?'

In the long pause that followed, he got up and made ready to go. But then he did his best to explain how deeply influenced he'd been by their first meeting in Boulogne, and how he'd found her company so invigorating and fascinating. He couldn't bring himself to admit that only the day previous to arriving in Boulogne that Sunday, he'd been in the arms of another woman. Somehow, and he couldn't fathom exactly how or why, the torrid interlude with Amy in Capel seemed quite irrelevant to his initial meeting with Marion Brenchly.

All he could try and explain to Marion now was the immediate excitement he'd felt when he had been ordered to return to Etaples. How the opportunity to see her again had gripped and dominated his thoughts.

She also got up, but instead of going to where he stood, she moved towards the front door, then turned and gazed at him.

'I'm flattered by all this, Thomas, of course I am. But it doesn't alter the fact that I have a husband near here. A husband to whom, despite these last few weeks, I thought that I was reasonably happily married. Now, as I said, I'm a bit off balance now. I think it would be for the best if you went back to your camp. I....'

'Please.... Please, Marion,' he interrupted. 'Tell me that you'll let me see you again before I go back to Arras at the end of the week'

'I should say no – but I can't. I'd never forgive myself if I didn't see you again. And the way this ghastly war is going, that's probably what the alternative would be. Come here again on Wednesday evening.'

*   *   *   *

He knelt on the floor in front of the army blanket. It was dark. The windows of the instruction hut had been mostly blacked out from the watery sunshine outside.

He carefully ran his fingers over the scattered components, almost caressing them, to register their position on the blanket in front of his knees. One by one his mind recorded their positions: magazine pan, barrel and receiver group, operating rod assembly, trigger housing and pistol grip, feed cover, feed arm assembly, butt stock, gear casing…now, two small items yet to locate… Yes! Cartridge… and the charging handle. All parts present and correct.

'Very well, gentlemen', said the sergeant instructor, 'When I say *"Go"*, then assemble your weapons. Ready…Go!'

Thomas deftly picked up the first two parts of the machine gun, slotting them together, and then continued rebuilding the Lewis. Just as he finished the task the hut's curtains were being swept apart by orderlies, and the sergeant instructor was rapidly moving among the six officer trainees scattered about the hut's dusty floor.

'Not bad, gentlemen. Not bad at all. Certainly it was a big improvement on yesterday's efforts. You'll be doing this exercise several more times today. It's got be like the Lord's bloody Prayer. Remember, before we finish the week here, you have to demonstrate that you can strip, clean and then reassemble a Lewis in night-time trench conditions – and then fire off three pans of ammo with acceptable accuracy.'

At the end of the day, Thomas filed out of the hut and headed straight to where he could hitch a lift back to base camp. It was Wednesday, and he desperately wanted to wash the sand and grit of the firing-range out of his hair and put on some decent clothes for his visit to Marion's.

He'd spent the previous evening in town, drinking rather too much with the three other officers sharing his tent. It was only towards the end of this afternoon that his head had recovered from the splitting headache with which he had started the day. Nonetheless, he'd performed well enough in his training. Two more days of instruction and testing and he should be a qualified Lewis gun officer.

He waited until seven o'clock before setting out for her house, managing to buy some flowers and a bottle of wine near the fish market.

When she opened her door to him he gasped at what he saw: She was wearing an electric blue silk blouse, and a close fitting black skirt trimmed with silver buttons. Her hair was gathered up and held at the back by a Spanish style comb. Her make-up was restrained and subtle, emphasising her beautiful eyes. He was momentarily rendered speechless as he rather clumsily offered her the bunch of flowers.

She smiled, but said nothing as she laid the flowers on a window sill before turning back to him. He finally opened his mouth to speak, to try and articulate an apology for his behaviour two days earlier. But there was no opportunity for any words to come. She had now moved very close, and her arms were around him, her hands gently cupping the back of his head. She put her lips on his, very tenderly. He responded, embracing her, kissing her, feeling his heart pounding and a strange tingling sensation in his legs that seemed to reach down to his very toes.

Then he felt her warm tears running down his cheeks. He felt her tremble as his lips caressed the lobe of her ear, and she pressed herself against him.

'Make love to me, Thomas…please…forget anything I said when you were last here. I want you to love me, now, tonight. For god's sake stay and love me…'

He was woken by the bell of a neighbouring church clock, striking eleven. He felt her warm thigh straddling his, and her arm across his shoulder. He made to get up and out of the bed, but felt her grip on him steadily tighten.

'Thomas,' she sighed, 'you can't possibly leave yet. We haven't finished the Third Act. This is simply the interval.'

'I mustn't outstay my welcome, and they might take a snap roll-call back at camp,' he replied. 'For some reason they've been tightening up on discipline recently. Morale has been a worry for the army there, so far this year.'

'Very well, but you can manage another ten minutes. There is something I have to explain to you.'

Needing no further persuasion he slid effortlessly back into the sheets, pulling her towards him.

'Let's not worry about explanations, Marion. I'm sure they can't be that important.'

'No, they are to me,' she said firmly, pulling herself up onto an elbow, 'I need to explain to you why my fidelity to Paul seems to have gone out of the window this evening. I want to be honest and open with you. It's important to me.'

She raised a finger towards him and gently traced patterns over his face.

'It's only right you know this, Thomas. You see, yesterday I finally managed to make contact with Paul again. More than that, he agreed to come across to Etaples. It was my day off, you see, and we were able to spend several hours together.'

He interrupted. 'I see. So what does that say about this evening?'

'No, you must let me finish. I simply have to be level and straight about this. You need to understand. I tried very hard to reconcile Paul to my being out here. I truly hoped that he would see reason and forget his prejudices. Had he shown some scope for compromise then I would have tried to get our marriage back to some sort of normality. If he'd done so, Thomas, then you wouldn't have been here this evening. I'd determined that, if necessary, I'd get word to you that our agreement to meet here tonight would have to be broken. I'd steeled myself not to see you again.'

'I see,' he muttered. 'Then I take it that your husband didn't respond as you'd hoped. Does that mean I'm here now as second best?'

By now she was out of bed and pulling on a robe.

'That's a cheap remark, Thomas. I hope you didn't mean it.'

'No, of course I didn't. I'm really ashamed that I said that to you. Please forgive me.'

She sat on the edge of the bed, taking his hand in hers.

'Thomas, I simply wanted you to know the truth. I still love my husband, despite his behaviour. But yesterday he forfeited any exclusive rights to my affections. I don't feel any shame about this evening. You've made me wonderfully happy these last few hours. I'm so glad that you came. Now please tell me that this hasn't just been a young soldier's casual affair with an older woman, scorned by her husband?'

He pulled her across him and kissed her with a passion he'd never quite experienced before.

'Marion, you're utterly irresistible to me. I think that my being sent back to Etaples was a wonderful stroke of fate. I'm totally besotted with you. What's more important is that you've been the best medicine I could have hoped for. I've completely got over my ghastly attack of nerves.'

'And it hasn't made any difference... the fact that I told you how I would have reacted if Paul had been more reasonable?'

'Not in the least,' he said, looking intensely at her. 'I'm touched by your honesty, but it was quite unnecessary. And anyway....'

'Yes? Anyway what?'

'I need to search my conscience, too. I'm not married as you are. But I did have a brief involvement with another woman, just before I embarked for France last month. It was an old friend and colleague who I met by chance in Folkestone. She'd been widowed, earlier last summer.'

'So, are you now feeling guilty about taking up with me this evening?'

'I should be. I know that. But somehow everything seems insignificant compared with what this bloody war is doing to us all. I arrived here a few days ago in a state of shock. Your husband is probably acting quite out of character. You are vulnerable and lonely. None of us is being true to ourselves. We're all – as you said about yourself the other night: disorientated.'

She put a hand around his neck, pulling his face to hers and pressing a gentle kiss on his lips. 'Let's not talk any more like this, Thomas. Let's just enjoy each other in the little time we have. I want you so much...'

* * * *

He stood smartly to attention, but couldn't resist a slight smile of satisfaction as the Lewis gunner's chevron was handed to him and his hand was shaken by the young major who had welcomed them to the Machine Gun School at the beginning of the week.

'Well done, gentlemen.' said the major. 'Please stand at ease. You'll all be rejoining your various battalions tomorrow. Hopefully, your new expertise with the Lewis will be appreciated by all the men under you, and by your commanders. We must all now hope that this war can now become a more mobile affair this year, and that we can get up and out of the godforsaken trenches. If any infantry offensive is to be successful in 1917, then the Lewis gun will have a major part to play. For now, good luck to you all, and good shooting in your new role as Lewis gun officers.'

Thomas filed out of the hut for the last time. He collected his valise and greatcoat and headed for the transport to take him to the railway station.

He'd taken his leave of Marion Brenchly the previous night. He now had to readjust to his return to Arras and his place in the war's next chapter.

Chapter 16

She stopped the staff car for the third time that morning and sighed with frustration. 'It's no use, Colonel Fenwick, I'm sure that we've taken a wrong turning. There were so many different roads leading out of Hesdin – and to be honest, I simply don't know which one we're on.'

'Don't worry yourself, Amy. We can't be far out of our way. I saw the river just over to our left when you turned that last corner. We need to keep to the course of the River Canche all the way to a village called Frevent. After that, received wisdom is that we head south to Doullens to pick up the main road for Arras.'

'So what do you suggest that I do for the moment?'

'Stay on this road until we get to the next village. We should be able to get our bearings from there. Meanwhile, I'll try and do some serious map reading – but geography was never my strong point at school.'

Amy restarted the engine and engaged gear, pondering on the previous few days' events. The Channel crossing had been without incident, though because of the darkness she had had no idea whether Simon Mockett's new destroyer had been close by her hospital ship or not.

They'd docked at Le Havre before making connection by train with the Base Camp up at Etaples, which was to be their source of supply for the pioneer field hospital, not far from the front line further to the east. But after only one night in Etaples, the colonel had been ordered to head straight for the chosen site of the field hospital, a village six or seven miles south west of Arras.

Amy was ordered to act as his driver and general assistant. If all went according to plan, the colonel would stay on at the building chosen for the hospital. Initially, it would be Amy's job to return to Etaples periodically and oversee the transfer from there of all the necessary equipment and supplies for the hospital. However, the immediate challenge was to find Frevent, somewhere further along the Vallee de la Canche. It was not proving to be easy. Amy was happy to be seduced by the attractiveness of the rural surroundings; it seemed difficult to believe that there was a world war going on not too far away, but she did not wish to appear inefficient as the driver – and she felt hopelessly lost.

Finally they came to a village, where her companion took their map and spoke to a local man who was re-painting the front of the village bakery. After a short conversation and some animated direction from the local, Fenwick rejoined her in the car.

'I'm delighted to say that we are definitely on the right road. This little place is called Fillievres. It's another twelve or thirteen kilometres to Frevent – say eight miles. When we get there we'll try and get something to eat and drink.' He folded the map and tossed it on to the back seat. 'Wake me up when we reach a decent bar, or restaurant, if they run to one.'

Amy glanced at her watch. It was half past noon. She did some basic calculations: half an hour or more to Frevent, an hour's stop for lunch, another hour or so to their destination, if her memory of their planned route had served her well. She drove confidently onward, reassured now by occasional glimpses of the river they were following. The colonel began to snore gently.

* * * *

Meanwhile, in Arras, Thomas searched the sea of strange faces before him. Was he in the right part of the cellar complex? The surroundings certainly looked familiar. Surely his brief trip to Etaples couldn't be playing such bizarre tricks with his memory now that he was back in the city - but where on earth, or more to the point, below earth, was his platoon?

'Can I help you, sir? You look lost. Missing your unit are you?'

He turned to see the ruddy face of a sergeant from the Signals Corps.

'Yes I'm afraid that I am, Sergeant,' Thomas said. 'They were all snug in here last week when I left them. They must have changed billets.'

'Not much doubt about that, sir,' said the sergeant. 'We arrived here last Monday. But the whole city is upside down at the moment. We are expecting the big spring push to start any day now. Word is that it might be this weekend.'

'No idea where I should start looking, then?'

'None at all, sir,' replied the sergeant crisply. He smiled broadly: 'Perhaps you should go back to Etaples.'

'Nice thought, Sergeant, but I don't think my CO would be too sympathetic. No... nothing else for it. I'll go and find the billeting officer. His office is just off the Grande Place somewhere.'

An hour later he was back in another part of the cellars, being guided by one of the army's city messengers who was carrying a large rucksack of mail and other documents.

'It's a long hike to where your battalion is now, sir. You'd never find it on your own,' said his guide, as he led the way down a steep flight of steps, which led to a large circular tunnel.

'Where in hell are we?' asked Thomas, standing on a ledge and looking down at water running along the tunnel bottom.

'Hell is the right word, sir,'chuckled the messenger. 'You're looking down at the Crinchon Sewer. This is the city's main drain. We have to follow this for quite a distance. It will eventually take us to the beginning of the cave complex. The city's cellars have been holding almost thirteen thousand men. The caves themselves accommodate another eleven to twelve thousand. Your battalion was moved deep into the caves last week.'

Thomas didn't answer. He plodded on behind the guide, trying to gauge the distance they were covering.'

After about four or five hundred yards there was a dog's leg in the sewer. The guide paused, and pointed upwards.

'This is where we take a left turn, sir. We're almost below the main railway station now. Jerry loves shelling the station. This particular part of the sewer has been a godsend for getting our troops safely through to the rest of the tunnel system and then into the caves.'

Soon Thomas realised that they had now left the sewer and were heading along a broad tunnel. There were electric lamps and water pipes running along the walls.

He touched the messenger's shoulder: 'I was told that there was a railway line down here, too.'

'Quite right, sir. Though it's a tramline, strictly speaking. You'll see the start of it just up ahead in a moment. It connects with the St Sauveur caves, about another six hundred yards away. That's where your battalion is now.'

After another twenty minutes walk Thomas realised that the tunnel had widened out into what was the first of a series of vast caves. Straddling both sides of the tramline were all the signs and activities of a waiting army. Storage depots with piles of equipment, cooking braziers, wash rooms and toilet facilities, signposts with familiar names such as *Glasgow, Edinburgh* and *Carlisle*. A silent world far below the shell-bursts way above.

They stopped at a door with a sign which had *Caves Major* written on it. The messenger turned and said: 'This is as far as I need take you, sir. The major will direct you to your battalion. Good luck. I hope they don't keep you buried down here for too long.'

He'd disappeared before Thomas had time for a proper thank you and farewell, and then the door suddenly opened.

'My goodness, it's Winson!' said a surprised Bill Falcon, the adjutant, almost colliding with him. 'What's up, didn't they let you outstay your welcome at the machine-gun School?'

'I'm afraid not, sir. But the good news is that I passed muster there, and can now handle a Lewis blindfolded.'

'Well, hopefully that won't be necessary, but it's good to see

155

you back. You've missed nothing here these last several days. Our battalion has been totally confined to one of these wretched caves. Apart from an occasional view of the sky from one of the ventilation shafts, the men have had nothing to distract them. But things might be happening very soon now, maybe in a day or two.'

'The big push, sir?'

'Perhaps. But follow me now – I've finished my business here, and I'll show you where your platoon is. We'll look into the hospital on the way. There's someone I want you to meet.'

* * * *

Beaumetz at last! Amy breathed a sigh of relief. She turned the car off to the right, leaving the main road to Arras, cleared the village and crossed a railway line, then gently brought the car to a halt. She paused for a moment, turned around and smiled at the serene sleeping face of the colonel. Looking at her watch she realised that they were a little ahead of their schedule. It was just short of three o'clock, and they should be only two kilometres away from their destination. She also realised that she could hear the muffled sound of distant heavy artillery. Getting out of the car she looked to the north-east, where the outskirts of Arras were now only seven or eight kilometres away. Within the last few hours the war had drawn so much closer to her.

She returned to the car and found the colonel rubbing his eyes, yawning and saying:

'Do you think it's much further, Amy? Do you want me to do some more map reading for you?'

'I think you'll be pleasantly surprised, sir,' chuckled Amy. 'But perhaps I could have a quick look at the map myself for a moment?'

She glanced briefly at the map and then pointed to a minor road off to the left, and just ahead of them.

'I think that must be our final turning for Rivière and the château. Yes... look down there. That's almost certainly the château, just on our side of that bit of woodland. Do you see it?

The distance and direction is right. We turned off the main road for Arras just before you woke up. I'm certain this is Beaumetz just behind us.'

He gave her a measured, somewhat dubious look, recovered his map and pored over it for a moment. He looked about him and then turned back to her, smiling broadly.

'Well done, Amy. I'm sure you are right. I'm sorry that I nodded off in the car again. But, as it has turned out, it's clear that you are a far better navigator than I am. Just as well, too. I'll probably have to pack you straight off back to Etaples as soon as we've sized up the situation down there.'

She clambered back into the car and they set off on the last short leg of the journey. Within five minutes they had arrived and were looking up at the rather faded grandeur of the château and what was to be the pioneer field hospital for victims of neurasthenia.

As they drew up an RAMC orderly scurried out of the front doors, saluting nervously as he stopped in front of them.

'Colonel Fenwick, sir?' he asked.

'Yes, I'm Fenwick. This is VAD Nurse Nicholls.'

'I'm Corporal Weston. I'm all there is at the moment.'

'All there is! What do you mean, Man? Are you telling me there's no one else here?' demanded the colonel impatiently.

'I'm afraid not, sir. Sergeant Pearson and I arrived here yesterday with some advanced supplies and equipment. The sergeant's gone into Arras today to try and arrange for an army plumber and electrician to come and sort out some of the facilities here. It's all a bit primitive, I'm afraid, sir.'

Fenwick looked at Amy anxiously then strode into the château, with her and the orderly in hot pursuit. Half an hour later, having completed a full inspection of the building and scribbling copious notes, he sat down and drew a deep breath.

'Well, at least we have a telephone here, Amy – we must be thankful for small mercies,' he said, resignedly. 'We must hope that the sergeant gets back soon with the maintenance men.' He looked at his watch, then continued: 'All being well, the rest of our medical staff should start arriving tomorrow. But the supplies and equipment already here aren't nearly enough. I'm going to make out a further inventory of things, which we really must have here by the weekend. I'll do this straight away, and then tomorrow, I'm afraid, I'll have to ask you to get directly back to Etaples with the inventory and pull out all the stops to have everything despatched here without delay.'

'Do you really think I've got enough clout to achieve that on my own, sir?' Amy asked anxiously. 'Will they listen to a VAD and take notice?'

'Don't concern yourself over that. The telephone line between here and the Base Camp will be red hot by the time I'm finished with it this evening. Anyway, I'll be sending you directly to a woman who pulls most of the hospitals' supply strings. She'll organise things for you.'

'A woman, you say, sir?' Amy queried, somewhat incredulously.

'That's right, and she's fully empowered to give me all I need to get this place up and running. She's a civilian, by the way. Her name's Brenchly. Marion Brenchly. You two should get on like a house on fire.'

* * * *

Bill Falcon paused outside the entrance to the underground hospital, brought out his notebook and turned a few pages to refresh his memory of various diary entries before turning back to Thomas.

'You remember that business with the Jerry plane that crashed near Warlus before we arrived in Arras?'

'Only too well,' said Thomas. 'The CO pulled my leg over the fact that none of my men shot down the other aircraft as well. The problem was, I thought he really meant it!'

'Yes, I well recall the way you looked on that occasion. Scalded cat comes to mind. Well, anyway, the pilot you brought out of the aircraft has survived. He's badly burnt about the face, but the medics think he'll recover eventually. He's down here. I had to write up a full report on the incident, and I've already spoken to him. He was anxious to meet the person who rescued him that day, so I think we should grant him that wish before we have to leave the caves. Follow me.'

Falcon led Thomas through a side tunnel and into a medical ward with ten beds along each side. Every patient in the beds was heavily bandaged.

'It's a special burns unit,' explained Falcon, after speaking briefly to a male nurse. 'The pilot's name is Oberleutnant Luther. Here he is.'

Thomas found himself peering down at a head, which seemed to be almost buried in thick layers of bandage. He could see two holes for the man's eyes, and another for his mouth. The patient was clearly awake, and slowly raised one of his arms as he recognised Falcon. He then began speaking, in what appeared to Thomas to be nearly flawless English:

'Good day, Major Falcon. How are you?'

'Very well, thank you, Oberleutnant. Do you feel well enough to meet another visitor?'

'I think so. But I hope he won't have too many questions for me. My lips are very sore today. They changed my bandages earlier.'

Falcon reached out and patted his arm reassuringly. 'We won't stay for long. I can imagine how tiring and painful it must be when they have to redress your burns. But I want to introduce you to Lieutenant Winson. It was he who led the party that rescued you from your aircraft earlier this month.'

Thomas heard a muffled sob, and then realised that tears were welling in the orifices in the bandage where the patient's eyes were. He took hold of the hand that was slowly held up to him.

'I am so pleased to have the chance to meet you, Lieutenant,' said Luther. 'I shall forever be in your debt. Thank you so much for all you did. I hope one day to be able to smile again. When that day comes, I hope that you will be able to see my smile.'

Thomas smiled himself, albeit bashfully, saying: 'It was the least we could do. I'm sure that your soldiers would have done the same for one of our pilots, had he been in your position. I'm glad you are recovering now, that's the main thing. But tell me, where did you learn to speak such fluent English?'

'I lived in England for several years. I spent two years at one of your schools in Durham. My father was a visiting lecturer at one of your universities. We only left England in 1912. I studied modern languages in Dresden before the war broke out. Then... then they taught me to fly... I, I...' He broke off and began to sob gently.

Falcon touched Thomas' arm and pointed to the ward's exit. Then he bent down and patted Luther's arm soothingly: 'We won't tire you any more. I'm glad you were able to meet Winson here. You must get some rest now.'

As they made their way out of the hospital complex, it was explained to Thomas that the crash of his aircraft had left the oberleutnant not only badly burnt, but severely mentally traumatised as well. Apparently the pilot had had to grapple feverishly with the damaged Fokker after being scalded by the leaking coolant from the radiator. Since being admitted to the hospital he had relived the crash over and over again in his mind.

'It'll take God knows how long for him to recover from the anguish and stress of that crash,' said Thomas.

'You're right, of course,' replied Falcon. 'At least we infantry keep our own feet on the ground. Pity it has to be in a bloody trench somewhere. Ah well, let's take you back to your platoon.'

* * * *

That Saturday evening, after a week in the caves below Arras, claustrophobia was beginning to take its toll. Thomas decided that he needed some fresh air and a change of scene. He persuaded the adjutant to let him go through the caves to the reserve trenches, to liaise with some of the Lewis gun teams belonging to another regiment. He took Broadbent with him for company, and they managed to work their way through a further complex of tunnels and galleries until they reached one of the ways out into the British reserve trenches.

Fresh air there, however, was in short supply. The air was thick with acrid fumes of explosive blowing back from No Man's Land. A relentless allied barrage of the German lines, which had lasted for the whole of the Invictas' current stay in the caves, was continuing. The enemy trench systems were being comprehensively pounded by thousands of shells. Enormous eruptions of soil and smoke and trench debris could be seen for miles ahead, and the distant atmosphere seemed to buzz and whine with the shrapnel hurtling through it.

Thomas wondered how effective this enormous barrage would be in terms of dislodging and demoralising the Germans who, over the previous nine months, had systematically re-positioned and consolidated their main lines of defence to create even deeper and better protected trench and dugout systems against the Allies' anticipated spring offensive.

Arriving late during the initial Somme offensive the previous summer, he had not been part of the catastrophic attacks on the first day of that July. What had been beyond doubt about the offensive then, was that the combined allied ordnance had simply not been up to the task of seriously dislodging the enemy in his deep dugouts and underground shelters. Would it now be any different on this occasion? He fervently hoped so. Word was that within less than thirty-six hours the massed allied assault would begin. Would the massed German machine guns reign supreme again, or would the massively increased number of British shells, which had been falling on the enemy since the beginning of the week, have weakened him enough for the allies to make real advances out of the city and into the open countryside of Artois? Thomas and his colleagues would know soon enough. Then Broadbent interrupted his thoughts:

'So tell me more about this German pilot you rescued. I gather he was pleased to see you again.'

'Yes, it's an intriguing business. I'd have liked to get to know him better but, apart from the fact that he's clearly still very weak from his physical injuries, the mental strain of that crash has affected him very badly. We were only with him for a few minutes.'

'Well, he's not the only one with a problem of mental strain,' replied Broadbent. 'Several of Nine Platoon's men are unfit for duties still. Seeing poor old Armstrong and a number of others blown to pieces last week has taken care of that.'

'I'm not surprised. It was a ghastly incident. I don't mind telling you, it put the wind up me. It seemed to hit me later that night when I was on the train to Etaples. Delayed shock, I suppose.'

Broadbent didn't answer, but shivered momentarily before taking one last look over the parapet, and then he turned back toward the entrance to the caves.

Thomas followed, pulling his greatcoat about him, trying to think of better times ahead, after their imminent challenge had been dealt with.

* * * *

'I think you should wait here with the car, Corporal Weston. I don't want to get back here later and find that some other kind soul has requisitioned it,' Amy said, authoritatively.

'Can't I even go and get a cup of tea, miss?'

'Definitely not, there'll be plenty of time for that later. You heard what the colonel said before we left the château this morning: "Guard Mrs Nicholls and the car with your life".'

Without waiting for an inevitable riposte, she strode away smiling to herself at the newly found influence she had. Hopefully, she would quickly locate Mrs Brenchly and sort out the problems with the new field hospital's missing equipment.

The previous night had been an uncomfortable one, sleeping on a bare floor in the château, with only a travelling rug from the car to provide some warmth. As she left that morning, the plumber and electrician, spirited away from other duties in Arras, had resumed their struggles to try and provide running water and power to some parts of the building at least.

Now here she was in Camiers, near to Etaples, where the complex of military hospitals seemed to have grown beyond the army's wildest dreams. She walked and walked, stopping and asking innumerable nurses, orderlies and others just where she might track down the indispensable Mrs Brenchly.

Eventually she found herself knocking on a door to a wooden hut, one of scores that were still multiplying.

'Come!' said a powerful female voice.

Amy entered to find a slim, very attractive woman listening intently to her telephone. The woman finished her telephone conversation, looked up and said:

'Yes, my dear, how can I help you? Would you like it yesterday, or the day before perhaps? Incidentally, I'm Marion Brenchly. Forgive my little joke.'

Amy wasted little time in introducing herself and explaining where she had come from. She then pulled out the sealed envelope, which the colonel had entrusted to her to deliver that morning.

Mrs Brenchly read the enclosed papers carefully, put them in an in-tray, and then looked up at her visitor, speaking softly:

'So how is Rupert these days?'

'Rupert?'

'The colonel, of course! Didn't he tell you that we were close friends? We're almost neighbours back in Blighty, and he and my husband were at school together. Incidentally, please sit down.'

'I assumed he had some influence with you,' said Amy. 'He made it clear to me that I should seek you out personally. He didn't think anyone else would be able to expedite the help he needed so urgently.'

'He was quite right. Everyone is chasing me this week. I think we can assume something pretty dramatic is about to happen within the next day or so. But don't worry, Rupert isn't asking for the moon, desperate as his letter makes things sound. I'll arrange for the supplies and equipment to be drawn this afternoon. I'll also do my best to organise some reliable transport for them. What I don't have too much control over is what happens between here and your new place near Arras.'

Amy thought quickly: 'If the transport can leave today, my companion Corporal Weston and I could accompany it to Rivière. I think that might put Colonel Fenwick's mind at rest.'

'Good idea! You display all the initiative Rupert has credited you with. Have you been with the VAD for long?'

'Not long at all,' laughed Amy, 'I was a village schoolmistress until a few weeks ago. The colonel press-ganged me from Netley to be part of his new field hospital team.'

Marion turned back to the letter in her in tray, read it once again and then looked at Amy intently, and said:

'How would you like to have some lunch with me? This is going to be a long day for you. We could forget the war for half an hour or so. I'm sure that there are plenty of other more convivial thing we could talk about.'

Chapter 17

The Easter Monday quickly proved itself to be no Bank Holiday for the Invictas. Thomas and his men, together with thousands of other troops had spent several hours, since soon after the previous midnight, filing through the cave system and communication trenches to reach the allied front line to the east of Arras. Their period of rest and recuperation was well and truly over.

Now as the early dawn approached, they stood shoulder to shoulder in a trench, awaiting the time of five-thirty in the morning when their attack was due to begin. When the moment finally came it heralded a weird few seconds of anti-climax. No whistles were blown, no other apparent signals given, the massed ranks of men simply started to climb out of the trench to begin the advance through No Man's Land toward the enemy.

Within seconds, and for mile after mile to left and right, the skies above the German trenches were lit up with distress rockets. The defenders were signalling desperately for more support as it became evident that the British attack had begun.

Thomas had earlier emphasised to the platoon Lewis gun team how he wanted to keep in close contact with them throughout the day. He was conscious of his new role in maximising the efficiency of the company's four such weapons. But easier said than done: within what seemed little more than moments, his comrades were starting to scatter, as they hurried forward, dodging into and between shell holes and other breaks in the terrain. The battlefield was already incredibly crowded with so many men ducking and diving through the cratered landscape ahead of them. Thomas just managed to keep in contact with Private Turner, who was shouldering the Lewis gun, and he briefly glimpsed Smithers, Hughes and two others struggling along with the necessary Lewis ammunition drums.

But within a further short time he realised that many of the other men about him were not of his platoon or company or battalion, even. The chaos of the battlefield was already manifesting itself and, as they began to draw near to the first of the enemy trenches, high explosive shells, fired from behind the German lines, began to burst overhead. Other heavier shells were now bursting in No Man's Land and Thomas shivered with terror as, fifty yards away, he saw some men's dismembered bodies flying up into the air. Then suddenly he found himself jumping down into one of the front-line German trenches, his eyes darting from side to side looking for grey uniforms. But the trench was deserted. Already the enemy was in full retreat.

By now he realised that he had lost touch with the rest of his platoon. He was quite alone except for a few other Tommies from a totally different regiment. He found a communication trench and, together with his new companions, gingerly made his way along this towards what must be one of the enemy support trenches. Finally he was relieved to see Sergeant Jackson and several others from his platoon just ahead of him.

To make matters worse, the weather had deteriorated badly. Snow was alternating with sleet, and the ground conditions were increasingly wet and sticky. It seemed obvious now that the tank support, which they had been led to believe would bolster the attack, was not forthcoming.

Thomas took a rapid head count and said: 'Well, we must push on. We've a long way to go before we get to our first main objective. Hopefully, we'll make contact with the rest of our men later in the day.' He turned to the assembled company. 'All fit? Then forwards again, men – and look out for those grey uniforms. We must run into the buggers before much longer.'

The enemy artillery barrage had now gathered more strength, but more allied troops of various units were running side by side with Thomas' men as their advance continued. Then, rounding another corner, they momentarily stopped in their tracks. Grey-coated, dishevelled and demoralised German troops were beginning to stagger out of a huge bunker, arms raised and badly shaken.

'I put a Mills bomb in there two minutes ago,' said a Tommy in front of them, 'how many of these bastards survived the blast, I've no idea.'

'Be sure to check the survivors for concealed weapons,' said Jackson, 'Then get them away back down one of the communication trenches.'

Suddenly, one of Thomas' men shouted out: 'Look, sir – it's Mr Porter, and some of Eight Platoon!'

Gerry Porter and a dozen of his own men waved a welcome as they approached, looking as disorientated as Thomas himself felt.

'It's good to see a familiar face again, Winson. Any sign of Standish and our other platoons?'

'No, unfortunately not. Do you think they may be behind us?'

'Not if I know Lieutenant Standish. It's my guess he'll be a long way ahead of us. Let's see if we can find him.'

'Absolutely. I'm almost less worried about the Germans, or exactly where we are in their trench system, than I am by this snow that's falling so heavily. We must keep moving to stay warm, and anyway, we can't have covered more than half a mile from our start position. It's another half mile or so to what they call the Blue Line trenches – assuming we can find them in this bloody awful weather.'

Their now painstaking advance continued for almost another two hours. In that time Thomas managed to keep most of his platoon together, though Corporal Jenkins and several other men from his section were nowhere to be seen. Broadbent and his platoon seemed to have disappeared without trace. The distances covered now reduced dramatically as the enemy finally began to resist with renewed energy, and German artillery reorganised and unleashed many more shells into their own now captured trenches. Eventually Porter gave a little cry of triumph and slapped his hand on Thomas' shoulder.

'Look ahead there! It's Standish. We've finally caught up with him.'

Thomas took another look around him, still dismayed by how many men from his platoon were still unaccounted for. Also, it was obvious that the enemy troops ahead were now beginning to resist fanatically. Standish meanwhile, looking shaken, and wiping some blood off a superficial wound to his face, was not prepared to hang back. He ordered them to continue the advance, and the Company realised that it was now attacking another support trench still held by the Germans, and where resistance was heavy and fierce. Standish instructed his men to try and maximise the use of communication trenches as their best way forward, rather than run too much risk from both artillery and machine gun fire, which were now turning the ground above the trenches into an absolute killing field.

Then suddenly Thomas realised that he and the group of men immediately with him had actually burst into the German support trench and found themselves directly alongside several Germans, who were standing on their firing step, fully engrossed in discharging their weapons into other British troops who were also trying to attack the same trench with a full frontal advance.

As he threw down his rifle and snatched at the revolver from his deep jerkin pocket, Thomas saw Hughes, just in front of him, reverse his own rifle and slam its butt end into the side of the head of a German officer, who had been firing a handgun over the top of the trench. Many single shots rang out in the trench as chaos reigned for several yards either side of them, then Jackson began to lob Mills bombs further along the trench beyond their own section, while Smithers did the same in the other direction. Within moments none of the Germans in Thomas' immediate part of the trench remained standing. The officer clubbed by Hughes was out cold. His subordinates, seven in number, were all dead or dying.

Gradually now, more of the Company began to appear, albeit in dribs and drabs, together with numerous other men from other regiments. Then finally Jenkins and the last remnants of Winson's own platoon appeared. Jenkins bore bad news: Broadbent had been badly wounded and had been carried back towards a dressing station.

By four o'clock what was left of the battalion was mostly reunited and losses were being calculated. It was too soon to differentiate between killed and wounded, but it gradually transpired that the battalion's casualties appeared to be in the order of twenty-five per cent. They had advanced approximately one mile from the British front line.

Orders eventually came down from the battalion commander to occupy that enemy trench before night fell. Even as this work began, another brigade of men was passing over their position to continue the allied push. The snow continued to fall unremittingly.

*   *   *   *

As darkness fell that night, two successive explosions were heard from other parts of their trench. These didn't result from shellfire. The explosions had emanated from deep within German dugouts. Four men exploring the dugouts had been blown to pieces by delayed action mines left by the Germans. A runner from battalion HQ scurried past Thomas and his men, warning everyone not to enter any of the other dugouts.

'That's bloody nice, sir, I'm sure,' moaned Hughes, still fingering the revolver he'd taken from the German officer earlier. 'I thought at least we'd be able to get out of this snow and get our heads down somewhere warm and dry tonight.'

'No chance of that now,' said Thomas, and turning to Jackson he continued: 'make sure everyone has heeded the warning. Check that everyone from our platoon is clear about this - nobody is to enter any of the dugouts. Even the entrances may have trip wires. Smartly, please, Sergeant.'

As Jackson disappeared around a corner, Thomas began to

take stock of the scene and, having set up platoon sentries and overseen the positioning of the Lewis gun, he met together with Standish and Porter. Clearer facts were beginning to emerge about the casualties sustained that day. More than one hundred and sixty men and several officers from their battalion were reported as casualties. Thomas' platoon was now only thirty strong, with one section corporal missing. Several men were showing signs of tiredness approaching exhaustion. With an increasingly thick layer of snow on the bottom of the trench, and no safe prospect of alternative shelter, the night would prove to be a punitive one.

After precious little sleep and a very necessary schedule of intermittent work through the night, to ensure the men's blood was kept flowing, the dawn came to reveal a freezing cold and dramatically white landscape. Half a mile to the south of them, on the Arras to Cambrai road, a huge mechanised allied advance continued. Thousands of men and hundreds of tons of supplies were moving forward to sustain the momentum of the allied attack. News began to circulate of a definite, sustained penetration of the German lines. This seemed to be supported by columns of cavalry joining the road traffic. Thomas suddenly realised that his men were spontaneously cheering, buoyed up at the thought of some really mobile, open warfare at last.

Finally, towards the end of a second afternoon in their trench, it was their turn to rejoin the advance. As darkness fell, they were led through the snow and painstakingly undertook a journey leading over broken and very difficult terrain now cleared of the enemy, but badly littered with broken barbed wire and all the other debris of warfare. They criss-crossed many more trenches, shell holes and other obstructions, cursing and panting under the weight of their equipment and weaponry. Eventually, after covering what Thomas estimated as another mile or so, he and his men were halted and told to dig in.The digging was both difficult and very unpleasant. The near frozen ground was hard to shift and riddled with debris from the two days of battle. Bodies, or fragments of bodies, were all too frequently encountered beneath their trenching tools. For many of the conscripts who had only been in France for a matter of weeks it was their first close hand experience of death.

Then, just as it appeared that their makeshift trench would be enough for that night's shelter, Standish suddenly appeared and called Thomas and Porter to him.

'This is going to sound totally absurd, I'm afraid, but we've just received new orders.'

'Don't tell me,' said Porter, 'we're to go back to the caves or, preferably, to that lovely little hotel I know just outside the city.'

'I only wish you were right. Unfortunately, we do have to leave here and go further forward.'

'Surely there will be some hot grub for the men before that?' said Thomas.

'No there won't be', Standish replied, 'the colonel's been instructed to move us on immediately - another three miles or so.'

'Three miles,' gasped Porter, 'in these conditions that'll take us most of the night.'

'I can't help that. Now, inform the men. We have a long trek ahead of us.'

* * * *

A long trek indeed it was. After something like three miles of slow, strenuous walking, and several hours later, they realised that another new dawn was breaking. Again they were ordered to stop and dig in. The men were now morose, disaffected and reluctant to dig with any kind of enthusiasm. When Standish reappeared he made it crystal clear that their new position was a very perilous one: 'I'm sorry men, but you have no choice but to dig again, dig hard, and make sure that before daylight you can at least be under cover from enemy fire.' He paused and pointed to the south: 'Now, there's a village a few hundred yards away. It's name is Monchy-le-Preux. It's five miles from Arras, where you were only a couple of days ago. It's been a huge advance and we've done well to get so far. But the Germans are in Monchy, and they have strong positions immediately east of the village, too, and as soon as they can see you they'll start shooting again. We've no other cover – so if you value your lives, then bloody well dig!'

The men needed no further persuasion. For the next half hour the trenching tools were but blurs in the half-light. Everyone, officers included, working flat out on the improvised trench dug at intervals between available shell holes, desperately securing some shelter from the next inevitable enemy artillery barrage and storm of machine gun fire.

As the last reliable cover of darkness faded, they abandoned their tools and ducked down into a trench less than three feet deep. Their new position was in full view of the enemy machine gun posts sited just outside Monchy, and of others within several of the village buildings, too. German snipers were already beginning to assert themselves, with one of their bullets ricocheting off Private Williams' steel helmet.

'Get all your bleedin' heads down!' bellowed Jackson, 'Nobody's to attempt looking over the trench top unless through a periscope.'

Meanwhile Thomas had crawled into a shell hole with Hughes, Smithers and Turner. They started to break out the ammunition drums for the Lewis machine gun.

'Shall we try and get the Lewis into a firing position, sir?' asked Smithers.

'No, we can't risk it unless absolutely necessary. The damned Germans are far too close, and they're on higher ground. We have to wait to see exactly what our orders are for later today. In the meantime, keep your heads well down, as the sergeant's just reminded us. Turner, you crawl back and tell the sergeant we want a periscope here in the Lewis' position. If Jerry counter attacks, then you want to be among the first to know about it.'

Barely had he spoken than the unmistakeable noise of a tank could be heard in the distance. The noise gradually increased and, once Turner had returned, Thomas trained the periscope over the lip of the shell hole: 'It's a British tank - and there are waves of infantry all around it. They're heading for the outskirts of the village. It's a full scale attack!'

Fresh, massed infantry was moving across the ground on all sides of them, all heading directly for the village. German machine guns had now opened up en masse and were starting to have a devastating effect on the advancing men. The solitary tank was firing its six-pounder gun, attempting to dislodge some of the enemy machine guns from in and around the village.

Thomas handed the periscope to Turner, instructing him to note any significant change of events on the battlefield. He then slithered out of the shell hole and wriggled and crawled his way along the shallow trench to where Jackson and several other men were lying, some of them nibbling at iron rations, others trying to sleep, others rubbing their hands to try and keep warm.

'What about the grub we found in the Jerry trench last night?' Thomas asked of the men.

'It tastes like the proverbial, sir. The men won't eat it, hungry as they are,' replied Jenkins.

'That and the remains of our own iron rations are all we're likely to see today, Corporal. You need to make that clear to the men.'

'Well, let's hope this attack on the village is successful, then. If Jerry has to leave there in a hurry, and we're drafted in later today, then we might end up sitting pretty in a billet with full bellies before bedtime.'

Thomas grinned, but looking along the other men's faces he couldn't discern much optimism. Another day of this, he thought, and his men would be beyond any real ability to fight effectively.

Then they heard other sounds – this time horse traffic. Jackson was looking through another periscope: 'Blimey, Mr Winson. It's the cavalry. They're heading into the north west side of the village. Our infantry must have broken through!'

Thomas took the 'scope and gasped at what he saw next. Cavalry units were attacking in force alright, but were taking many casualties from machine gun and artillery fire as they approached the village outskirts.

So it went on for another two or three hours. On several occasions German aircraft swooped over their heads, machine-gunning targets towards the village, and all Thomas and his companions could do was lie and wait, as there was no safe opportunity to elevate their heads or weapons enough to retaliate. Enemy snipers continued to take a toll of anyone who raised a head above their pathetically shallow trench.

The morning dragged on and became another afternoon and, with the weather remaining as extreme as ever, the men grew ever more hungry, cold and lethargic, unable to move their limbs much at all in such a hazardously exposed position. Finally it began to grow dark again and, with the darkness, so their digging was renewed.

* * * *

For all the next day, too, they remained where they were. No movement beyond their trench and shell holes was possible. No word was received about the outcome of what had clearly been a major allied attack the previous day. No further orders beyond those to stay put were received from the battalion HQ – wherever that might have been.

In an excruciatingly cramped position, and with little else to occupy him, Thomas' mind began to wander back over the events of the last two months. He variously found himself mentally transported back to Amy's cellar during the bizarre bombardment of Capel, then to the train out of Boulogne and the ghastly accident involving the young Aussie soldier, then to the horrors of the trench where young Armstrong had been blown to pieces little more than a week earlier. He determined to clear his mind of such depressing preoccupations, and focused his thoughts on the peace and exquisite pleasures he'd experienced the previous week in Marion's little house in Etaples.

Finally, as night fell yet again, word filtered through to Thomas that Standish had been summoned to go into the village for a meeting with the other company commanders and the CO, who had set up his HQ in the cellar of a house in the village square.

Two hours later Thomas and Porter were called to meet with Standish and be told what the outcome of that meeting meant for them.

'The situation in the village is ghastly,' began Standish.

'What do you mean?' asked Porter, 'from what we could make out through the periscopes yesterday, it looked as though the tanks and the cavalry had made all the difference. The infantry got into the village – are you telling us that they can't hold out there?'

'The cavalry got into the village too,' said Standish. 'Unfortunately the enemy artillery slaughtered them before they could consolidate and make any sort of breakthrough on the other side of Monchy. It became a blood bath. The village is full of dead horses, and the streets I walked through were pretty well still running red.'

'What about those tanks we saw? Didn't they tip the balance?'

'Yes, to some extent… three or four tanks did get through, and the CO reckons they were a big help initially. They knocked out enough of the Jerry machine guns to enable the infantry to clear out the remaining Jerries from the buildings. But that's as far as it has gone. Apparently, High Command now believes that if we don't launch another attack on the enemy positions east of Monchy at dawn tomorrow, then Jerry will be sure to counter attack. They're well-situated in two wooded areas outside the town and they've loads of artillery support.'

'So who'll be the attack force at dawn?' queried Porter.

'It might have to be us.'

Thomas was aghast: 'Surely you can't be serious. Our men are dead beat. They simply haven't got another attack left in them. Four days in this weather, three nights in the open under snowfall, hardly any decent food and precious little sleep. The battalion simply isn't up to it. The CO must realise that. Are you telling me that he hasn't asked Brigade HQ to have us relieved with fresh units?'

'Winson's right,' argued Porter, 'if we attack tomorrow, it'll be like committing suicide. We're already down to barely three quarters of our number.'

'The CO doesn't need any convincing of that. He's in full agreement,' said Standish wearily. 'He has asked for us to be relieved but it's a request that could well be refused.'

'For God's sake,' said Thomas balefully, 'the men have been in these conditions for too long. They're nothing but exhausted, almost frozen to the marrow, and damned near to their physical and mental breaking point.'

'All the company commanders have told the CO exactly that,' replied Standish. 'He has listened to us and he's doing his damnedest. Now, we have to hold on here until we know more. Inform all the sergeants that the men must get what rest that they can. If the worst comes to the worst and we do have to attack, then make sure that the men get a decent measure of rum during tomorrow's stand-to.'

Thomas and Porter slithered back into their shell crater and then reluctantly informed their platoon sergeants of the ominous news.

'Is there any point in our trying to get some more sleep?' asked Porter. 'It's about nine o'clock.'

'We must certainly nap if we can. I just don't want to end up like two officers I once saw on the platform of Arras railway station a few weeks back.'

'What had happened to them?'

'They'd gone to sleep the night before on a couple of spare stretchers.'

'And?'

'They froze to death.'

'My God, Thomas, you are a Job's comforter. Suddenly I don't feel quite so tired.'

'Don't worry, Gerry. You get some kip. I'll keep an eye on you. You can spell me later.'

As the next two hours dragged by, Thomas tried to fill his mind again with thoughts of Marion and the start of their affair in Etaples. He'd often wondered what it meant to actually fall in love. Now he really felt that he knew the answer. He steeled himself against even thinking of what the morrow would bring. He simply concentrated all his thoughts on being back behind the lines, on being back in Marion's embrace, looking into her beautiful eyes, caressing her lips …

'Sir! sir!' It was Sergeant Jackson, his war weary face alight with the good news he bore for Thomas.

'What is it Sergeant?'

'Mr Standish has just heard from HQ in the village, sir. Our battalion is being stood down. A relief battalion is already on its way here. We've orders to make our way across to the Arras road and head back to the caves.'

'Thank God for that,' said Thomas, already shaking Porter from his sleep. 'Alright, Sergeant inform the men to get themselves together, and then…'

'And then what, sir?'

'And then give the men their ration of rum.'

'Rum, sir? But we're not attacking.'

'That's right, Sergeant. We're not attacking and, as I see it, it's a cause for us to celebrate that our men aren't being needlessly slaughtered at dawn. They will appreciate having some fire in their bellies with a five-mile trudge through the night back to Arras facing them. I'll take full responsibility for contravening the orders about when to issue rum.'

'Very good, sir.'

'Naughty boy, Winson,' said Porter grinning, once the sergeant had gone. 'So how will you explain the missing rum to the quartermaster once we get back to the caves?'

'We have to save weight somehow, Gerry,' replied Winson, returning the grin. 'Certain situations require certain sacrifices. Now, for God's sake let's leave this hell hole.'

Despite all their debilitation from their four-day ordeal in the snow, freezing water and the terrors of the German trenches, the battalion was overjoyed to be heading away from the forward edge of the battlefield. Eventually, five miles and several hours later, by which time the sun had almost risen yet again, they were descending into Arras' cave complex once more. Stepping carefully over the bodies of hundreds of other sleeping men, they collapsed onto the floor as one.

When Thomas next opened his eyes it was late that night. He felt as though he had been reborn.

Chapter 18

'Is that all for today, Mrs Brenchly?' asked the clerk. 'I've checked that all today's requisitions have been dealt with. There are no other urgent requests that I know of.'

Marion Brenchly looked at her watch and gasped. 'My god, Hazel, it's nearly eight o'clock. I didn't mean to keep you here until this hour. You must think me an absolute slave driver.'

'Don't give it another thought. It's been a hectic week. None of us knows where the hours have gone.' She paused, then stepped forward and put her hand on Marion's arm. 'You really deserve this next few days off. You must try and relax and recharge your batteries. Will you be able to see your husband for some of the time?'

'I very much doubt that,' Marion replied nervously. 'He's probably caught up in this latest push. Even if he's still at Montreuil, I'm sure he'll be burning midnight oil running around after the top brass there. Perhaps I'll get to see him when things quieten down again. You run along now – and remember what I told you about Mr Granger, my replacement. His bark is far worse than his bite.'

Once she was alone, she gave her desk a quick tidy and then penned a brief note for Granger. She knew that he would be a safe pair of hands for the next three days. She also knew that every graveyard was full of people like herself who had been regarded as indispensable. No, she'd earned a good rest and she fully intended to get out of Etaples, enjoy a change of scene and try to sort her emotions out.

As she let herself into her house later that night she wondered if Thomas was still alive, even. When he'd left her ten days ago, she realised that he would be going back to Arras and an inevitable battle of major proportions. She was better placed than most others to gauge what the levels of casualties had been during the last week; the drain on army supplies, both military and medical, had been phenomenal.

Over that last week the staggering influx of medical casualties to the hospitals at Camiers since Easter Monday had taxed her own energies to an enormous degree. She had checked and double-checked the casualty lists on several occasions since the offensive began. So far Thomas' name had not turned up, but she realised that he might be anywhere on the battlefields - alive, dead, or even a prisoner. She shuddered at the thought of it.

After a restless night she packed a small suitcase and walked the short distance to the fish market area and waited patiently for the promised staff car that was to be her transport that day. She smiled at the thought of renewing her friendship with Rupert Fenwick. They had communicated frequently during the previous week since Amy Nicholls had been to Camiers to sort out the supply problems for his new field hospital. Now, having heard that Marion was long overdue a few days' break from her work, Fenwick had persuaded her to visit him at Rivière, remember old times and let him display his gratitude to her for so rapidly helping him to successfully provision the hospital.

Soon she found herself travelling in a car that was part of a huge supply column heading away from the army base camp, en route for Arras. The major offensive had necessitated a huge replacement operation, of both men and material. She took pride in the efficient way that everything seemed to be consolidating, especially the movement of the medical supplies, which was very much down to her own efforts.

By early evening her driver explained that he had turned off the main road to drop her in Rivière. As the sun was setting she stepped down in front of the château to find herself being welcomed by Rupert Fenwick.

'Marion! It's wonderful to see you again. I caught sight of you through my office window, and you really are a sight for sore eyes. How many years is it since we last saw each other, for heaven's sake?'

'I think it must be five or six years, Rupert. I remember you spending that weekend with us soon after they made you a consultant. I'm only sorry that we didn't manage to get together again before the war broke out.'

'I know, I know,' he said. 'I volunteered my own services to the army almost immediately after war was declared. Since then normal life has pretty well escaped me. But you, Marion, who'd have thought that you, my favourite actress, would be doing such a fantastic job for us? How on earth did you manage to cut through so much army red tape?'

'That's a long story Rupert, and I'm not going to bore you with it all today. Now, I have two requests.'

'Your wish is my command, Ma'am.'

'Fine, I'd like a strong cup of tea and then, if possible, a hot bath – can that be organised?'

'I'm sure it can. Now, come inside. I'll show you to your room. We've quite a good annexe at the back of the main building. It's tucked well away from the medical wards. I want you to have a good rest while you're here. Lord knows we're so much in your debt.'

As they went through the main entrance hall of the château, Marion recognised a familiar face exiting from a side door.

'Why, hello again,' she said, 'It's Mrs Nicholls. It's really good to see you again so soon.'

'Welcome to the Rivière Ritz,' replied Amy, smiling broadly. 'The colonel here told me that we should expect an honoured guest today. Incidentally, please call me Amy.'

'Thank you – and please call me Marion.'

Fenwick looked at his watch. 'Amy, I think you've just finished your stint in the ward. Could I ask you a favour? Would you take Marion through to the annexe. I've arranged for her to be in Room '2'. Could you show her the bathroom and generally help her to get settled?'

'Of course, Colonel, it'll be a pleasure.'

* * * *

Thomas cradled the silver revolver in his hand, running a finger over the beautiful mother of pearl embellished handle. He looked across at Hughes, who was smiling back at him with a mischievous glint in his eye. Several other members of the platoon waited for Thomas to speak.

'I must say it's a really lovely weapon, Hughes. I suppose you'll expect to keep it.'

'Any reason why I shouldn't, sir? The German officer I took it from can't expect to get it back now, can he?'

'No, of course not. I just wondered if you might be interested in selling it?'

'Why, do you want to buy it, sir?'

Thomas smiled. 'I think it's worth more than I could afford to pay for it. But I do know that the colonel is interested.'

There was a lot of animated conversation between Hughes and his friends before Thomas continued: 'I have to go and see the adjutant and colonel this afternoon. Will you let me show them the revolver? I suspect the CO would be interested in having it as a regimental souvenir.'

'It's fine by me, Mr Winson. If the price is right, I'd be glad to get some money to send home.'

Just then a medical orderly from the underground hospital caught Thomas's attention:

'Mr Winson, sir?'

'That's right. What can I do for you?'

'It's your adjutant, Major Falcon, sir. He's visiting some of your men. He asked me to come and find you.'

'Of course, I'll come straight away.'

Falcon was waiting for him near the hospital entrance. He was clearly deep in thought and busy jotting in his notebook. Thomas was well aware that many of the battalion had been hospitalised in the two days since returning from Monchy.

'Not bad news I hope, sir?'

'Well it certainly isn't good, Winson,' replied Falcon, 'the medical officer I've just spoken to is spending as much time dealing with cases of bronchitis, pneumonia and rheumatism as his colleagues are with men who were actually wounded in the attack on Monchy.'

'It's hardly surprising, really, is it, sir. We're only flesh and blood, after all. Four days in those freezing wet conditions were bound to take a heavy toll of the men.'

'Try explaining that to the colonel. I have to go back and tell him that we have a sick list as long as your arm. If the battalion's needed back in action soon, we'd be hard pressed to find four hundred men.'

'May I ask why you sent for me, sir?'

'Of course, I mustn't bore you with my administrative problems. There's another reason why I needed you here. It's bizarre, really, Winson; an extraordinary business altogether.'

Falcon ushered him over to a bench seat, turned back several pages in his notebook and resumed: 'Do you remember that German flyer that I introduced you to down here. The one you recovered from his crashed aircraft. The one whose face was badly burned?'

'Of course, Oberleutnant Luther, wasn't it?'

'That's right.'

'What happened to him? Did he die?'

'No, but apparently he's had some sort of complete mental breakdown.' Falcon got up and paced about for a few moments before resuming his seat and continuing:

'The daft thing is, Winson, his breakdown has apparently manifested itself in some form of enormous guilt complex about the war.'

'How exactly do you mean, sir?'

'He's reportedly been doing little for this last week except sob incessantly about what he sees as his crimes against the British, and against our flyers especially. He says he wants to try and atone by disclosing all he knows about German air power, and their strategy and tactics.'

'That will be welcome news to the Royal Flying Corps, then, won't it sir?'

'It's a bit more complicated than that, Winson. That's where you come in to the picture.'

'How do you mean?'

'Well, the strange thing is that this character Luther is insisting that he'll only unburden himself to you. He won't talk to anyone *but* you. The RFC is so keen on extracting as much information from him as they can, that they want us to go along with the scheme. It's like something out of *"Alice In Wonderland"*.'

'I'll talk with him if that's want you want.'

'It's not as simple as that. He's no longer here. But you come with me now, and we'll go and report back to the colonel.'

* * * *

She picked nervously at the food on her plate, waiting for his reaction. She knew exactly how close Rupert Fenwick and her husband had been. She very much hoped her host would display a sympathetic attitude to the problems she'd disclosed. When he finally spoke it was to disarm her with his honesty:

'To be absolutely candid with you, Marion, nothing you've said has surprised me. I always did think that you and Paul were never well-matched. Even as a lad he was old before his time, and a drier stick you wouldn't wish to meet. You on the other hand... you're such a lively, artistic lady. I'm frankly surprised that your relationship has lasted as long as it has.'

'Was it really that obvious?' she asked.

'It was to me. Paul never really appreciated your talents. I suspect that he's now so out of time, and out of touch with the home front realities of this war that he can't bring himself to understand just how much of a huge contribution that you and

184

countless other women are now making. You really mustn't have any guilt feelings about what's happened between you these last few weeks. If Paul had one iota of common sense he'd realise just what a fool that he's making of himself.'

She reached over and took his hand in hers.

'Do you really mean that?'

'Of course I do. So much so that, if you want me to, I'll try and make contact with him and try and win him round to seeing your side of things.'

'I'm afraid that things have probably gone too far for that,' she muttered, getting up from the table and moving over to a window, trying hard not to show the tears running down her cheeks.

He looked nervously at his watch, resisted the temptation to ask any more questions and moved briskly to the door.

'Marion, I must start my rounds of the wards. You get some sunshine and fresh air this morning. Amy Nicholls has a half-day off today. She's suggested walking you along the riverbank this afternoon. I'll see you for some dinner this evening.'

She wiped her eyes, glad to escape any further embarrassment. Her morale had been boosted by Rupert's unexpected response. She was now quite certain in her own mind that her husband no longer deserved her love. Then, as her thoughts started to wander towards Thomas, there was a knock at the door. On opening it she found Amy standing there.

'Good morning, Marion,' said Amy smiling broadly, 'I'm hoping to persuade you to join me for my afternoon off today.'

'Yes, Rupert said we might walk together. Do you know the countryside hereabouts?'

'So far I've had absolutely no opportunity to explore beyond the château grounds, it'll be a new experience for me. Well, are you game?'

'I certainly am. I've done nothing but look at office walls, stock rooms and warehouses in Camiers for the last several weeks. Let's get some country air together. Knock on my door as soon as you are free this afternoon.'

As soon as Amy had left her alone, Marion returned to her room and sat quietly for half an hour gathering her thoughts. She was determined to declare that her marriage had clearly foundered. She took out her travelling stationery wallet and began to write to the man to whom she had been wife for twelve years:

Dear Paul,

As by now you must be aware, I have made every effort to contact you and arrange a meeting. You have refused to see me, telephone me or even write to me. I have now reached a point where I feel desperate about the breakdown in our relationship, but you have simply turned into a personal issue all that I have been trying to do for the war effort.

You seem incapable of seeing things in any light other than your own. The fact that you have rejected every one of my advances to you over these last few weeks makes it clear to me that any love you may have once had for me is now quite dead.

I have felt very alone and vulnerable during all this time, but I cannot have been anywhere in your thoughts, otherwise you would have found some means of reaching out to me.

You must now understand that I will make no further effort to contact you. I have lost all the feelings that I once had for you – I consider our marriage to be over.

Marion

* * * *

Colonel Drummond fondled Hughes' revolver for a minute or more, then looked at the young private standing in front of him:

'Mr Winson has told me you are prepared to sell me this gun, Hughes.'

'That's right, sir.'

'What do you think would be a fair price for it?'

186

'I wouldn't like to hazard a guess, sir.'

'Very well - what would you say to twenty-five pounds?'

Hughes gasped and turned nervously to look at both Thomas and Major Falcon.

'Why, that's more money than I've ever seen in my life, sir.'

'So, Hughes, will you accept my price?'

There was little further hesitation. Within seconds Hughes had pocketed the money, saluted the three officers and beat a hasty retreat.

The colonel opened a drawer in his desk and put the revolver inside it.

'We'll present that to the brigadier as a regimental offering when he visits tomorrow,' he said. 'Now, down to business, Gentlemen. The adjutant's told you about this nonsense concerning the German pilot, Winson?'

'He has, sir.'

'And what do you think about it?'

'I'm willing to go along with what the RFC wants, if that's your wish, sir.'

Drummond scowled and sat up in his chair.

'It's hardly *my* wish, Winson. The man's an out and out traitor to his country and the uniform he wears, as far as I can see it.' He paused before continuing: 'However, the RFC are convinced that they might glean some vital intelligence from this man Luther. God knows our own fliers have apparently taken a savage beating during this offensive. So, I've agreed to second you to an RFC officer for two days to interrogate Luther. The officer will be here first thing in the morning to take you to where Luther is being treated. That's all. The adjutant will give you further instructions first thing tomorrow.'

Thomas returned to his part of the caves, first stopping off at the hospital where so many of his battalion's men were recovering from exposure and other wounds.

Quite soon he found himself in conversation with an army doctor who was just coming off duty from the ward where some of Thomas' comrades were being treated:

'May I inquire after Corporal Jenkins, Doctor?'

'You may; he's one of many cases of PUO.'

'PUO? I'm sorry,' replied Thomas, 'I don't know what you mean.'

'It means Pyrexia of Unknown Origin. Pyrexia is from the Greek word pyresso – meaning: *"I am feverish."* Corporal Jenkins is suffering from what you chaps call Trench Fever.'

'Will he be alright, do you think?'

The doctor shrugged his shoulders.

'I hope so. It depends if he contracts pneumonia or some other really nasty infection. Hopefully, that won't happen.'

'May I go in and see him?'

'Of course, but only stay a short while, and don't overtire him. He needs all the rest he can get. Most of them do. They've clearly been through hell.'

Thomas found Jenkins awake in his bed, but looking totally exhausted. The corporal complained of feeling dead tired, with pains all over his body and a hacking cough on his chest. He managed a weak smile, and slowly raised his hand as Thomas sat down beside him.

'How are you, sir?' whispered Jenkins. 'Not much of a voice, I'm afraid.'

'I'm well, thanks. But don't try to talk. I'm under strict orders not to tire you any further.'

'Any news on Mr Broadbent?'

Thomas paused; he didn't want to depress Jenkins any more than he could help.

'We don't have much information as yet. He apparently suffered severe leg wounds that first day. We're still waiting for more news.'

Jenkins nodded and looked about him. He slowly raised a finger and pointed at a bed opposite him.

'That man was with the battalion that came to relieve us at Monchy,' said Jenkins.

'Did you know that the Germans counter-attacked them the following morning,' he went on. 'He was one of only seven survivors from his whole battalion. It could so easily have been us, couldn't it?'

Thomas smiled weakly, put his hand on Jenkins' arm and said: 'Well, it *wasn't* us. Now, you are safe and warm down here, and the only important thing for you is to get better. I'll come back soon and keep an eye on you.'

Jenkins had already slipped off to sleep before Thomas had finished speaking. Thomas quietly stood up and returned to his part of the cave to try and catch up on some more sleep himself.

Well before dawn on the following day, he got up, packed a few spare clothes in his valise and, together with his servant Walters, began the trek back through the caves and cellar complex to the exit, which led up into Arras' Grande Place. There, as arranged by Falcon, he rendezvoused with the RFC officer who was to take him to find Oberleutnant Luther.

'Morning – Lieutenant Winson?'

'Yes, I'm Winson.'

'Very glad to meet you. I'm Flight Lieutenant Travers – Mark Travers. I'll be working with you for the next couple of days. An unusual assignment for us both, isn't it?'

'It certainly is,' replied Thomas, 'but it's preferable to being up to one's ankles in snow and ice in a trench.'

Travers grinned as he took Thomas' valise and put it in the rear seat of the small car he had waiting.

'Yes,' he said, 'I can't say I envy the infantry's lot. Were you caught up in this latest show?'

'Yes – my battalion attacked Monchy. We were pulled out on the fourth day,' replied Thomas. 'And you, are you a flyer?'

'Yes I am, but I'm working for RFC Intelligence now.'

'So,' said Thomas, 'where are you taking me? It'll be light in less than half an hour. If we are going, we shouldn't waste any more time. There'll be some stray German shells falling soon.'

'We have about half an hour's drive,' said Travers crisply, 'jump in.'

As the car pulled away, Thomas turned and waved his farewell to Walters. He wasn't sorry to be free of the caves for a while, but was horrified by the devastation all around as they picked their way through the city's south-east environs.

'I take it that Luther is still in a hospital,' said Thomas, 'he had horrific burns to his face.'

'Yes…but…well…'

'So where exactly are we headed, then?'

'I'm just about to pick up the main road for Doullens and Abbeville, but we turn off after about six or seven miles. Luther is being treated in a new field hospital for victims of the sort of mental breakdown he's had. He's in an old château, in a place called Rivière'.

Chapter 19

Travers paused briefly at the entrance gates to the small château, then got out of the car and looked about him.

He called back to Thomas, 'No notice up. No indication that it's the hospital we want – but this has to be the place.'

Thomas didn't answer; his eyes were fixed on a solitary walking female figure in the middle distance. He strained his eyes, trying to make sense of the image.

'Are you alright?' queried Travers, climbing back into the car. 'You look as though you've just seen a ghost.'

'Forgive me!' shouted Thomas. 'I must speak to that woman at the end of the drive. I think I recognise her.'

He jumped out of the car and ran across a lawn toward the château's main entrance. As he approached her she turned, gasping loudly as their eyes met.

'My god! Thomas! I can't believe that it's you.'

'I couldn't believe my eyes either, Amy. What in heaven's name are you doing in France? It is you, I hope. Either that or I've got trench fever of some sort and haven't realised it.'

By now they had embraced momentarily and were holding each other at arms length, looking intensely at each other, trying to make sense of the situation.

'Your mind isn't playing tricks on you,' she finally said, 'but just look at my uniform. Meet one very inexperienced VAD trainee nurse.'

'VAD? Nurse? But you're a village schoolteacher – at least you were a few weeks back.'

Amy chuckled, 'I'm afraid that the village school seems a million years away now, Thomas. Soon after all that excitement, when you and I were almost blown to Kingdom Come, I applied to join the VAD, and here I am.'

Their conversation was interrupted by Travers, who had parked the car, and who now joined them. He smiled, touching his forage cap, waiting for an introduction.

'I was right, Travers,' said Thomas, turning to him. 'I did know this lady. Amy Nicholls, meet Lieutenant Travers; he's just driven me here from Arras.'

Amy shook Travers' hand, saying to Thomas, 'And what on earth are you doing here? You are not here as a new patient, are you?'

Before Thomas could speak, he felt Travers gently squeezing his arm, and then pre-empting the reply: 'No, Miss Nicholls, the lieutenant here is no new patient. We're both here on an intelligence matter. I'm afraid that neither of us can discuss it with you. I'm sorry that I have to appear so secretive, but I'm sure that you will understand.'

She paused only briefly before replying, 'Only too well. Lieutenant Winson and I were almost arrested as spies back in England only a couple of months ago.' She paused for dramatic effect before continuing: 'It's alright, Lieutenant Travers, just my little joke. Thomas will explain it to you later. Now, I'd better take you both inside and find Colonel Fenwick for you. I'm sure that Thomas and I will find some opportunity later to catch up with each other's news.'

With that she led them both into the château's entrance hall and knocked at a door with Colonel Fenwick's name on it. She entered, spoke briefly and then came out and ushered them in.

'Lieutenants Travers and Winson, sir,' she said, before winking at Thomas, turning on her heel and exiting quickly.

Fenwick rose from his chair to greet his visitors and extended his hand to both of them: 'Welcome to Rivière. I'm Fenwick.'

'Thank you, sir,' said Travers. 'The people back in Arras are extremely grateful to you for your cooperation in letting us come here to see your patient Luther.'

'I'm not sure that I had much choice in the matter. But it has been emphasised to me that when you meet with Luther it will essentially be an interview on his terms, not any kind of interrogation by you.'

'Absolutely, Colonel. This is precisely why Winson is here with me.'

'Exactly so,' replied Fenwick, opening a medical file in front of him, 'nonetheless, you will understand my insistence that Luther's medical condition is my paramount consideration. Despite the poor devil's appalling burns, which will take ages to heal, he has had a complete mental breakdown. On good days he can be quiet and rational, on others he is in an awful state. However, I did see him this morning and he seemed calm and keen to meet with his rescuer again. Incidentally, Winson, we didn't know your name until today. Luther kept telling us about the man who pulled him from his aircraft, but his amnesia for certain names meant that you were a mystery figure as far as we were concerned.'

Thomas now spoke up, 'I really feel a bit of a fraud in all this, Colonel. It's true that I led a detachment from my platoon to find Luther's crashed aircraft, but beyond that I didn't do very much. We subsequently met briefly again when he was in the caves hospital beneath the city. But, honestly, our conversation then was very short. Why he is now choosing me to act as some sort of intermediary between him and the British really strikes me as very bizarre.'

'Bizarre it may be,' cut in Travers, 'but if Luther's offer to disclose important military intelligence is genuine then we have to accept it and on whatever terms he might dictate.'

'Do you really think that what he might be able to disclose to you can be so important?' asked Fenwick, looking down at his file.

'We simply don't know until we hear what he has to say to us,' replied Travers. 'What I can tell you, Colonel, is that the

RFC are already referring to this month as "Bloody April." Our current losses in the air war are, frankly, terrifying. Our pilots' life expectancy after arriving in France is currently averaging only three weeks or so. The German superiority in the air is such that any intelligence we might gather from Luther could be crucial.'

'Very well,' said Fenwick, 'let's not waste any more of your time. I'll take you to Luther straight away. We've put him in a private room so that you'll have total privacy.'

Before they got to the room where Luther was waiting, Travers reminded Thomas of the conversation they had had during the drive from Arras. How they couldn't assume that Luther would agree to a third party being present for the disclosures he wanted to make or, even if he did, that he might insist on Thomas being the principal receiver and respondent in whatever conversation might develop. All they could hope for was that Luther would accept Travers as an informed third party, perhaps more importantly as a fellow flier, some sort of like soul.

As it happened their fears were quickly allayed. Luther, his face still swathed in bandages, but sitting up in an armchair, immediately warmed to Travers after being introduced by Fenwick. He questioned him briefly about his own flying experience before turning to Thomas, looking at him and refusing to let go of his hand.

Finally Thomas broke what seemed an interminable silence: 'So, you see, Oberleutnant, they let me come to see you again.'

'Yes, but you must call me Dieter. And you...?'

'I'm Thomas. I'm glad that you want to meet me again, but, to be honest, I'm not sure why.'

Luther muffled a sob before saying, 'It's very simple really. This war has totally sickened me. I'm so ashamed of what Germany has done to France and Belgium. Our people don't just want to have an empire like the British. I think that they want to rule the whole of Europe, too.'

'Well, you're out of the war now, Dieter,' said Thomas, 'your priority is to get over your wounds.'

'You simply don't understand what is going to happen next in this war, do you?' Luther asked.

'What is going to happen, then?' asked Thomas.

Luther eyes appeared to be searching both their faces as he continued, 'How would you feel if the war suddenly came much closer to England? What would you say if I told you that, probably within only a few weeks from now, our air force will be bombing your coastal towns of Kent, and probably London, too?'

'You mean with more Zeppelin attacks?' said Travers now leaning forward intently.

'No, not Zeppelins. Our people have already realised that they are far too vulnerable to be the future of any serious aerial bombing. I'm talking about a new range of twin-engine bombers. Bombers that will fly across the Channel from the Belgian coast carrying a bomb load big enough to lay waste to your towns and possibly London itself.'

'But weren't you a fighter pilot, flying an Albatros from the Douai area?' said Thomas.

'Oh yes, and a very effective one, too. I have terrible nightmares about the number of your comrades I have shot out of the sky.'

Travers persisted, 'But how do you know about these new bombers, Dieter?'

'It's frighteningly simple. Throughout much of February and March I was helping to test fly them.'

'And what were the bombers called?' asked Thomas.

'Travers here will know them as Gothas. Gothas have been flying as one form or another for the last two years. I was helping to test a new type, the 'G-IV'.'

'And is the new model really capable of bombing our towns in England?' Travers asked.

'It soon will be,' said Luther, 'most of the aircraft's technical problems have been overcome now. The word is that the 'IV' will be built in hundreds. It won't fly much faster than the earlier Gothas, but it will be able to fly much higher. I think that even with its bomb load, it will be able to reach England and drop its bombs before your aircraft in England will have time to get high enough to intercept it.'

Thomas and Travers looked at each other intently. Luther was clearly well-informed. They had to gather as much information from him as they could.

An hour later Thomas and Travers emerged from Luther's room. Thomas' head was swimming with facts about aerial warfare. Travers' brow was heavily furrowed with worry and he was still scribbling furiously in the notebook he had produced during the long interview. He subsequently made his apologies to Thomas and scurried away to find a quiet place where he could properly write up all the data they had gleaned about the new Gothas. They agreed to meet later over lunch.

Thomas returned to the car to retrieve his valise and find out where he and Travers were to be accommodated that night. As he returned to the château he met Amy again. She was just about to take a short stroll around the grounds of the château and offered to show him where his room was. She led him around the side of the building towards an annexe at the rear.

'I hope you found the session with Dieter fruitful?' she said, taking hold of his free hand.

'I'm awfully sorry, Amy. I had little choice but to come here. Now I am here and sharing such an extraordinary reunion with you, I'm simply not allowed to talk about why Luther wanted me here.'

'Don't let that concern you, Thomas. I've been looking after Luther since he arrived here a few days ago. I've shared a few of his nightmares during that time. I know exactly why you and the RFC officer are here. I wondered whom the mysterious father confessor figure might turn out to be, and poor Dieter had no memory of your name. Now I know, and what on earth were the chances of it turning out to be you of all people?

'Anyway, here we are, this is where you and Lieutenant Travers will be sleeping while you are here. There is another visitor in the room around the corner. You'll no doubt meet her later. Now, I must dash. Perhaps we can have a proper talk together later when you are off duty – hopefully this afternoon, but I have to leave for Camiers by three o'clock.'

Before he had time to answer she was gone. He put his valise down on one of the two beds in the room, removed his tunic and boots and lay down on the other bed to ruminate about Luther's warning of the aerial bombing soon to afflict England. Within minutes he had begun to doze off. When he woke, to feel a gentle shaking of his arm, he expected to look up and find that Travers had arrived. Instead he suddenly found himself blinking - and then looking up into the unmistakably azure eyes of Marion Brenchly.

* * * *

Travers put down his knife and fork and pushed his plate away. He lit a cigarette, inhaled deeply and gazed intently at his companion.

'You seem disturbed by this business with Luther, Winson. I would have thought it would give you immense satisfaction to be some sort of instrument in the process of his coming over to us.'

'It isn't Luther that's bothering me. I've had two almighty shocks today. To be honest, it's rather more than I feel I can cope with.'

'Well, one of the shocks clearly wears a nurse's uniform. What else is it that has shaken you up?'

Thomas rose from the meal table and wandered over to a window from where he could look back at the annexe building. After a few moments pause he turned back towards Travers, smiling as he spoke: 'No offence, old chap but my personal life has been in a bit of a turmoil these last few weeks. I won't deny that the nurse I introduced you to this morning is part of that, but if you don't mind I'd rather not discuss my other reason for being a bit disorientated.'

'Of course, I didn't intend to pry. Shall we try our luck with Luther again? If he's up to it, of course.'

'Should we clear that with Fenwick first?'

'I already have. Fenwick spent some time with him straight

197

after we left him this morning. He thinks we can have another hour with him, as long as Luther himself is agreeable.'

'What else do you think Luther might tell us that could be of value?'

'A great deal, I suspect. He's not only a fighter ace, but a test pilot to boot, remember. He probably also knows what other new German fighter aircraft are currently being developed. It would help us enormously to know what our fliers will be facing later this year, and next if the war continues for that long.'

'From what you said to Fenwick this morning it sounds as though your people are taking an almighty hiding already. I have to say, last week when our battalion was completely pinned down outside Monchy, the air was swarming with German aircraft, many of them shooting at us. I didn't see one British fighter trying to intercept them.'

Travers nodded, saying, 'Yes, things have been very bad for us, but within another month or two we should have some new aircraft of our own. Sopwith has a terrific new fighter almost ready for us. We should soon be able to meet the Boche on equal terms. Until then we must take as much advantage of Luther's disclosures as we can, so let's get back to it.'

They quickly made further progress. Luther disclosed that he had also been involved in the flight-testing of a newer version of the Albatros aircraft. Travers greedily absorbed all the technical details, which Luther had remembered with what appeared to be total clarity.

On leaving the room Travers explained to Thomas that the type of Albatros in which Luther had crashed, and which had already taken such a heavy toll of British and French pilots, would soon reappear in even deadlier form.

'That's pretty depressing news for the Allies,' remarked Thomas.

'I don't think so. By the time the beast is in service we will have our own replacement aircraft. From what Luther divulged in terms of the new Albatros' technical specifications, we should be able to match it, both in terms of performance and armament.'

Thomas looked at his watch, thought for a moment and said: 'Would I be right in thinking that you now need a little time to yourself to write up this latest information?'

'Yes, you would be right,' replied Travers with an easy smile. 'And would I be right to think that you need a little time to see your nurse again?'

'She's off to Camiers in less than an hour. I'd like to see her before she goes.'

'Of course you must see her. I'll crack on with my report. Good luck.'

Thomas quickly found Amy. She was pleased to relate her various adventures of the previous two months, particularly how, after deciding to volunteer for nursing, she had been enlisted to work with neurasthenia victims.

'Neuras-what?' asked Thomas.

She smiled and said: 'It's what you and your comrades call shell shock. But the army doesn't like the term any more. It certainly doesn't cover Luther's problems for example, does it?'

He didn't answer, preferring not to get into further discussion of war casualties, however they might be officially classified.

Then the realisation came over him that he was finding it extremely difficult to have a normal conversation with Amy. He knew it was a guilt issue, regarding the fact that Marion Brenchly was also at Rivière. It was impossible to forget the fact that, after such a passionate, albeit brief encounter with Amy in February, he had so desperately sought the affection of Marion so very recently in Etaples. Trying to come to terms with these two women being in the same place at this moment in time was confronting him with problems with which he felt quite unable to grapple. Then he felt her hand on his arm.

'Thomas, I simply have to go now. My transport for Camiers is due to leave in just a few minutes. It's amazing to have met you again, and in such bizarre circumstances as these. God bless.'

He barely had time to look up before she was gone.

* * * *

199

A few hours later he was in the arms of Marion again. They had wasted few words. Their meeting together earlier in the day had been extremely brief – barely long enough for both of them to get over the shock of meeting again so soon and in such strange and unexpected circumstances. Now, as she cradled his head against one of her breasts, she gave vent to all the emotions, which had been pent up for the previous week.

'I was physically sick when we parted in Etaples, Thomas. I couldn't bear the thought of losing you so quickly. When the announcement of the Easter Monday attacks reached us in Camiers, well... my blood just ran cold. I knew that you would be involved in the action around Arras. I haunted the office where the casualty lists were posted, praying that your name wouldn't be on them. I think my worrying about you took me to the very brink of exhaustion.'

'So that was what brought you here, not just to liaise with the colonel who runs this place?'

'Yes. Rupert - Fenwick that is - guessed that I was close to the edge. We're old friends and, of course, he's very skilled in such matters. He also knows of my problems with Paul. Incidentally, I've written to Paul and told him that I feel our marriage is finished.'

Thomas turned slowly onto his side and looked into her beautiful eyes. 'Are you sure that's what you really want, Marion? This bloody war makes it almost impossible for any of us to make rational decisions about such things. Your husband may have been a victim of excessive strain, too, remember.'

'I doubt that. I think that under the surface he and I simply inhabited different worlds. It took meeting you to make me realise that. I'm now totally sure that before meeting you I'd never known what it meant to be hopelessly in love with someone. I may not know too much about you, Thomas, but I do know that you liberated my true passions that last night in Etaples. It's hopeless for me; I'm completely smitten with you, and I'm not being remotely theatrical now. Can you understand what I'm saying to you?'

He didn't answer, but pulled her face to his, kissing her tenderly, before sitting up in the bed. Finally he spoke: 'Marion, I think that I fell for you that very first night in Boulogne. I was desperate to be with you in Etaples, especially after witnessing your husband's behaviour there. When I was sent back to the town to do my machine gun training, and I'll be quite open about it, my first priority was to somehow see you again. Thank God I succeeded.'

'I thank God you did, too.'

His face darkened. 'Unfortunately, Marion I'll probably have to rejoin my battalion as soon as tomorrow. I wasn't on the casualty lists last week, but a frightening number of my comrades were. We must both be realistic about this, you especially. If you are serious about cutting loose from your husband you must understand that my future as a subaltern is about as tenuous as it gets out here.'

'Do you really think that makes any difference to how I feel about you, Thomas? I can't stop loving you now. When you go back to the lines will you feel any less desperate about me, if I really do mean so much to you now?'

'There hasn't been one day since that night in Etaples when I haven't felt desperate about you.'

'Then consider this conversation over and make love to me again, otherwise I'll simply be sick once more. An officer and a gentleman would never condone that, would he?'

Chapter 20

He woke before daybreak and slid quietly out of her bed. Marion lay motionless, her dark hair barely appearing above the bed covers. He switched on his torch to see the time, and then silently crept out of the room to go and wake Travers.

But Travers' bed was empty, and his RFC uniform and other belongings had gone. Then Thomas' eyes lit on a note fastened to the pillow of the other bed.

The neatly written note explained that Travers had received a telephone call late that previous night. That he had been urgently summoned back to Arras to make a full report there regarding Luther's disturbing disclosures about the imminent bombing campaign on England planned by the Germans.

Thomas read on and was pleased by the personal and kind remarks Travers had written about their brief liaison at Rivière:

...I'm sorry that our time here together has been so short. I would have liked to get to know you better. It intrigues me that Luther so wanted you to be here and be the true recipient of his information about the new Gotha bombers. However, you and I both have other work to move on to now. I expect to be flying again very shortly - hopefully in one of our new aircraft so that I can meet the Boche on equal terms again.

And you, Thomas, will no doubt soon be back in action

somewhere beyond Arras.

In the meantime, I'm delighted that you had the chance to renew your acquaintance with that lovely VAD nurse you introduced me to - lucky dog! Take care of yourself. I'd like to think that sometime in the future we might meet up again.

Best wishes, T.

He folded the note and left it beside his valise. Then he returned quietly to Marion's room. There he found her already half dressed.

He said, 'I hope I didn't wake you. I had to go and rouse Travers, the other officer I'm here with. As it happened, he'd already gone.'

She didn't answer initially, but smiled warmly as she curled her arms about his neck and kissed him passionately.

'Marion,' he said gently, sitting her down on the bed, 'my companion has already been spirited away back to Arras. I'm almost certainly going to be recalled there myself this morning.'

'Of course', she replied, kissing him again. 'My time is up, too. There'll be ructions in Camiers if I don't start back today. But it doesn't matter. Last night was wonderful. I couldn't believe it when I found you here yesterday.'

He briefly turned away before continuing. 'Marion, there's something I have to explain to you.'

'Do either of us really have to bother with any explanations when our time together is so short?'

'Yes... I really must explain this to you. There's been this extraordinary coincidence. It involves one of the VAD nurses here. Her name is Nicholls.'

'Nicholls? Do you mean Amy?'

'Are you telling me that you know her?'

'Well, yes. We did some work together to get this place set up and properly supplied. She came to Camiers. We seem to get on well together. She took me for a long walk here a day or two ago. Thomas, what is this leading up to?'

'Tell me,' he said, 'has she mentioned me to you since I've been here?'

'No, should she have done?'

'I'd like to think not, but I must be completely honest with you now.' He paused. 'Marion, when you and I were together back in Etaples, I mentioned that I'd had a brief involvement with another woman just before leaving England. The woman was Amy.'

'Good heavens, Thomas. I can now well understand why you are a bit uncomfortable about things here. I thought that I'd had a shock finding you in the château. For you, it must have been quite traumatic, bumping into both Amy and me. But now, you must tell me - were you in love with her?'

'There wasn't time for either of us to get to that stage. What happened before I left Folkestone was all so sudden.'

Thomas related the events of that fateful February weekend at Capel, and how previously he and Amy had worked together before the war. He explained how Amy's dead husband had been one of his closest friends before 1916.

'I'm glad you've told me this, Thomas. Not because I think you have anything to be ashamed of. From what you described about the shelling of Amy's village, and how tenuous you must both have thought that life had become, what happened between the two of you that night was pretty understandable.

'Having said that, Amy and I will undoubtedly have more contact with each other in Camiers. She is the supply link between the hospital here and our depot there. I know that she journeyed there again yesterday.'

'Exactly. I won't have the opportunity to explain to her about you and me now, will I?'

'Well, no, and I think that she should have some explanation. It certainly wouldn't be right for me to explain things to her. When you are back in Arras you should write to her. Will you do that?'

'Of course, but you must tell me now. Does what I've just told you make any difference to us? It's you that I love, Marion. You do believe that, don't you?'

She flung her arms about him smothering him with her kisses.

'You know I do, you silly, gorgeous man. And anyway, and I hope this won't dent your confidence too much, although she certainly never mentioned you to me, but from what she did say, there is some naval officer in the background somewhere. I've no idea of his details but he definitely sounded as though he might be more than just a friend.

'But now, you and I really have to say our farewells again, Thomas. Promise that you'll write to me. I must know where you are and how you fare back at the front.'

* * * *

Within half an hour Thomas had been summoned to Fenwick's office and given a telephone number to call in Arras. He quickly found himself talking to Captain Falcon, the adjutant, who wasted no time in informing him that he was required back at battalion HQ with immediate effect. Apparently his transport was already en route between the city and Rivière.

He quickly gathered up his few remaining belongings and returned to Fenwick to take his leave. The colonel looked at his watch and then ushered him into a chair.

'Well, Lieutenant, what have you made of this strange business with our patient Luther?'

'I don't know exactly what Travers has been able to tell you, sir, or how much I should divulge about Luther's disclosures. I'm in a difficult position as far as the intelligence goes. All I can really say is that our journey here doesn't seem to have been wasted.'

'I think that you can unburden yourself in terms of any embarrassment you might feel about the confidentiality aspect, Winson,' said Fenwick, as he drew slowly on his pipe. 'Luther has been divulging all sorts of things to us, usually in the dead of night, through his nightmares, ever since he arrived here several days ago.'

'Of course, sir, I didn't intend to appear.....'

'Forget it. You and Travers had an important job to do. It's over now. I only wish that I knew what the future held for Luther himself.'

'Hopefully, he will recover, eventually.'

'Physically, perhaps. With regard to his mental state, well, we simply don't know.'

'Now that he's got things off his chest, Colonel, perhaps his mental state will quickly recover.'

Fenwick looked long and hard at Thomas. 'If you really think things will be that simple then, with respect, you delude yourself. I find his particular neuroses extremely disturbing. But there might be some truth in your opinion. We must be positive with all our patients.'

The colonel turned and looked out of the window. 'Ah, I think this might be your transport from Arras.' He turned back and offered Thomas his hand: 'Good luck, Winson. Try and stay clear of the rest of the German air force.'

He went outside to find that his car was being driven by Hughes, the young Lewis gunner. 'Morning, Mr Winson. I was the only one they could spare to get you back to Arras.'

'I'm sure it will be a smooth journey,' said Thomas with a smile, 'and how are things back in the caves?'

'Not so good, I'm afraid, sir. A lot of the men are still laid up with trench fever, or bronchitis.'

'How is Corporal Jenkins?'

'He seems to be on the mend now. There's bad news about young Lieutenant Broadbent, though. They couldn't save his left leg.'

Thomas sighed and said, 'Is he still in the caves hospital?'

'Not any more, sir. They put him on a hospital train yesterday. He'll be heading back to Blighty by now.'

Thomas didn't answer, reflecting sadly on the fate of the two fresh-faced officers he'd first met only a few weeks back. Armstrong, blown to pieces in the trenches just outside the city, and now Broadbent, sent home minus a leg. He took some comfort from Hughes' news that Corporal Jenkins was on the road to recovery.

By now they were approaching the south-western edge of

Arras, and Thomas was mindful that it was broad daylight. 'Are we going to have to pick our way through shell bursts, Hughes?'

'I hope not, sir. The city's been a lot quieter since Easter Monday. Jerry's guns have been kept too busy holding up our advances east of Arras.'

'Any news of how the advance has gone on since we came back from Monchy?'

'From what news we pick up in the caves, it seems that Jerry is too well dug in on the other side of Monchy. I've not heard of any real progress by our chaps.'

By now Hughes was negotiating the last turns into the city's Grande Place. Within the hour they had descended into the caves and Thomas found himself reporting to Major Falcon.

'It seems that you had a fruitful time at that field hospital, Winson. Royal Flying Corps are well pleased. I suppose you are sorry that your little excursion was so short-lived.'

'I can't pretend it wasn't a bit of a pleasure getting out of these caves, Major.'

'Quite - but you may well find that we won't be in them for very much longer. We've had considerable numbers of replacements now and that, together with our own recovery rate, means that we are almost back to six hundred officers and men.'

'Very sorry to hear about Broadbent losing his leg though, sir.'

'Yes, Standish's company's losses have been heavy these last few weeks. That brings me onto another matter. Standish will be taking over another company in a day or two. With a replacement platoon commander for Broadbent, and he's freshly arrived from officer training, the CO wants you to take over 'B' Company. You'll be acting lieutenant, as of today. Congratulations, Winson.'

'Thank you, sir,' said Thomas, shaking the major's outstretched hand, 'but surely Lieutenant Porter is senior to me. Shouldn't he be taking over the company?'

'In terms of service he may be senior to you. The fact is that you have been appointed as company commander, because that's what the CO decided. I'm sure that Porter won't have a problem with that. Neither should you. Now, I'll remind you that you are still our battalion Lewis gun officer. We have another task for you tomorrow. The CO wants you to give all the battalion's assembled officers a short lecture on how to get the most effective use out of every platoon's Lewis gun.'

'With respect, major, what about the sixteen teams who actually fire and maintain the weapons. Surely they should be included?'

Falcon paused, scratching his chin. 'I take your point, Winson. I may have to convince the CO, however. He might want officers and men treated separately. I'm sure that I don't need to elaborate on what he might see as the political reasons for that.'

* * * *

The following morning Thomas found himself in a large chamber in the caves' system, standing in front of twenty or so officers and two men from each of the battalion's sixteen Lewis gun teams. A worrying number of the faces were quite new to him.

The CO sat in the front row with Falcon alongside him. As Thomas rose to his feet, behind a trestle table on which lay a Lewis gun, he saw Falcon wink at him.

'Gentlemen,' Thomas began, 'if you are already a trained Lewis gunner, and have remembered all that you were taught, then much of what I say will not come as anything new. However, when we went to Monchy last month, we never really had the chance to use this weapon effectively. We were all too busy leap-frogging over Jerry's trenches, or later keeping our heads down in those ghastly shallow trenches once we found ourselves outside the village.

'Hopefully, things will be better during our next attack. If we can only find the opportunity to use the Lewis when attacking, then we can pin down the German heavy machine gun crews and make life a lot easier for the rest of our own infantry.

'To the officers here today, I can only impress upon you the importance of all of you having some knowledge of the weapon. Last year when I was in Trones Wood we lost most of our Lewis teams to enemy fire. Those of us who survived had to learn to use the gun ourselves very quickly indeed. If you ever need to do the same then I hope that the following tips will prove useful.

'Firstly, the Lewis' drum magazine is its biggest weakness. It's open to everything that can come up from underneath; dust in dry conditions, liquid mud in the wet. It may sound daft but, for the magazine, cleanliness has to be seen as next to godliness. Do your very best to keep the elements out of the magazine and the carousel around which it revolves.

'Next, make sure that every team carries ample numbers of spare springs for the gun's return mechanism. Also, cooling jackets in these guns only remain effective up to a certain point. There won't be time or opportunity to change overheated barrels. So, for the uninitiated, if you want the weapon not to overheat and to be able to keep firing, then restrict bursts of fire to eight to ten rounds. That way she should fire faultlessly all day....'

He continued to speak for another ten minutes, pausing only to occasionally pick up various parts of the weapon to illustrate points he was making. At the end of that time he sat down, somewhat embarrassed to realise that the officers and men had begun applauding him.

Colonel Drummond stood up, added a few words of his own before nodding to the adjutant to have the men dismissed. Within the hour orders came through for the battalion to make ready for another departure from the caves into reserve trenches behind Monchy.

By the next night they were acting as carrying parties. His men moved laboriously through the trenches, each carrying two sandbags full of rations and a two gallon can of chlorinated water; this in addition to their own weapons, ammunition and equipment. As they slowly made their way towards the support trenches, they had to negotiate ways past various other working parties. Some men were baling and scooping water from trenches, others were revetting trench sides with angle irons and expanded wire, some men were raising duckboards to try and keep their feet above rising water.

Without a guide Thomas realised that, in darkness, they would never have been able to navigate the seemingly endless labyrinth of trenches. To and fro, to and fro they went. The men reduced to being beasts of burden as the long nights dragged on. After several nights of relentless carrying of rations and equipment they were sent back to a rest area for the inevitable de-lousing, showers, change of clothing and some decent cooked food.

There, Thomas took stock of his situation, wrote an explanatory letter to Amy, and a very different one to Marion. He knew that it would soon be his battalion's turn to be involved in another of the inevitable attacks being made on the enemy just east of Monchy.

All too soon the time came for his company, now under his command, to head towards the front line trenches. It was the evening of May 3rd. The Buffs and East Surrey regiments had been attacking the enemy ahead of the Invictas, and involved in intense fighting since before first light that day. Later, at 10.30 p.m., Thomas' company together with 'A' Company, were ordered to make another assault on the enemy trenches under cover of darkness. They had barely clambered over the parapet of their trench before sustained machine-gun fire began to scythe through their ranks. Within seconds, and immediately after seeing Hughes to his left drop the Lewis ammunition he was carrying and fall headlong into a shell hole, Thomas felt a terrific thump, though astonishingly no apparent pain, on his right shoulder. The impact spun him round several times before he fell headlong into a depression in the ground, crashing his left shoulder into something hard and unyielding.

The pain in his left shoulder was so acute that he felt he must lose consciousness but, despite an overwhelming giddiness, he somehow kept his awareness of the sky above him. This sky was now lit up by a myriad of bursting flares fired up by the Germans from their front line trenches. The incessant chatter of their machine-guns continued for what seemed an eternity, the whine of the bullets punctuating the otherwise still night air.

Eventually the area around him and the air above fell eerily quiet. The flares had all but stopped illuminating the sky. He could still hear sporadic gunfire and occasional explosions in the middle distance, perhaps two hundred yards away. Then he realised that as he had moved so few steps after leaving his trench, his own lines must be immediately close by. But try as he might, the excruciating pain in his left shoulder precluded him from even attempting to lift that side of his body. He was also now feeling pain in his right shoulder and he could feel a sticky mess spreading beneath the epaulette of his tunic. Then he heard a feeble cry for help from just a few feet away. 'Who is it?' Thomas whispered. 'Identify yourself.'

A weak voice answered: 'Private Hughes. Sixth Invictas. I'm in a shell hole. I've been shot in my leg.'

Agonisingly slowly, and fighting the acute pain from his left shoulder, Thomas, lying on his back and pushing with his heels, edged towards the place where Hughes' feeble words had appeared to come from. Then, as another enemy flare lit up the sky above, he froze, waiting quite motionless and silently praying that his low silhouette would not be seen and recognised by an enemy sniper. He found himself looking sideways down into the shell-hole where Hughes now lay. As the flare's light died away he remained on his back, trying to resist renewed giddiness and a powerful inclination to faint.

'Please help me... I've been hit by more than one bullet. Get me out of this bloody hole before I bleed to death,' Hughes moaned.

'Hold on Hughes, it's Mr Winson. Our trench is only a few yards away. I saw the parapet in the light of the last flare. I'm going to get some help. Don't try and follow me. I promise I'll get a stretcher-bearer back here very soon.'

With a superhuman effort Thomas painstakingly wriggled on his back in the direction of the trench. There, once he had identified himself, strong arms reached out in the darkness and, inch by inch, holding him only by the underside of his body, eased him down onto the fire-step. Before he would allow stretcher-bearers to give him any aid he insisted on watching them retrieve

Hughes from the nearby shell-hole. Half an hour later they were in a first aid post and medical orderlies were thrusting dressings onto their wounds.

'We'll get you back to the advanced dressing station very soon, sir,' said one of the orderlies, 'they'll give you both an anti-tetanus inoculation and then move you on to a casualty clearing station a few miles behind the lines.'

Mercifully, by comparison with conditions after a mass major offensive, the medical infrastructure had not been overwhelmed that night. Neither Thomas nor Hughes had to wait too long after further treatment at the advanced dressing station, before being loaded into a field ambulance and taken back to a suburb of Arras and a church hall, which, with now reduced shelling of the city, was being used as a casualty clearing station.

By now Thomas was exhausted by the pain in the left shoulder and, after another two hours had passed, he asked a nurse if she could give him anything to ease the pain.

'I'm afraid we can't offer you any morphine,' she said. 'The surgeon will be along to see you soon, and you must remain conscious for that. You have a bullet wound in your right shoulder, so an operation will be needed for that. I'll call Sister to look at the other shoulder. She won't be long. Try and relax a bit, if you can.'

He lay there for what seemed another eternity, with no prospect of sleep, through being in such pain. At last he realised that his stretcher was being lifted, and he gasped in agony as two orderlies lifted him onto a trolley. Then he felt his tunic being cut away with enormous scissors and, finally, a nurse began to clean the wound to his right shoulder area. The sister came and looked at his other shoulder. 'My word, young man, your left shoulder is up around your ear. How on earth did you manage that?'

'I fell over when I was shot last night. Have I broken it?'

'I think you would be in much less pain if you had broken it. No, I suspect that you have a really nasty dislocation there. It's one of the most painful of injuries. When we anaesthetise you for surgery, we'll see if we can re-set it. I'm sure that's what the surgeon will confirm for you.'

By now dawn had broken and some bright sunlight was coming through the hall's windows. His trolley was shortly moved again, this time to an adjacent room occupied by a surgical unit. A further examination was made by a surgeon, then Thomas realised that he was being approached by an army chaplain.

'Don't alarm yourself young man. I'm not here to read you the last rites. I'm strictly C of E, you're going to recover and, anyway, today I'm doubling up as an anaesthetist. Now, I want you to breathe steadily, close your eyes and think of home...'

Chapter 21

She rose from her chair, went over to the window and peered out at the dismal scene in front of her. Nurses and army orderlies scurrying between huts, ambulances and supply lorries trying not to lose traction on the muddy tracks, the occasional walking wounded grimacing against the harsh wind and driving rain. Finally she turned around and confronted her husband. It was their first meeting for two months.

'You seriously dare to ask me why we have to meet here in my office?' Marion said coldly, trying not to let her voice shake. 'You, who were almost violent with me when I last saw you in Etaples? Your behaviour was unstable then and I'm not prepared to risk another outburst from you today. My clerk is in the next room. If you dare to raise your voice to me, she'll call the military police that we have here. I'll never let you treat me like that again. Do you understand?'

Paul Brenchly sighed deeply and fidgeted nervously with his with hat. 'Marion, I've thought very hard about our situation. I've also spoken to some fellow officers who know something of what you are doing here. Perhaps I was somewhat unreasonable when you first arrived from England...'

'How dare you patronise me like that? I don't give a damn what your staff officer brethren think. From the way this war's going at the moment, they need to look at their own house before making judgements about me. It seems to me that the whole staff

214

set up at Montreuil needs to be flushed through with chloride of lime.'

'Marion, please. I'm not here to discuss the war. I'm here to try and understand why you want to end our marriage. Surely one bad disagreement between us isn't enough for that?'

'It wasn't just one bad disagreement. You chose, over a period of several weeks, to eliminate me from your life. You ignored all my letters. You refused to answer all my attempts to contact you at staff headquarters. Do you seriously believe that that was normal behaviour on your part? I arrived here at Camiers with a very difficult job to do. If everyone else had treated me with the contempt that you displayed, then I would have been back in England within a month. I implored you to try and accept that I really wanted to make a contribution to this war. Your reaction was appalling. I needed your support and understanding, but all I got was your insulting and belittling comments, and then complete ostracism for the next two months. If a man really loves his wife, then he doesn't even think of behaving like that.'

'I do love you, Marion. I thought that I was acting for the best.'

'No, Paul, you weren't. You were only thinking of what was best for you. What you saw as being best for your career, the estate back home, keeping me firmly in what you thought was my appropriate place. I also realise now that we are such different people, and it has taken this wretched war to reveal it. I'm also now convinced that we have never truly been in love. Look at me now and tell me differently.'

He didn't answer her and could only shuffle awkwardly in his chair. Marion returned to her desk, glanced down nervously at her diary and wiped a tear away from her eye. 'I really must ask you to leave now, Paul. We've said all that can be said. It's better if we go our own way. I've made a new life for myself here and in Etaples. As soon as they can spare me for a week I intend to go home and clear things up there. The way our situation is now, I shall want to build a new life for myself once this bloody war is over.'

'You're still my wife, Marion,' he said, but with little emotion.

215

'If I am, then it's in name only. Putting it bluntly, your only real marriage is to the army. Now please go.'

He needed no further goading and left her without another word. She put her head in her hands and sobbed uncontrollably.

* * * *

Thomas regained his consciousness somewhat violently, feeling a strong pair of hands lifting his head and back up so that he could vomit into a pan that had been hurriedly positioned beneath his chin.

He felt the waves of nausea flooding over him, a vicious headache and sharp, though very different, pains in both his shoulders.

'There we go then, much better out than in,' said the nurse holding the pan. 'It's nasty stuff, anaesthetic. Once you've got the effects of the fumes out of your system you'll soon start to feel your old self. Your operation is over and done with now. You've got a broken collarbone on one side. A bullet ricocheted off that, and a dislocation of the shoulder joint on the other. The good news is that we've reset the joint - it took three of us to do it. A real nasty dislocation that was, and a proper tug-of-war as well, with two of us on one side pulling on a sheet wrapped round your upper torso, while the surgeon pulled on your arm from the opposite side. I'll bet it feels awful, doesn't it?'

He nodded weakly, not daring to attempt to speak, so sick did he still feel. Eventually he was able to sink back on raised pillows, as the nausea began to pass. 'Now you try and rest', said the nurse gently. 'A little later on the doctors will probably give you a sedative so that you get some proper sleep. Try and relax now.'

Some time later a doctor appeared by his bedside and checked his pulse rate and temperature. 'It may sound silly saying this, Lieutenant, but you've been quite lucky. A bullet broke your collarbone as it ricocheted off the bone and then exited through the muscular tissues just to the side of the neck. A nasty exit wound;

you've got a much bigger hole at the back than at the front but, hopefully, not too much serious damage to the nerves there. If the bullet had been another two or three inches to the right, the wound would probably have been fatal. Your other shoulder was dislocated, probably as you hit something solid when you fell. Now, we can't keep you here much longer. I'm going to inject you with a sedative. A few hours from now, you'll wake up somewhere else. Good luck.'

'Wait! Please,' said Thomas, 'can you please ask the nurse to inquire about a private soldier named Hughes? He was brought in here with me. He was in my company. He had leg wounds.'

'I'll do my best. Now, let's have that arm.'

When he came round again he thought that he was having another giddy turn. The ceiling above him seemed to be swaying from side to side. Then he looked to the right of him and realised that another cot alongside him was swaying, too. Then he saw that he was no longer in a room but on a train. A train stripped of its seats and full of swinging cots. It was dark outside and the train was moving very slowly. Then he became aware of powerful artificial lights outside the train windows, of the sound of grinding brakes, of whistles blowing and of clouds of escaping steam.

He felt a reassuring arm on his chest. 'It's alright, young man. You're on a hospital train. We're just pulling into Boulogne. You'll be tucked up in a proper bed again very soon.'

He looked up at the nurse who had spoken to him. 'Boulogne? Are we going to England, then?'

'Not his time! No, you don't have your Blighty wound yet, I'm afraid. You are going a couple of miles out of the city, to a hospital at Wimereux. You'll be well taken care of there. Try and rest a little more now. There'll be an ambulance for you soon.'

* * * *

Amy braced herself and drew a deep breath before knocking at the door. She had been trying to rehearse in her mind what she

217

should say when she next met with Marion. The letter she had received from Thomas a few days ago had been more of a surprise than a shock. The disclosure he'd made about his love affair with Marion hadn't upset her. What she had found so extraordinary was the way that the fates of the three of them had come together so dramatically at Rivière. She was also aware that Marion was married to a staff officer based in Montreuil. More particularly, Amy was fascinated as to how, in the space of just ten or twelve weeks since he had disembarked from Folkestone, Thomas and Marion's lives could have become so closely entwined, bearing in mind that he was on active service at the front, and she had such a demanding job in Camiers.

Her curiosity was short -lived. Marion, after nervously inviting her into her office, embraced her and did her best to make her as welcome as she could. On her part, Amy reassured her that her own brief encounter with Thomas in Capel had been but a transient thing, not binding on either of them. It had been two old friends, in desperate circumstances, finding an abrupt comfort and solace in each other.

Having broken the ice so suavely, Amy was content to sit back while Marion related the circumstances of her first meeting with Thomas in Boulogne. Then how their two paths had later crossed again during the terrible scene with her husband by the quayside in Etaples. Marion also went on to explain how Thomas had sought her out a few weeks later after he had been sent back to the town to undergo his Lewis gun course.

'To be honest with you, Amy, Thomas was probably experiencing battle fatigue that week. He'd just undergone a horrendous experience in the trenches, and was clearly suffering from some nervous debility. I didn't take too much notice of it when he kissed me after we'd had a meal together. Basically, I put him off on that occasion. But then, after my husband, who I'd not seen or heard from for weeks, rejected me again, well…. it left me feeling pretty vulnerable, too. When Thomas came back to my house a couple of nights later… I…well… not to put too fine a point on it… I was ready for him. What happened between us that night was simply a huge relief to both of us. I wanted him to love me, and I've been head over heels ever since. '

'And the coming together again at the château, that really was sheer chance?'

'It was - you have to believe that, Amy. It was the most incredible shock to me to find him there and, of course, at that time I had absolutely no idea that the two of you had been anything but friends. Of course, Thomas knew that he had to tell you about me.'

'It really isn't important now Marion. Thomas wrote to me immediately after he got back to his unit. He explained everything, especially your own reaction when he broke the news to you about the two of us. Now, have you heard anything more from him?'

'No, not for some days now,' said Marion, fighting back her tears. 'I know roughly where his battalion is. I'm able to ascertain that from the supply line data we have here. The battle he's involved in seems to have become another stalemate. I hope and pray that he'll survive. I simply can't bear the thought of losing him now.'

* * * * *

The ambulance drew to a stop and waiting orderlies opened the rear doors. He felt his stretcher being lifted and carried up some steps into a dimly lit entrance hall.

'Here we are then, sir,' said one of the orderlies, 'Number Fourteen General Hospital, Wimereux. Hardly the Ritz, but this is where you'll be for the next week or two, I'll wager.'

Thomas smiled wanly at the two orderlies as they lowered his stretcher to the floor and then immediately returned to the ambulance for their next patient. A sister appeared next, accompanied by two nurses. She read the label attached to his pyjama jacket, before examining the dressing on his right shoulder. 'Well, Lieutenant Winson,' she said with a wry smile, 'to be injured in one shoulder is unfortunate. To be injured in both is positively careless. However, we'll try and forgive you for that. Now, how are you feeling after the ambulance ride?'

'I ache badly in the dislocated shoulder, but apart from that, I'm not too bad, thank you, Sister.'

'Good man. We'll move you into a ward straight away. It's very late and you need some more sleep.'

The ward, despite the fact that by now it was in the early hours of the morning, was not a quiet place. Several patients in other beds were groaning or uttering muted cries in their fitful sleep. At one point in the night, another officer in the bed opposite to him began calling out for his mother. His cries gradually became quieter and, after another half hour or so, Thomas fell into an uneasy sleep. When he awoke it was already daylight outside, and the bed opposite was now empty.

His mouth was now very dry and he called out for some water. It wasn't a nurse who came to his aid but another army chaplain. He was a rotund, benign looking man with a twinkle in his eye. He tried to raise Thomas up in the bed before a squeal of pain warned him to stay clear of Thomas' shoulders.

'Very sorry, old chap. I didn't mean to hurt you,' said the chaplain. 'Now sip this slowly.'

While he was slaking what seemed to be a fiendish thirst, Thomas eyes caught sight of what appeared to a note sticking out of his top pyjama jacket. He asked the chaplain to take it out and read it for him.

The chaplain took out a pair of spectacles and read the note aloud:

'Private Tim Hughes operated on for two flesh wounds in right leg. Seems to be recovering from his operation, no bad loss of blood. Being sent to Base Hospital in Boulogne.
Nurse Lewis, Arras

Ps: Next time you come to our casualty clearing station, please don't carry Mills bombs in your tunic pockets. It makes us nervous!'

'Is Hughes one of your men?' asked the chaplain, smiling wryly at the note's postscript.

'Yes, we were wounded alongside each other as soon as we left our trench. I'm glad he's not too badly injured.'

The chaplain finished giving him the drink and then squeezed his arm very gently. 'The doctors are just about to start their rounds. I'll come back and see you again very shortly. Perhaps you'd like to dictate a letter for your parents.'

'I'm afraid both my parents are dead.'

'In which case, I'll write to someone else for you. I don't doubt that there's someone else who loves you very dearly.'

Thomas turned his head away, suddenly feeling very sorry for himself. He felt a strange mixture of emotions: relief at still being alive, and apparently not too seriously wounded; pleasure that Hughes also seemed to have had a narrow escape from death; anger that his stint as company commander had been so short-lived, and frustration that Marion could have no idea of where he now was. He could feel the warm tears trickling down his cheeks and onto the pillow next to his eye.

'I'm sorry,' said Thomas, as a tear ran down his cheek. 'I know that there are plenty of other men here who are far worse off than I am. I'm just feeling a bit sorry for myself.'

'Of course, don't give it a second thought.' The chaplain looked at his watch and continued: 'The doctors aren't due just yet. Now, who am I writing to?'

In less than half an hour the chaplain had written out four brief letters for him. One to Marion, one to Amy, one to his aunt in Folkestone, and a final one to Major Falcon. Meanwhile, Thomas reflected that he was secretly glad not to have a Blighty wound, feeling confident that, finding himself relatively close to Camiers again, it might not be too long before he would see Marion once more.

In fact his wish was granted much sooner than he could possibly have hoped for. That same afternoon, and without telling Thomas, to avoid possible disappointment, the chaplain had managed to get a telephone message through to Marion's office explaining the situation. The following morning she appeared at the entrance to his ward, accompanied by the beaming chaplain. Thomas felt his spirits soar as she bent down to kiss him.

'You silly, boy,' she whispered in his ear, 'what on earth have you done to yourself?'

'I made the mistake of climbing out of a perfectly good trench. Jerry didn't seem to approve of it. I lasted about three seconds before getting shot.'

'And, from what I've been told, you didn't even manage to fall over properly,' she said, smiling through her tears.

'That's true, but the good news is that I'm not going back to England yet. So, I shall insist that, while I'm so close to you, you visit me as often as humanly possible.'

'Just try keeping me away.'

Two days later, after being telephoned by Marion, Amy arrived in Camiers and went straight to Marion's office.

'You will go and see Thomas, won't you Amy?' said Marion, with just a trace of doubt in her voice. 'Can the colonel allow you a little extra time to get up to the hospital in Wimereux? Do I need to ask him on your behalf?'

'No, there's no need. As it happens I've just been granted three days leave. I'm spending it in Boulogne. Popping up to Wimereux from there will be no trouble at all.'

'Any particular reason for choosing Boulogne to spend your leave in?'

'Yes, there is. A certain naval officer is there for a while. His destroyer is berthed in the port for a few days for some reason. He telephoned me at Rivière and asked me if I could get up there and see him. The colonel has been wonderful. I'm being allowed to knock the days off my first home leave, which isn't due for a long while yet. I managed to come across here today in a supply lorry. I'll get an afternoon train up to Boulogne.'

'Where will you be staying while you are there?'

'Oh, Simon will have seen to that.'

'Simon?'

'Yes. Simon Mockett. Commander I must call him, I suppose,' she said, smiling.

'It was he who organised my joining the VADs. Our paths first crossed soon after that weekend when Thomas and I were almost blown to pieces outside Folkestone. Simon was a naval intelligence officer of some sort. He came up to Capel on navy business - at least that's what he told me. It later turned out that he had ulterior motives.'

Marion smiled. 'And to think that only a few days ago I was so worried about how you would react to Thomas' news about me and him.'

'Well, Marion there is a war on you know.'

* * * *

The doctor peered down to look closely at his bullet wound, sniffing quietly as he did so. 'H'mm. No sign of infection so far, but there's a lot of tissue repair needed at the back of the shoulder. It should heal naturally, but it won't be quick.'

'And what about the other shoulder?' asked Thomas. 'What exactly happened to it?'

'What happened was that, when you impacted with whatever it was you fell on, the top of your arm bone violently lost contact with the socket of your shoulder joint. The ligaments in your shoulder will have been torn. When those ligaments heal they'll do so in a position which will probably be unhelpful to holding the shoulder in a proper position. After suffering one shoulder dislocation, many people are prone to the injury repeating itself. But that won't necessarily be the case for you.'

'So how long will I need to be in here, do you think?'

'Difficult to know for sure. What I can say is that you'll probably need many weeks for the two wounds to heal. After about twelve weeks or so, the dislocated shoulder should be reasonably recovered. You might be fit for light duties within a couple of months from now, but you certainly won't be up to digging trenches or carting heavy loads up to the line for some time after that. But then you are an officer so that won't be an issue, I suppose.'

Thomas didn't see much point in telling the doctor how often he had dug trenches and shouldered loads of railway sleepers with his men.

'Once we have finished with you here,' the doctor continued, 'you'll probably be moved off to a convalescent hospital somewhere. In the meantime, both your arms will need to be in slings for three or four weeks. Those shoulders will need lots of rest and recuperation.'

No sooner had the doctor moved on to the next bed than Thomas saw the ward sister in animated conversation just outside in the corridor. As the sister entered the ward to whisper in the doctor's ear, Thomas realised that the other person outside was none other than Amy. The doctor briefly turned and winked at him. The sister beckoned Amy in.

'I can't believe you've come all the way from your château just to see me,' Thomas said, as he kissed her.

'You're quite right, I didn't. But I am in Boulogne on three days leave. I'm a bit bored, so thought I'd look in on you.'

'You're a very generous hearted lady, Amy. I'm not sure that I deserve this.'

She smiled. 'Don't be silly! As it happens, I was with Marion only yesterday. As far as your women go, Thomas, I think you display endearing powers of discrimination.'

He blushed momentarily as she brought out a gift of some handkerchiefs for him. 'Anyway, I'm not here on my own,' she went on. 'I've brought another visitor to see you. I wonder if you'll recognise him.' She got up, went to the ward's entrance, and returned with Simon Mockett.

Thomas smiled, 'Shouldn't you be busy in Folkestone harbour?'

'Not any more. I'm back at sea. They've given me a new destroyer to play about with. Now, how are you feeling, Thomas?'

Two days later, after another welcome visit from Amy and Simon, and after they had gone their separate ways, he was pleased and surprised to get one letter from Major Falcon and another from Jenkins, now convalescing just outside Arras. To read of the battalion's misfortunes, however, left him badly demoralised. On the night when he had been so precipitantly wounded, his battalion had suffered devastating casualty rates. Their attack, though bravely pushed, had been a complete failure. Although one group of sixty men actually got as far as the German trenches, they were quickly cut off and later all captured. With regard to the rest of the force, over two hundred and fifty rank and file and eleven officers, Thomas among them, had been casualties. The battalion had been so much reduced that it had to be reorganised into just two companies. Standish had survived, unwounded. Porter had been blown up, but was recovering from shock and minor wounds. The other newly joined platoon commander in Thomas' company was still missing.

As his own days in the hospital at Wimereux ran into a week, and then two, Thomas felt his strength returning and the pain in both shoulders gradually diminishing. He was glad that both his legs were uninjured and that he was able to exercise them in a garden behind the hospital building. A combination of decent food, sea air, and frequent visits from Marion all helped to hasten his recovery. In the middle of his third week, however, he received tragic news from Folkestone. The letter he opened was not from his aunt Josie, whose house he'd stayed in before his embarkation in February, but from another relative in the town.

It told him that his aunt and uncle had both been killed in a German bombing raid on the Kent coast. Apparently, several enemy aircraft had succeeded in flying from a base on the Belgian coast. Unsighted and flying at high altitude they had dropped enough bombs on Folkestone to kill scores of people who were queuing for scarce food in the town's main shopping area. His aunt and uncle had died instantly.

Thomas folded the letter and immediately cast his mind back to his meeting with the German pilot Luther at Rivière. Luther's prophecy had been realised: the war was no longer restricted to mainland Europe and the Middle East. It had now arrived, horrifyingly, in England, too.

Chapter 22

It was a glorious June day. He strolled lazily along the water's edge, the ripples in the sand firm beneath his feet. In the sand dunes above the beach he could hear several children at play. He breathed deeply, feeling invigorated by the crisp sea air. He longed to be in a sailing boat again, feeling spray on his cheeks and a heaving deck beneath his feet. He flexed his two arms, knowing that it would be some time yet before he would be able to control either the halliards or mainsheet of a sailing craft.

He looked at his watch, realising that lunchtime approached and that his appetite remained as keen as ever. Turning back up to the top of the beach and striding over the dunes towards the road he wondered how much longer he would be able to enjoy such coastal delights.

By the end of the previous month he had left the hospital at Wimereux and been sent to a convalescent centre in the sleepy seaside resort of Hardelot, just eight miles south of Boulogne. The bullet hole in his right shoulder had largely healed without complication, and the collarbone was mending, though the wound remained tender. The dislocation in his other shoulder had caused more problems for him, however. He was still suffering moderate levels of pain and a continuing lack of mobility in that arm and shoulder. All the indications were that it could be some more weeks before a medical board might declare him fit enough to return to active army duties. While he missed his comrades in the battalion, he was aware from the letters he received that his fellow officers and men, after they had taken such a savage mauling east of Monchy, were still, mercifully, well behind the lines and being rested. Jenkins had made a full recovery from trench fever and had returned to England after finally agreeing to be trained as an officer. Colonel Drummond, the CO, was still recovering from wounds received on the same day as Thomas. Hughes was now recuperating at Deauville further down the coast, but Privates Smithers and Turner, who had both been with the group sent to rescue Luther from the plane-crash site near Warlus in March, had been killed, probably by the same machine-gun that had wounded Thomas and Hughes.

Such was the war of attrition and stalemate that continued in the maze of trenches a few miles outside Arras. The year was rapidly showing ominous signs of becoming every bit as bad as 1916. Thomas could see no end to the wastage of good lives. Short of some major technological breakthrough that would enable infantry to defy the enemy machine guns and artillery barrages, it seemed that men would simply go on being sacrificed by the thousand, for no more than the gain of a few yards of enemy held terrain.

He put the whole wretched business out of his mind. It was Friday and his heart sang at the thought of Marion making the short journey up from Camiers later that afternoon. She had reserved a room at a small hotel in the extensively wooded area just back from the village. She had done this for the last two weekends. The regime at the convalescent centre was liberal enough for him to absent himself for hours at a time without any real difficulty. He intended to make the most of their time together.

But as he entered the room that served as the officers' mess at the centre, he was astonished to see there none other than Travers, the RFC officer who, a few weeks earlier, he'd accompanied to Rivière.

'Good, Lord,' said Thomas, 'what on earth are you doing here in Hardelot?'

'I'm returning from a temporary posting in England. My

contacts in RFC intelligence heard about you being wounded, and ending up just outside Boulogne. I was given a few hours and a motorbike and the opportunity to look you up before heading to find my new squadron near Doullens. Have you heard about last month's bombing raids on the Kent coast?'

'I heard about them alright, I lost an aunt and uncle in the raid on Folkestone.'

'I'm dreadfully sorry to hear that. Were they close to you?'

'Very close, and very dear. They were almost like parents to me.'

'It was the raid on and around Folkestone that whisked me back to England,' said Travers. 'They sent me to an airfield at Bekesbourne, just outside Canterbury. We started special patrols in new, two hundred horsepower 'SE5' aircraft. The German Gotha bombers made another attack, this time on London, but they've not been back since.'

Thomas searched Travers' facial expression. He had a distinct feeling that there was something that he wasn't being told. He thought it unlikely that Travers could make such a detour to Hardelot, unless there was another agenda for it. His instinct proved to be well founded. Travers looked about him, clearly now becoming more ill at ease. For a few moments nothing was said. Then Travers asked: 'Is it alright if we go somewhere a little more private? I've something on my chest.'

They went out into a walled garden, now almost deserted, as every other patient had gone into the dining room for their lunch. Travers sat down on a bench seat and gestured Thomas to join him. 'Thomas, I haven't misled you in the sense that I have been given a special dispensation to make this visit to you down here. But it wasn't just the kindness of my superiors' hearts that's enabled me to be here. I'm afraid I bring sad news.'

'Well, don't go on keeping me in suspense. We get enough suspense in the trenches, wondering if the next Jerry shell has our name on it.'

'Very well. Just before I left Bekesbourne I was called up to London to meet with the RFC intelligence staff who had evaluated the information given to you and me by Oberleutnant Luther in April. I'm afraid that the sad news I bring you today is about Luther himself. I'm sorry, Thomas, but Luther is dead.'

'Dead? Did he die of his burns? I thought that, physically at least, he was on the road to recovery.'

'No,' said Travers, 'I'm afraid that he took his own life. Apparently he cut his wrists.'

Thomas rose from his seat and wandered away for a few yards. He found himself looking hard at the brickwork of the wall in front of him, as though there might be some answer there to the questions now racing through his mind. Travers was immediately at his side.

'Thomas, we were well aware that the balance of Luther's mind had been left badly disturbed by his air crash.'

'Not so well aware that we weren't happy to pump him for the information he had about the Gothas.'

'He volunteered that information quite freely. He asked to see you especially. He no doubt felt better after telling us what the Germans were planning.'

'If it's as simple as that,' said Thomas, 'then why have you come out of your way to tell me this news personally? Are you hoping that it will make me feel a little less guilty?'

'Thomas, for heaven's sake, there's no question of you or I needing to feel guilty. It would simply have been quite wrong for you to have discovered this news by any other means.'

'So perhaps you're saying,' snapped Thomas, 'that your visit to me makes the RFC feel a bit better, then?' He didn't wait for a reply but went back to the seat and sat down, suddenly feeling very tired. He looked up at Travers' sad face, and continued: 'I'm sorry. I'd no right to snap at you like that. I'm less upset by your news about Luther than I am by the bloody cruel irony of it all.'

'I'm sorry, I don't follow you. What irony?'

'Quite simply the fact that Luther told us all he knew about that new breed of German bombers, but it didn't save my aunt and uncle in Folkestone, did it?'

'No, indeed it didn't. It didn't save a lot of other folk, either.

The important thing is, Thomas, that you and I did our best at that moment in time. It takes more time to defend against these things. We've got measures in place back in England, now. We have our own new aircraft, able to fly high enough and fast enough to meet the bombing threat. You must believe me, that Luther's information was crucially helpful to us. I'm sorry that you, the instrument of his revelations, became a victim in the sense that you lost loved ones at home. It's war, Thomas. How many other good friends have you and I both lost these last two or three years? Now, Luther is dead. Your aunt and uncle are dead. But you and I are still alive. Let's try and keep it that way. Now, we'll go and see your nurse and try and get permission to get out for a decent lunch together at that interesting little hotel down by the seafront. I want to buy you a stiff drink, too - several if need be.'

* * * *

Thomas and Marion lay entwined in the four-poster bed. She felt his hand gently caressing her neck while his lips brushed against the lobe of her ear. She sighed deeply and turned to kiss him. The gentle early evening sunlight began to cast soft shadows on the far wall of their bedroom.

'Thomas?'

'I'm sorry,' he replied, 'I simply don't have the energy left for conversation.'

'I'm not surprised. We've only been here for four hours and you've three times made love to me with a passion which has almost left me breathless.'

'That's because I'm worried that they might be expecting me back in Hardelot for supper,' he replied, smiling mischievously.

'Nonsense! You have those nurses wrapped round your little finger. They seem to let you get away with anything at that place. No, there's something else on your mind today. I won't complain about it. Lord knows you've certainly not neglected my needs this afternoon. But something else has been driving you today. Won't you tell me what it is about?'

He rose from the bed, poured them both a glass of water and then began to unburden himself of the story of Travers' news. She quickly interrupted him: 'Thomas, you don't need to go on. I had a telephone call from Amy Nicholls yesterday morning. She asked me to break the news about the German flier to you. How on earth did the RFC officer find you here to tell you himself?'

'He was invited to come here by the intelligence branch he used to work for. I can only imagine they felt a little sheepish about Luther's suicide. I really can't think why. We're all busy slaughtering Germans wherever we can find them. What's another dead German flyer, after all?'

'Thomas, I know nothing about that business which took you to Rivière. But whatever it involved, I'm sure that you acted honourably. You shouldn't feel bitter about it.'

'Perhaps. I certainly did nothing under duress, so I really mustn't blame anyone else for what finally happened there. Now, let's change the subject. What's the situation now between you and your husband? Have you told him about us?'

She paused, sipping her water before beckoning him to return to the bed and hold her. 'No, I haven't told him,' she said. 'What would it achieve? It might anger him to the point of trying to track you down and doing something really spiteful to you. It wouldn't make me feel any easier to tell him of our affair. Paul and I haven't been man and wife for longer than I care to remember, so I don't really feel any guilt about my behaviour. And, anyway, with this war to contend with…'

'You're going to say that I could soon be dead, anyway, so why need we bother to come clean about our affair?'

'Thomas! That's a cruel and spiteful thing to say. I can't bear you really believing that I could think that.'

He threw his arms around her and pressed her to him. 'I'm dreadfully sorry, Marion. You're right - it was unworthy of me to say that. For god's sake say that you forgive me.'

'I think that I could forgive you almost anything. But, you must tell me, would you feel more at peace if I told Paul about us?'

He paused long and hard before answering her: 'If you are

truly convinced that, whatever might happen to me, you'll never go back to being his wife, then I think that we should tell him. If I survive the war, I'd want you to divorce him sometime in the future. For the peace of mind of both of us then, perhaps, he should be told now. I doubt that he'd try and take revenge on me militarily. I fail to see what he could do in that respect. Anyway, he surely has pride enough not to want to publicise the affair.'

She agreed that the following week she would try and go to Montreuil, meet with her husband and explain her situation to him. For the rest of that weekend she and Thomas made the most of their time together. They walked in the forest, through the country lanes and along the sand dunes. They savoured the sea air, the birdsong in the woods and the wine and food in the hotel dining room.

The following weekend, now in July, Marion returned to Hardelot. She explained that she had seen her husband and admitted her infidelity to him. However, she hadn't yet identified Thomas as her lover. Brenchly had taken her news stoically. A few days later she received a letter from him informing her that he had asked to be relieved of his staff duties at Haig's headquarters, and had requested a posting to active duty at the front.

Three weeks later, the day before he was due to present himself before a medical review board in Etaples, Thomas, together with Marion, journeyed to Boulogne. They had received a sudden, surprise invitation to attend the wedding of Amy and Simon Mockett. Simon had a week's leave, and Amy had agreed to take just three days off from her duties at Rivière. The neurological hospital in the château was busier than ever with all the casualties from the continuing Arras battles.

Much to their mutual pleasure, Thomas and Marion discovered that the venue for the wedding reception was none other than the Hotel Metropole, the place where they had first met each other almost five months earlier. Towards the end of the day, and before she and Simon left to begin a brief honeymoon, Amy took the time to find a quiet corner in the hotel and tell Thomas of the circumstances of Luther's suicide. As Thomas had already suspected, the staff at Rivière had found it impossible to keep the news of the bombing of the English coast towns from Luther. That news had provoked an agonising guilt complex in the German pilot and an acute sense of failure that his warnings had not been timely enough to save all the British civilians who had subsequently lost their lives. Thomas felt much better when she had finished, no longer feeling so guilty in the affair himself. They embraced each other warmly. 'Thomas,' she said, 'promise me that you will do your best to make an honest woman of Marion. She and I have become such close friends these last four months, and I know that she loves you very dearly.'

He smiled as he said: 'I know that only too well. I also know that today Simon and I are probably the luckiest men in France. You've been a wonderful friend to me, Amy. God bless you, and I hope that you have a wonderful marriage.'

The following morning he was driven down to Etaples to hear what now awaited him as regards his future. The three doctors who sat facing him had few questions. They established that both his shoulder injuries were now greatly healed. That he should avoid heavy use of the shoulder joint that had been badly dislocated, but that he was now fit to resume restricted active service, with the proviso that he should not try and use a rifle or attempt to carry out anything more than light efforts with his left arm and shoulder. The recommendation was that he should return to his battalion and be restricted to light duties for a few more weeks, probably in an administrative role with Battalion HQ. He was granted a week's leave after discharge from the convalescence centre. Later that evening he was making himself at home in Marion's townhouse in Etaples.

The next seven days simply flew by. Although Marion had to visit Camiers on a daily basis, she had organised her office to the point that she was able to spend a good proportion of her time with Thomas. The August weather was not kind to them, however, and disturbing news was coming back from the area of the new allied offensive in Flanders. The battle of Ypres was rapidly becoming bogged down in a sea of mud. Thomas was relieved to hear that his battalion had not been sent to be part of that battle.

The precious hours the two of them were able to spend together were not wasted. When possible, they enjoyed some time on the coast at Le Touquet, or roamed the wooded parts between there and Etaples. Thomas did a lot of cooking, often of fish, after visiting the nearby market. Each evening found them relaxing in Marion's parlour, enjoying good wine and her collection of gramophone records.

At the end of the week she saw him off at the railway station and he started yet another prolonged journey back to Arras, and then on to where the Sixth Invictas were now based. This position proved to be hardly changed from that near which Thomas had received his wounds three months earlier. For much of the time he had been away, the battalion had been largely involved in attack after attack on the enemy lines. Inevitably, each time they had then been counter attacked, and this apparently futile series of engagements had resulted in no significant gains by one side or the other.

After he had handed over to the town major the letter from his medical board in Etaples, he found himself assigned to Brigade HQ just outside the city. After another week he was sent to a training camp further south and given the task of coordinating Lewis gun practice and maintenance there. By now, from brief visits to Arras, and meeting one or two people he had known earlier in the year, he had learnt that his battalion was now so depleted of the men he had served with from February to May that it bore little resemblance to what he remembered. Eventually, several weeks later, and after moving yet again to an administrative post at a huge Divisional Rest Camp, he was summoned to appear before another medical board. There he was told that he was now deemed fit for active service in the full sense of the word.

Later that week when he walked into the officers' mess at Avesnes-le-Compte, more than eight months to the day since he had first arrived there, he felt like a veritable Rip Van Winkle. All he could see was a mass of totally strange faces, though it had been made clear to him that his own battalion was nearing the end of a month's rest back at Beaufort Farm, only three kilometres away. He ordered a glass of wine, and then reached into his valise for his writing pad and envelopes, to pen a letter to Marion.

'Good Lord! Who do we have here? It's a ghost from the past.'

Thomas looked up and found himself smiling at the sight of Gerry Porter. 'Gerry!' He said, jumping to his feet, 'what a pleasant surprise. I was wondering if they'd sent me to the wrong address. Yours is the first face I've recognised since walking in here ten minutes ago. How are you? I heard that you'd been blown up. Did it take them long to put you back together again?'

'Not long enough is the short answer. I had a pretty miraculous escape - no shell splinters at all. Within a couple of days I was back in the trenches.'

'I hear the battalion's had a very rough time,' said Thomas.

'Very rough, July and September especially.' We all thought that the abortive night attack in May was bad enough, but it's been horrendous outside Monchy ever since. Plenty ventured, but bugger all gained. It's been a sheer waste of men. They had no choice but to stand us down and rest us for quite long periods in between the fighting. There have been so many new officers and men that's it's virtually a new battalion you're coming back to.'

'Is the CO back now?' asked Thomas.

'Yes, last month, Standish's back, too. He went down with trench fever in August.'

'So, I suppose you've been made a company commander, too, by now.'

Porter grinned awkwardly and said, 'No, I'm afraid that the CO doesn't see me as a leader. He's probably right. I never was very good at giving orders.'

Thomas looked at his watch. 'I really must make tracks and report to the farm. Are you staying here?'

'No, I'll go back with you. There'll be so many introductions in order, you'll be glad of my help.'

* * * *

235

Captain Falcon beamed as he shook Thomas' hand. 'Wonderful to have you back again after so long, Winson. Are you fully recovered now?'

'Yes, almost fully healed thanks, sir. I don't think that I'll be much use with a rifle butt for a while longer, but no doubt I'll get back into using a revolver again.'

'Good man. We're on standby here, but something big is afoot. We have no idea what it is yet, but what I can tell you is that much of our training since coming back here has involved close cooperation with the Tank Corps.'

'I can't think of a better way of going back into action than being protected by a nice fat tank, can you, sir?'

'It has to be an improvement on the last four or five months. I've simply forgotten what it means to have any sense of continuity as far as the Sixth is concerned. We've more or less had a total turnover of officers and men since you were last with us.'

'So what will my own role be here, sir?' Thomas asked.

'The colonel definitely wants you as a company commander for the next show, whatever that might turn out to be. As from today you're promoted to acting captain. You'll be taking over 'A' Company. You know Porter, of course. He'll be one of your platoon commanders. The others are virtual novices as far as combat goes, I'm afraid.'

'Will I know any of the other company commanders, sir?'

Falcon paused for a moment. 'You know Standish, of course. But it may be that he will be assigned to brigade HQ before we go into action. Anyway, Winson, there's another matter. You clearly have some influential friends out here. We received a letter by special delivery for you, only this morning. It was brought across from a field hospital only seven or eight miles from here. Actually, it was the place you were sent to from Arras back in April. Do you remember? You went with an intelligence officer from the RFC.'

'Rivière, sir?' said Thomas taking the envelope from Falcon.

'Yes, that's the place. You'd better read the letter now. If it's a matter of real importance, and I suspect it must be, as someone has pulled staff strings to establish where to find you so quickly, it may be that you'll need my help in case you need to make a speedy reply.'

Thomas assumed that the hand-written note, whose envelope simply bore his name, must be from Amy. He opened it to find the worst of news:

Dear Thomas,

Colonel Fenwick has been wonderfully kind, and is enabling me to make contact with you without the delay of going through the normal postal delivery arrangements. He managed to trace your new whereabouts through his contacts in Arras.

I'm afraid that I have some terrible news from Camiers. Two days ago the Germans bombed the hospitals there. Marion was badly wounded. I had to go there earlier today and was told that she had to undergo surgery for multiple shrapnel wounds. Apparently she is to be repatriated to England as soon as possible. She had already been moved by the time I tried to find her whereabouts in Camiers. It was impossible to discover just how seriously she had been injured.

I know that you must be desperately upset to receive this. I wish that there was something I could do to be of more help. I will do my best to learn which hospital she goes to in England. As soon as I know more, I will contact you.

God bless,

Amy

Thomas suddenly felt totally cold and empty. Feeling the tears welling up in his eyes, he saluted the adjutant, turned hurriedly away and made his exit. Once he had recovered his composure he found the nearest quiet and private place and read the letter over and over again. Having killed scores of civilians in England, including his two best-loved relatives, the Gothas had now been turned on the wounded lying helpless in military hospitals.

He found himself running a hand over the scar tissue of his right shoulder. Suddenly, for him, the war had taken on a disturbing personal dimension. Now, he simply wanted to wreak his own personal vengeance on this terrible German war machine. His right shoulder might remain a hindrance as far as rifle use was concerned, but he knew that a Lewis gun equipped with a spade grip for his hand would be well within his capability. He went off to find one and to get in some firing practice...

Chapter 23

Travers glanced up through the cutaway in the upper wing of his Sopwith Camel fighter aircraft, searching the sky for enemy aircraft. He then stared all around him, checking the air space over and over again for any signs of German reconnaissance planes. Nothing – the enemy air force was clearly not remotely interested in the landscape beneath him. Strange… the Germans' main Hindenburg defence line itself was almost immediately beneath him now. Massive trench works and swathes of barbed wire defences dominated the fields for mile after mile. Two or three miles to the east he could make out the bridges over the Scheldt Canal, a small area of woodland and then, several miles away to the north, the buildings in Cambrai.

He dived lower now, making his way west to cross the British front line, and circled the now familiar villages of Gonnelieu and Goudecourt. He peered down at the rail terminus and the busy activity, which had been a feature for several days now: tanks – scores of them - being unloaded and marshalled and then carefully hidden from sight in the nearest woodland.

It was very obvious to Travers now why he and his flight of Camels had been detailed to deny any access by German reconnaissance aircraft to the skies above this area. Something very big was building beneath him. The British army was clearly planning to make a massed attack on the Hindenburg Line using tanks as a spearhead. He turned his head and waved acknowledgement to the flight of relief aircraft now appearing on his starboard side, then signalled his own pilots and broke off west, to head back to the airfield and afternoon tea.

* * * *

Amy knocked at Colonel Fenwick's door. He opened it himself, waved his orderly out of the room and bade Amy to sit herself down. He returned to his desk and held up a letter just received from London.

'I've got new orders for you, Amy. The powers that be want you back home.'

'Back home, sir? Is there something wrong?'

'Quite the contrary, it seems that we in the château here have become victims of our own success. The army authorities are so impressed with what we've been able to achieve out here with neurasthenia victims that they want more of the same.'

'So why send me home, sir?'

'So that you can help with the organisation of more field hospitals out here. You remember Captain Danvers back at Netley Hospital? Well, he's Major Danvers now. He'll be heading up a new training unit at Netley, and then acting as liaison between there and three new field hospitals to be created in France. He wants you back to help him.'

'You know that I'd be more than happy to stay here at Rivière and support you, Colonel.'

Fenwick smiled. 'I'm very touched by that, Amy, but Danvers is absolutely right to request that you go back. He was generous enough to let me have you when I was so desperate for help earlier in the year. And, frankly, you are now the best placed person to help advise him on the organisation we've built up out here. Anyway, I've no say in the matter - to be honest, I'm basically being instructed to send you back.'

'When do I leave then, sir?'

'Tomorrow morning – but take heart: you get a week's leave before you have to be in Netley. Go home. Get this place out of your hair. See friends and family if you can.'

Amy took his proffered hand, smiled and then wiped a tear from her eye. 'You've been really kind to me, Colonel. I've learnt so much from you. Is there anything I can do for you in England?'

He turned away, thought for a moment, and then sat down heavily, his face clearly troubled. 'There is, actually. You remember my friend Mrs Brenchly? She's in hospital – somewhere in Dulwich. If you could make a short excursion when you pass through London, and go and see her? I'm told that she's still desperately ill. Please visit her if you can. Let me know how she is.'

'May I ask if her husband has been able to see her, Colonel?'

'I really don't know. Apparently Paul Brenchly requested to be released from Haig's staff headquarters. He went to a front line posting, but where – I've no idea.'

Amy left without mentioning anything further about Marion Brenchly. She went to her room and started to gather her clothes and belongings together. Her life was about to take yet another turn.

*　*　*　*

As the brown painted London Omnibus ground noisily to a halt, Thomas rubbed his eyes and stared again at the driver, who was now jumping out of the driving seat.

'Well, if it isn't young Hughes,' said Thomas. 'The last time I saw you, we were sharing a shell crater together.'

Hughes turned, stood immediately to attention, saluted and smiled. 'Mr Winson, sir! You're a sight for sore eyes, if ever I've seen one. Welcome back, sir.'

'The surgeons obviously did a good job on you, Hughes. I heard that they took you off to Rouen. They obviously weren't Blighty wounds, then?'

'Afraid not, sir. I was lucky, though – just flesh wounds, they told me. After I was discharged from hospital they sent me to the coast at Deauville to get fully healed and recovered. I'd recommend it for a seaside holiday anytime.'

'And what about home? Did you eventually get back to Sheerness for a spot of leave?'

Hughes blushed - pleased and surprised that the officer had remembered his background. 'I did, sir, but I found it heavy going.'

'No family problems, I hope?'

'No, sir. My parents have kept well, and all my brothers and sisters, too. What hit me hard was finding out just how many of the local lads I knew have been killed since we were called up just over a year ago.'

'I don't doubt it. Between them, the Somme and Ypres have accounted for hundreds of thousands of lives,' said Thomas.

'Yes, sir, and Arras was no picnic, as you and I both discovered.'

Hughes was now looking down at his own feet, apparently trying to grapple with some thoughts which clearly disturbed him. He said, 'To be honest, Mr Winson, being back home for that spell of leave...I felt like a complete stranger. Nobody back there who hasn't been out here has any idea at all what it's like in the trenches. It must sound daft, but I was quite glad to get back to the battalion. The snag is, I hardly know anyone else in the Invictas here now, either. These last seven or eight months have wiped out most of the blokes who I started serving with.'

Thomas decided that a change of subject was needed: 'So, where are you off to with the wagon?'

'Out to collect the officers from Avesnes-le-Compte, sir. They won't be in any hurry to come back to the billets, though. You can lay odds on that. Would you like a lift there, Mr Winson?'

'Why not? While you're driving you can probably tell me something about all these tanks hidden in the trees.'

'No such luck, sir. I'd love to get my hands on one of those beauties, but you can't get anywhere near them. There's doubling of sentries day and night all around the woodland where they're parked up. The infantry aren't allowed near the tank corps, and vice versa. Perhaps I should put in for a transfer. I can drive just about anything else. Perhaps they'd let me try my hand with a tank. I'd feel a bloody sight safer inside one of those things than being in a trench or shell hole somewhere. Sorry, sir, excuse my French.'

Thomas laughed, dismissing Hughes' apology with a wave of his hand. 'I doubt you'd have much luck with a transfer in time for the next push. Anyway, you're too good with a Lewis gun for us to lose you just yet. I'm still the battalion's Lewis gun officer, remember? My word would be law–so stick to driving 'buses, Private Hughes and get me to the officers' club-I'm getting thirsty.'

* * * *

The hospital matron looked up from the letter she had been reading and observed Amy closely. 'It seems that you have quite a lot of influence with the Royal Army Medical Corps, Nurse Nicholls. I understand from this letter that you have made quite a difference at this field hospital near Arras.'

'I've simply been helping out there as best I can in an unqualified role,' Amy replied equably.

'Your modesty is a credit to you, but I'm left in no doubt by your superiors that we must accommodate your visit to Mrs Brenchly as best we can. So tell me, how were you associated with her in France?'

'Marion Brenchly had a crucial role administering the hospitals in Camiers near Etaples. I had to liaise closely with her to enable my superiors to get our new field hospital up and running. She helped us enormously – especially in cutting through army red tape.'

'Were you in Camiers when she was so nearly killed by the bombing?'

'No. I heard about it later – but… please tell me, can I see her? It's why I am here, after all.'

'Yes, of course you can. And your Colonel Fenwick is clearly a close friend of Mrs Brenchly – it's he who has written me this letter. I understand that you will be reporting back to him, but... I wonder...well, this is difficult...'

'What is difficult, Matron?'

243

'To be open and honest with you, Nurse Nicholls, we've been puzzled not to have heard directly from Mrs Brenchley's husband. We managed to establish that he is a staff officer in France, but we have failed in our attempts to communicate with him. We're anxious to inform him about other issues beyond his wife's very slow and difficult recovery from her wounds.'

* * * *

The artillery barrage had only lasted a few hours. Now it was beginning to roll forward and the British tank and infantry attack was only minutes away. The tanks' engines had roared into life a little earlier and, finally, as a series of flags began waving to left and to right, the iron monsters began to roll forward.

Thomas drew his whistle, gave a long blast and signalled to his company of men to begin the advance. The hundreds of tanks, all belching smoke and fumes, began to roll forward in unison, with the infantry in close pursuit. Within only twenty minutes or so the machines were approaching the German forward trenches. Astonishingly, the German artillery had not started to respond. He signalled his men to pause and crouch down as several tanks immediately ahead ground to a halt. They waited as tank crews released the chains securing facines, enormous bundles of tightly packed tree branches, which many tanks had had fixed above their front section. These facines tumbled forward into the German trenches to provide bridges enabling the machines to continue their relentless advance.

Less than an hour later and, miraculously, with few apparent casualties among their ranks, Winson realised that his company of men were virtually through the Hindenburg Line. It seemed to be the same on both sides of him. All the tanks, benefiting from the firm and gently undulating landscape, had made excellent progress. What few Germans they now saw were all in headlong retreat, clearly terrified and totally demoralised by the tanks, against which their machine guns had virtually no effect. The enemy barbed wire, together with all its supporting infrastructure had been totally obliterated, leaving wide, clear paths of advance for the allied infantry.

'Winson, Winson – hold on a moment!'

Thomas turned to find Colonel Kendrick, the battalion's acting commander running up to him.

'Winson, I'm taking Porter and six of his platoon with me. We need to capture a battery of guns just on the northern edge of the wood ahead of us. You proceed to the front edge of the wood with the rest of your company and go in as ordered. We'll rendezvous with you on the eastern side of the wood once you've cleared the Hun out of there.'

Thomas nodded his assent, turned back and hurriedly caught up with the rest of his men who were still close to the rear of the tanks. He now had a clear sight of the woodland ahead of him. The capture of Lateau Wood, an area of dense woodland about a quarter of a mile square, was the objective for his company. His orders were quite clear: to enter and clear the woodland of the enemy, and then to capture the German reserve trenches on the wood's eastern edge. This was part of the plan to enable the Battalion to occupy the high ground above the Scheldt Canal, supposedly denying the enemy any easy opportunity to mount a counter attack.

The tanks, meanwhile, were continuing their seamless advance. By now the woodland was only a few hundred yards distant. Sustained German machine-gun fire was causing a storm of bullets to rattle off and around the tanks, and some casualties were finally being sustained among the foot soldiers. Then, finally, the tanks were grinding to a halt, just yards short of the trees, with all their guns firing. Thomas gave another blast on his whistle, immediately hearing the answering whistles of his platoon commanders. As the tanks ceased firing, the Invictas plunged into the woods, throwing Mills bombs and firing Lewis guns, rifles and revolvers, as they crashed forward, dodging between the trees.........

*   *   *   *

245

He banked the aircraft low over the canal bridges, watching intensely as the German troops dashed back across them in full flight. The whole of the Hindenburg Line in the area over which he flew had apparently been comprehensively abandoned by the enemy troops. The British tanks, most of which seemed to be unscathed, had achieved a five thousand yard penetration of the German trench system. The subsequent advance of the British infantry had been unprecedented. Diving lower, he could now discern British troops coming out of the eastern fringes of Lateau Wood and beginning to infiltrate what, less than half an hour earlier, had been German trenches.

He soared up over the slopes above the Scheldt and looked north towards Cambrai, a few miles away, wondering if that whole city might soon be in allied hands. Then he dipped low again, circling a lone farmhouse on the other side of the wood, which appeared to be a focus of activity for British troops. Satisfied that the plan of allied advances had been fully realised in the sector that he had been patrolling, he turned the Sopwith Camel to make a final pass over the bridges of the canal.

The string of machine gun bullets struck the Camel just ahead of his own weapons mounted in front of the cockpit. Instinctively he pulled back savagely on the control column and then, halfway through the loop, executed a rapid barrel roll, feverishly searching the sky all around him. His efforts to evade any pursuing enemy aircraft were in vain, however. His engine was now belching smoke and flames. Travers dived to attempt to use airspeed to extinguish the fire, but a second later...oblivion, as the aircraft exploded.

Hundreds of feet below, Thomas and his company of Invictas momentarily looked up from their newly occupied German trench and watched as the aircraft's burning debris tumbled down onto the slopes below them...

* * * *

Her face, though drawn and pale, brightened briefly with a hesitant

246

smile as Amy approached her bed. She made a vain attempt to raise herself in the bed, but sank back again as the effort proved too much for her.

Amy took her hand, leant down and kissed her left cheek, which still bore a livid two-inch scar just above the jaw line. 'Marion, it's so good to see you again. We've all been so worried for you. It's wonderful to hear that you are at last beginning to recover.'

'People keep telling me that, Amy. The way I feel, though, I've yet to be convinced of it. I feel so weak from all these operations they keep doing.'

'Take heart, Marion. Matron assures me that you're no longer on the danger list. She hopes that the surgeons have finished with you now. You remain so weak because of all the blood you lost in Camiers. It probably sounds absurd for me to say this…. but you were lucky. Apparently the bomb fragments didn't damage any of your vital organs too badly. You suffered a lot of bomb splinter wounds, but you will recover – that the matron promises me. A few months and you'll be as right as rain.'

'I'm not really in a state to appreciate your kind words, Amy. I think that they are still using morphia on me. I just seem to be detached from things altogether. I can't begin to think straight.'

'That's hardly surprising. But you probably shouldn't waste energy on thinking about anything except getting better. Let your body recover. Your mind will get back to normal eventually. You've been badly traumatised, just like the soldiers we have at the château. You will get through this, believe me.'

Marion winked at her and managed another weak smile. 'Do you bring any news of Thomas, Amy?'

'Nothing really up to date, I'm afraid. I know that he rejoined his old battalion some time ago. He's back at the Front, and fully recovered from his wounds. I'll do my best to get word to him when I go back to France next week. I'll be sure to tell him about your recovery, Marion. Don't worry.'

'And my husband Paul? Is there any news of him?'

'Colonel Fenwick heard that your husband has left Haig's staff and has gone to the Front himself. More than that I simply don't know.'

'I'm afraid it's unlikely that Paul will want to see me again. I wrote to him weeks ago, making it clear that, as far as I was concerned, our marriage was over.'

'Marion... this is difficult, but I have to try and explain things to the matron. The hospital has been trying desperately to contact your husband. What would you like me to tell her?'

Marion covered her face with one hand, sobbing gently. She replied: 'Tell her the truth. What difference can it make now? This is clearly the worst year of this bloody war. Neither Paul nor Thomas may survive it. I'm not sure that I will survive it if they have to cut any more shrapnel out of me.'

Twenty minutes later Amy left a now sleeping Marion, took her leave of the matron and stepped out of the hospital into a Dulwich street scene full of tired, grey faces and hungry looking children. Food was becoming increasingly scarce in the shops, and the populace, even in this more affluent part of south London, was self-evidently worn out with the war effort. She wondered how much more the people on the home front could take.

Chapter 24

'Message from Battalion HQ, sir.'

He turned and read the brief note from Major Falcon the adjutant:

Come to Battalion HQ immediately for company commanders' conference.

Thomas skirted around the north edge of the wood, using the reverse slope to make sure that he did not fall prey to any sniper. Once clear of the wood it was a short half-mile to where the adjutant had set up his headquarters in a captured bunker within what, just the day before, had been part of the German Hindenburg support line.

As he approached the bunker's entrance he noticed, just a few yards away, Captain Standish kneeling beside one of several bodies. He was removing some personal effects from the pockets of Gerry Porter, one of the dead. Standish looked up, not attempting to disguise the tears running down both his cheeks. Thomas didn't intrude on his grief and looked at the other corpses. One of them was Colonel Kendrick, the acting CO. Another was that of a subaltern, unknown to him.

'They were killed yesterday morning,' said Standish. 'They succeeded in capturing a battery of guns on the north edge of the wood, but then they were shot down by remaining Bosche who were still hidden in the wood.'

'It took my company a long time to clear the enemy from that wood,' replied Thomas. 'There were several rearguard Bosche hidden among the trees. We flushed them out eventually, but not until long after the colonel had collared Gerry Porter and several of his platoon.'

'I'm sure that you did the best you could, Winson. No, apparently, once the colonel spotted that gun emplacement he was bent on capturing it to ensure that the tanks remained safe from the Bosche artillery. He would have probably got up to their position before you and your men could have barely started to penetrate the wood itself.'

'I'm very sorry about Gerry,' said Thomas. 'I know that you and he were very close.'

Standish stood up, saying: 'You're very kind. But I suppose it really underlines the fact that to make close friends in this war is simply not a good idea. Anyway, I know that you have been called to a conference here. I have to get across to the Brigade HQ, where I'm attached. Good luck, Winson.'

Thomas saluted, turned away and headed into the entrance to the bunker. There he was astonished to see Colonel Drummond, who he assumed was still recovering from wounds which had put him in hospital weeks ago.

'It's alright, Winson. You haven't seen a ghost. I'm still not in the best of shape, but they've decided to let me come back and resume command.'

'I'm very saddened by Colonel Kendrick's death, sir. He was a very brave man.'

Drummond looked to make a reply, but was interrupted by the arrival of the other company commanders.

'Many congratulations, gentlemen, you all played a blinder yesterday,' said Drummond. 'Thanks to the tanks, we secured all our objectives. Our basic losses were very light. Despite that, we lost our second in command, Colonel Kendrick – a very fine officer. But now we have to move on. Winson – what is your assessment of the situation immediately east of the wood?'

'To be honest, sir, I really think that, without significant reinforcement, our position is tenuous, to say the least. We're being expected to hold a very long stretch of trenches with less than half the number of men necessary. We're also holding trenches which face the wrong way. We'll need some time to adapt them to a defensive position. I must also ask you, sir, what is being done about the bridges over the canal? If the Germans decide to counter-attack us, the bridges will facilitate that very nicely for them. If we are to really consolidate our position above the canal, then those bridges should be destroyed.'

Before Drummond had the opportunity to reply, another person entered the bunker. Thomas turned and gasped. He suddenly found himself facing none other than Marion's husband, Major Paul Brenchly.

*   *   *   *

Simon Mockett looked pensively at Amy as she stirred her cup of tea. 'So… how did you find Marion?' he asked. 'Does the hospital expect her to recover?'

'They seemed to have stopped operating on her at long last,' she replied. 'But the extent of her wounds was horrifyingly bad. She's so weakened and depressed. But that's probably down to all the morphine she's been given.'

'Has her husband been able to get back to see her?'

'No. The hospital has been unable to contact him. Obviously, I haven't told them about the state of her marriage and the situation regarding Thomas.'

'No, of course not,' he replied, 'it's a difficult situation – but all too common these days. I have to deal with this a great deal. Many naval marriages have been broken by this war, too. I can give ample testimony on that.'

Amy smiled and reached out to take his hand. 'You're not trying to tell me something, are you, Captain?'

'Of course not you silly woman! I was referring to several of my crew. But I do have to remind you that you are due down at Netley Hospital this afternoon, and I have to rejoin my ship at

Chatham. Let's go and enjoy some lunch together in the remaining few hours we have with each other.'

Two hours later, after seeing Simon onto his train, Amy once again visited the hospital to take her leave of Marion. To a large degree it was a wasted visit. It was explained to her that Marion was sleeping deeply and still heavily sedated. However, the hospital matron had requested that, if Amy were to visit again, she needed to speak with her. Their meeting was brief, if somewhat shocking.

'Do sit down Mrs Mockett. I'm sorry that you were unable to speak to your friend Mrs Brenchly. Rest assured, I'll explain things when I see her later today.'

'Thank you, I have to travel down to Hampshire later today. I'm not sure how long I'll be there. But quite soon, within days, perhaps, I expect to be returning to France. It could be many months before I get the chance to see Marion again.'

The matron looked nervously at her. 'Mrs Mockett, when you were last here, I did explain to you that we were having no success in trying to get any response from Major Brenchly.'

'Yes, I do remember.'

'We've also had no success in trying to contact another close member of the family. We've sent telegrams to the family home, but have had no helpful reply from there either.'

'Matron...are you going to tell me that you think Marion is dying?'

'No, I'm not suggesting that at all. Ironically, what I want to tell you is news of a totally different nature. But, first, and it's only because of the special circumstances of this situation, I have to ask you to let me take you into my confidence. I believe that, once she is recovered, Mrs Brenchly will understand my actions in speaking to you about this.'

The matron reached into a drawer of her desk and took out a sealed letter, which she handed to Amy before continuing: 'As you can see, this is addressed to Colonel Fenwick in France. I'm not prepared to risk it to the army postal services, well organised and reliable as they may be. I'm well aware that the colonel is a close friend of both Major and Mrs Brenchly. This letter has an enclosure for Major Brenchly. I feel confident that if you get this letter back to the colonel, that he will have the necessary influence to get the enclosure delivered by courier.'

'Just as I got the colonel's own letter to you,' said Amy, smiling wryly.

'Exactly so. I'm using the same 'old boys' network, for want of a better term. But now, and I emphasise the confidentiality of this, I want to give you further news of Mrs Brenchly's medical condition…'

Just over an hour later Amy was on the train heading for Netley, penning a letter of her own. She was writing to Thomas to gently explain to him that he was, later next year, to become a father…

* * * *

It was pitch black as they slithered silently down the remainder of the grassy slope, pausing to take breath just short of the canal's edge. While there was every hope that no Germans would be found on their side of the canal, they couldn't dismiss the possibility that the enemy, just like themselves, might also be engaged in covert night-time reconnaissance activity.

Thomas signalled silently to his sergeant to keep still and mute. He huddled deep in a thick clump of reeds to check his compass bearing with one brief and shielded flash of his torch. He turned, for some moments quite unable to see anything of the sergeant in the darkest of November nights, but then crept back, eventually finding his companion, whispering to him as quietly as possible: 'We're about a hundred yards short of the bridge. We have to get close enough to see if it's actually manned by the Bosche at night.'

The sergeant nodded his reply and followed Thomas, both of them creeping stealthily a few steps at a time in their plimsoled feet. The night sky remained totally dark, with no glimmer of moon or starlight. They were both completely clothed in black, with their faces darkened with lamp soot. Their only weapons were cudgels, knives and revolvers.

Thomas had counted every one of his paces since they had turned to creep towards the bridge. He was certain that, by now, they must be within twenty or thirty yards of it. Closer, ever closer they inched, then they heard it – the unmistakable sound of spoon or fork on a billycan or metal plate. Next came the sound of muffled voices and footsteps on the metalled surface of the bridge itself. It was clear: the Bosche were present on the bridge under cover of darkness.

Their patrol mission complete, they turned and began the slow, difficult climb back up the slopes towards their trenches on the edge of the wood. On three occasions during their return, Thomas paused then, carefully positioning and shielding his torch, he flashed the pre-arranged signal in the direction of their own trenches: dash, dot, dot, dot, dot – the Morse-code for 6, the number of his battalion.

Eventually they heard the inevitable voice from the trench: 'Halt! Who goes there?'

'Mister Winson', replied Thomas, adding the required password.

Ten minutes later they were snug in a dugout enjoying mugs of tea laced with generous measures of rum.

Thomas looked at his watch, surprised at how much of the night had slipped away. It was already stand-to time, the half hour period before dawn, and the trench outside was becoming hectic with men taking up defensive positions behind the trench's parapet, preparing for any possible enemy attack. Gesturing to the sergeant to do likewise, he began to tuck into some bully beef sandwiches, which had just appeared. Then, barely twenty minutes later, as the first light of dawn fell on the trench outside, the field telephone rang: he was wanted by Colonel Drummond in the Battalion HQ, with immediate effect.

He entered the HQ dugout, accompanied by an officer and a sergeant from a detachment of the Machine Gun Corps, who had also been summoned from their positions just to the right of

Thomas' company outside Lateau Wood. Drummond addressed his opening questions directly to Thomas: 'So, what did you find out last night, Winson? Any Bosche on the bridges?'

'They were definitely there, sir. Certainly on the bridge I reconnoitred. It's obvious that they come out under cover of darkness, man the bridges and then melt back into the woodland on their side of the canal before dawn. It's hardly surprising. They've got the woodland just behind that bridge, and the grounds of the abbey, which are well hidden from us behind the trees. There's no telling how many men they could keep hidden there, should they wish to spring a sudden counter-attack on our positions. Aside from that, they are almost certainly occupying the bridges at night to stop our patrols from destroying them then.' He paused for a moment, gathered his breath and went on: 'With the greatest respect, sir, I must remind you that my men are positioned barely a thousand yards from that bridge.'

Drummond's penetrating eyes looked long and hard at Thomas, and then moved across to the machine gun commander.

'Well, Captain,' said Drummond, 'you heard that. How many machine guns have you got up near my company on that edge of Lateau?'

'Four, sir; the orderly sergeant here knows their precise dispositions and manning.'

'You heard my officer's worries about his men in the trenches to your left, Sergeant,' said Drummond. 'Can your guns cover those bridges? It's vital to us that they can. We're badly undermanned up there. Without your machine guns we'd stand little hope of holding Jerry back if he made a serious attack.'

'We can do that for you, sir. Our four teams are all within range of the two bridges. We can focus two guns on one bridge and the other two onto the second. We've got a clear field of fire to both.'

'Does that make your mind a little easier, Winson?' asked Drummond.

'I'm certainly glad that the machine-gunners are there, sir.'

The other captain and his sergeant were dismissed, leaving Thomas alone with his colonel. Then, a few moments later, the curtain into the dugout was swept aside and in strode Paul Brenchly.

'Ah, Major,' said Drummond to his visitor, 'Captain Winson here commands my company just east of Lateau Wood. He's reported to me on his patrol last night to reconnoitre the Vaucelles Bridge just below his position.'

Brenchly looked intently at Thomas's figure, still clad as he was in black boiler suit and with the remnants of the lamp-black on his face. 'And what did you discover, exactly?'

'That Jerry mans the bridge at night, sir.'

'It seems to me, Major,' said Drummond, 'that we should reinforce and attack over those bridges while the enemy is still recovering from our advance. Either that or we destroy the bridges to stop Jerry counter-attacking.'

'I've just come here directly from Brigade HQ, Colonel. You certainly aren't going to get reinforcements.'

'Why not?' asked Drummond.

'From what little I could gather, the Italians now have big problems on their own front, a thousand miles from here. The enemy has broken through their lines at a place called Caporetto. Apparently, we are currently dispatching all the men that can be spared to Italy.'

Drummond sprang to his feet. 'If we are not to get any reinforcements here, Major then, as a brigade liaison officer, you should get back to HQ and advise the destruction of the canal bridges.'

'That's partly why I'm here now, Colonel. I've been asked to go up and make an appraisal of our positions above the canal. Perhaps I can return there with Captain Winson here.'

* * * *

'Before we start our formal meeting with Danvers and the others,' said Colonel Fenwick, 'I'd like you to meet one of our more unusual visitors. Amy, let me introduce you to a genuine war artist, Lieutenant Jenkins. He's just with us for a day or so. He's been sketching some of our better and more amenable patients about the place.'

'This is a new experience,' said Amy, smiling at the visitor. 'Do I need to present you with the better side of my face?'

'I'm afraid that my work here is finished,' Jenkins replied, chuckling, 'though I'm sure you'd be a useful addition to the portfolio.'

'And where do you go from here?' asked Fenwick, 'Or aren't we allowed to ask?'

'Well… I don't think that's too much of a problem. Actually, I'm very excited. I'm being allowed to make some choices in what I produce for the War Office. I'm going on from here today to spend a day with my old infantry battalion, the Sixth Invictas.'

Amy almost choked at what she heard. 'My God! You did say Sixth Invictas?'

'What on earth's the matter, Amy?' Said Fenwick, 'You look as though you've seen a ghost!'

'Sorry, sir, it's just that I have a very close friend in that battalion of the Invictas.' She turned again to Jenkins: 'His name's Winson – Thomas Winson. Do you know him?'

'Know him!' echoed Jenkins, 'We crossed the Channel from Folkestone together last winter. I served under him for several months. I was just a humble corporal then. Then I got a bad dose of trench fever and was laid up in the caves' hospital beneath Arras. Next thing I heard was that Mr Winson had been wounded and taken off to a base hospital somewhere. I went back to Blighty soon afterwards. The army offered me a commission on the basis of becoming a war artist, and here I am. I have to thank Mr Winson, really. He got me doing some technical sketches while we were outside Arras. Apparently, the army authorities really liked them.'

'Amy,' said Fenwick. 'It'll be helpful to me to have a while here alone before the planning session with Danvers. You take the lieutenant away for a cup of tea. You can reminisce together for a while longer – I know that he planned to leave here this morning.'

She opened the door for Jenkins and beckoned him towards a rest room further along the corridor. 'Lieutenant, how sure are you that you will be able to get to the Sixth Invictas' current position? What if they're in the front-line somewhere?'

'I happen to know that that is exactly where they are. I'll be making the journey by motorcycle and sidecar. I need the storage space in it for my art materials and valise. Within reason, I'm authorised to go where I please, as long as it fits in with the War Office requirements.'

'And if you leave here today, when would you expect to make contact with Thomas' unit?'

'Well, I've already mapped out a route from here. I can't tell you exactly where I'm going for security reasons. But, barring accident or breakdown, I hope to complete the journey before dark today.'

'And you expect to actually make contact with Thomas?'

'Definitely, now that you've confirmed he's still with them. But - and I don't want to depress you, Nurse Nicholls - you must understand that I can't guarantee that Mr Winson hasn't become a casualty again.'

'Of course, I understand that. Nonetheless, in the hope that Thomas hasn't been killed, wounded or taken prisoner, I'd be very grateful if you could deliver a letter to him by hand. Will you do that for me?'

'Of course, it'll be a pleasure. If I have any mishaps, I'll ensure that the letter finds its way to him by army mail. Now, give me your letter. I really must make tracks.'

*   *   *   *

The two of them picked their way carefully along the path through the wood. Thomas paused every so often to speak to sentries, signalmen, stretcher-bearers, or anyone else they encountered while sheltered by the trees. Finally, Brenchly, who had remained silent since entering the wood, stopped and suggested that they both rest for a few moments. 'Lieutenant,' he said, 'since that last occasion when we met a few days ago, I've been trying to place you. I'm sure there's a familiarity about your face and voice, but I just can't recall a previous encounter with you.'

Thomas stopped in his tracks. He thought hard for a moment as to whether he should admit to the Etaples scene, which he remembered all too vividly from many months earlier. Eventually, rather than denying any knowledge of that, and with his curiosity over what Brenchly's reaction would be, he decided to refresh the Major's memory. 'Yes, Major. Your memory hasn't deceived you. We did meet briefly early this year. You were with your wife near the fish-market in Etaples.'

'Ahh…of course, you intervened in a bit of an argument my wife and I were having at the time.'

'It was more than a bit of an argument, Major. At the time I was concerned for your wife's safety. You appeared to me then to have rather lost control of yourself.'

'Yes…I'm afraid that I didn't behave well that day. I apologise for any offence caused to you. I'm afraid that I'd been under a lot of strain early in the year. I went through a disastrous period of failure trying to liaise with the French General Staff. Basically, I made a pig's breakfast of my work with them. I was relieved of duties with Haig's staff some months ago.'

They walked on in silence, Thomas anxious to avoid any possibility of the conversation throwing up any more personal issues. He had no inclination to enlighten Brenchly regarding his own subsequent involvement with Marion. Let 'sleeping dogs lie' was the best interpretation he felt able to put on this perversely chance meeting with her husband. He had far more important things to worry about now.

Fortunately, by this time they had reached the edge of the wood. It was still some distance to the trenches being held by Thomas' Company. He turned to Brenchly warning him to keep well down as they made their way along a communication trench. Finally he reported his return to the platoon sergeant, took Brenchly to a safe vantage point on the trench parapet and eased back a piece of sacking obscuring a spy-hole. 'There, Major. That's the bridge we reconnoitred last night. Now look along to your right – that's the other bridge that the sergeant machine-gunner mentioned. For what it's worth, it's my opinion that we need to at least double our strength up here to have any chance of repelling any counter-attack by Jerry.'

Brenchly hastily scribbled in a note-pad, looked at his watch, then asked Thomas if he could be shown the rest of the company's positions.

'Be my guest, Major, what you're in here is basically just back from part of the Hindenburg support line. The trouble is, everything in the trench is back to front. Before we arrived, Jerry was using these trenches to defend against any attacks coming through the wood. Now, I'll get the sergeant to take you along to both left and right. It's now noon. When you've seen all you need to, come back here to the dugout. We'll try and have something hot for you to eat. Meantime, if you'll excuse me I'm going to try and get a nap. We've been in these trenches without relief now for nine days, and I was out on patrol for much of last night. Now, don't forget: keep your head down. There are a lot of snipers in those trees across the canal.'

Thomas threw himself onto his bunk and was fast asleep within moments. His slumbers, though short-lived, were mercifully free of bad dreams. He woke suddenly to the sound of a sharp rapping on the doorpost of the dugout.

'Mister Winson, are you awake, sir? We've got a visitor.'

Hughes entered, beaming a smile. 'Look who it isn't, sir. It's Mister Jenkins. I can't call him Corporal no more. He's got two pips on his shoulders!'

'Well I'm damned,' exclaimed Thomas, jumping up, 'this is a turn-up for the book! What the devil are you doing here in officer's uniform? Don't tell me that you're a replacement platoon commander. We need a bit more than arty types around here.'

Jenkins laughed and sat on a stool, shaking Thomas' outstretched hand. 'Don't alarm yourself. I'm here to do some sketching. They've made me a war artist.'

'That's fantastic news...err...'

'Please...call me Marcus.'

'Fine, and please call me Thomas. Now, how have you been, and where have you come from? The last time I saw you, the doctors in the Arras caves weren't even sure that you would get over your dose of trench fever.'

'Well, clearly I did, but it was a very slow recovery. Then eventually a staff officer arrived at the caves to question me about my drawings of that Jerry 'plane which I'd sketched outside the city. Next thing I knew was that I was being offered a commission and the opportunity to become an artist for the army. I was granted extended convalescence leave at home so that my lungs could recover. It was wonderful to spend several weeks at home with my wife and daughter before coming back to the front.'

They were suddenly interrupted by a succession of overhead explosions. A few minutes later Hughes appeared again at the dugout entrance. 'Mister Winson, you'd better come quick. That Major Brenchly...he's been badly wounded. He copped some shrapnel in the chest.'

Thomas quickly went out into the trench and was beckoned along to the left, where stretcher-bearers were already lifting Brenchly onto a litter. There was blood and froth coming from his mouth. He looked helplessly at Thomas as one of the stretcher-bearers tried to put a wound dressing over a gaping hole in his chest. Brenchly then struggled to reach up and point at his breast pocket. Thomas gently took his hand then unbuttoned the pocket and found a letter inside. Brenchly nodded and mouthed the words: *My wife.* He then gasped, and breathed his last.

Thomas waved the stretcher-bearers away with the corpse and scurried back to the dugout. He immediately advised Jenkins that he should leave and return to a safer place behind the immediate frontal positions.

'But I haven't done any drawings yet, Thomas. It is why I'm here, after all. The Sixth Invictas used to be my battalion, too, remember?'

'Yes...that's as may be, but, with respect, your trench fighting days are over now. I'd hoped that the dead major was going to recommend the destruction of two bridges just below here.

Clearly he can't do that now, and our position in this trench is consequently more dangerous than ever. The Jerry shelling is now getting heavier, and our casualties are increasing. No, much as I'd enjoy your company, Marcus, you must get away from here.'

'Very well, but before I go, I've something to give you. Here, this letter was given to me by a VAD nurse - in a place called Rivière.'

Within another hour darkness had fallen. Thomas had doubled the sentries and sent a runner to advise the machine-gunners to do likewise. He then did the rounds of his company's positions and spoke to battalion HQ on the field telephone. Despite the increased enemy shelling, there was no specific news of any anticipated German counter-attack.

He lay on his bunk reading Amy's letter over and over again. His joy at the news of Marion's continued recovery and pregnancy was overshadowed by Brenchly's death, the all too brief reunion with Jenkins and the now increasingly parlous situation for the Invictas. He scribbled two brief letters of his own, one to Amy, the other to Marion. These he fastened in the top pocket of the private soldier's tunic he had decided to wear to disguise his officer status. His conviction that more hand-to-hand trench fighting with the Bosche was inevitable was now becoming obsessive. He found it impossible to sleep – even to doze fitfully. Finally, as the last of the night ebbed away he took his binoculars and joined his men for the stand-to period.

The enemy barrage commenced before first light. It was aimed, by the eerie light of overhead flares, at the areas around their trench and the woodland behind. It was astonishingly heavy yet brief for, as the night finally yielded to dawn, the explosions over and around them were suddenly interspersed with the shouts of men in the trench. 'It's a Jerry attack, sir!' shouted the nearest platoon sergeant. 'The buggers are pouring over the bridges!'

'Make sure all the Lewis teams are ready!' shouted back Thomas. 'Quickly now! Then check along to the right. Let's hope that the Machine Gun Corps are on their toes.'

He edged back momentarily to let Hughes, who was carrying Lewis gun magazines, get past him, when he suddenly felt a violent pain in his right wrist, and realised that blood was jetting out from the wrist onto the trench wall in front of him. In the next instant, he saw Hughes drop the stack of magazines, dive to pick up a Verey pistol, level the weapon to his left, and fire it in one apparently seamless action.

The trajectory of the Verey pistol's round was but two or three yards. It exploded violently in an incandescent storm-blast, completely severing the head of the German soldier who, seconds earlier, had leapt into the trench. In the next few moments, while the German's truncated body lay smouldering before them, a combination of rifle and Lewis gunfire from Thomas' men had brought down several other enemy attackers, staving off the initial assault on their position. By now the enemy artillery had fallen quiet, giving way to the reassuring sound of the British heavy machine guns off to the right. But despite all their combined efforts, there seemed no end to the masses of German troops storming over the canal bridges and up the slopes in front of them.

Then Thomas suddenly realised that a stretcher-bearer had bundled him into the dugout and was hurriedly binding a dressing onto his wounded wrist. 'You must use your other hand to keep pressure on this wound, sir. The bullet went through an artery.'

'Yes, yes...alright,' replied Thomas, 'but we must try and raise HQ on the telephone.'

Several efforts later the medic reported that the communication line with HQ was unserviceable. Thomas looked down at his wrist and, satisfied that the flow of blood had been temporarily staunched, he dived back into the trench to assess the situation. He was quickly reassured to learn that all the four company Lewis guns were still in action and that the trench had been held against the first wave of enemy assault troops. He immediately despatched a runner to Battalion HQ for further orders, as it was clear that a further sustained attack would almost certainly overwhelm their hopelessly undermanned position. Within the half hour the runner was back. He'd seen Germans already beginning to outflank other defences on the northern and southern edges of Lateau Wood. Battalion HQ had already had to shift position to better defend themselves and it was obvious that Thomas' company, too, should soon make a controlled retreat through the wood.

After another desperate half hour, following news that his company's strength was now down to less than sixty men, he issued the order to start pulling back into the wood. This in itself was fraught with danger, with enfilading German gunfire from outside the trees on both sides. They finally broke cover, heading across open ground to a temporary British strong point two hundred yards away. The controlled retreat had now become a rout, the Brigade HQ itself had also been evacuated, and Thomas, as morning gave way to afternoon, found himself just one of a long line of stragglers heading for a dressing station.

Later that day he learned that the battalion had been all but destroyed. The handful of officers who had survived the battle had been got away as wounded. Beyond this, barely fifty other ranks had escaped the ferocious German counter-offensive. Thomas' own wound, with extensive nerve and ligature damage was later deemed serious enough to require specialist treatment in a British mainland hospital. Before he finally succumbed to his exhaustion in a casualty clearing station, he opened again the letter from Amy. He was desperate to see Marion again and prayed that he would eventually be sent to a London hospital............

The End

Author's Note:

Although this book is a work of fiction, many of the places named and described were very real. I have done my best to keep faith with historical accuracy in terms of the military and, particularly, battle events described here.

The fictional 6th Battalion Invictas is based almost entirely on the 6th Battalion Queen's Own Royal West Kents, into which my father was conscripted in the autumn of 1916.

In terms of some of the main background events in the novel, they do follow actual happenings during 1917:

A snap German naval bombardment of the village of Capel, near Dover, did take place in that year.

Etaples and Camiers in northern France formed a major hub of British Army military and medical logistics during World War 1.

A 'shell shock' or neurasthenia centre did exist at Netley Hospital near Southampton. Field hospitals for shell shock victims in France were first trialled just behind the Western Front in 1917.

The caves beneath Arras did enable the allies to maintain an extensive and well-provisioned safe haven for thousands of troops very close to the German front lines.

German Gotha bombers carried out high altitude bombing attacks on English coastal towns in May of 1917. Scores of townspeople died in one raid on Folkestone.

After major stalemate on the Western Front in the summer and autumn of 1917, the battle of Cambrai in the following November saw the first successful mass use of British tanks against the German Hindenberg line of trenches. My father was one of a company of one hundred and twelve infantrymen who followed immediately behind the tanks. Ten days later, following a massive German counter attack, he was one of just twenty survivors from his company. Of his battalion of more than six hundred men, a total of barely any officers and only fifty men were left.

This is a historical novel, which I researched carefully to provide accurate background for this story. I wish to make special mention of the following sources of information:

First and foremost my father's own reminiscences of his combat experiences around Arras, Cambrai and the Somme. He was a quiet, modest man, not given to saying much about the Great War. But the few experiences he related to me about the close handed fighting in which he found himself during 1917 and 1918, provided the background to several of the most graphic and violent episodes related in this novel.

The original War Diary of the 6th Battalion West Kents, and the Regimental History for 1914-1919 proved very helpful.

Also, the very moving memoir of Alan Thomas, a company commander in the 6th Battalion West Kents: *A Life Apart* (Gollanz, 1963). My father would have certainly known Alan Thomas during 1917 and 1918 – possibly as his own company commander.

Philip Hoare's *Spike Island* (Fourth Estate, 2001) includes an excellent section on Netley Hospital's part in the treatment of WW1 shell shock victims.

For one general, but highly detailed account of the lives of British and Commonwealth soldiers in WW1, I would especially commend Richard Holmes' *Tommy – The British Soldier On The Western Front 1914-1918* (Harper Collins, 2004).

CPSIA information can be obtained at www.ICGtesting.com
Printed in the USA
BVOW022201160312

285402BV00002B/1/P